Quietwater Bridge, mid-morning

Deborah Rowland

For Melanie

First published in Great Britain by Deborah Rowland, 2022

Copyright © Deborah Rowland

Deborah Rowland has asserted her right under the Copyright, Design and Patents Act, 1988 to be identified as the author of this work.

A CIP catalogue record for this book is available from the British Library.

ISBN 978-1-916378-83-4

Typesetting and cover design by Linda Storey

First Quarter

1

Doesn't everyone want something? Aside from world peace, (and who wouldn't want that?), my quest for answers began the moment I returned from a tectonic weekend on the waterways, when time ticked by in slow-mo and talk was meaningful. Before then, I'd never consciously considered this business of wants, but now there was a mystery to be solved.

Back in the office I took a straw poll. All hope of inspiration evaporated as the reality of Fielding and Nair's employees' wanted list emerged: fatter bank balance; thinner thighs; cabbage butterfly-free cauliflowers (this was from Bob, part-time number cruncher and allotment fanatic); personal best at the next triathlon. Just as I was about to give it up and pop over to Jonty's Café for a chocolate cruffin, our mercurial bookkeeper Maureen Umber had looked up from behind her desk and said wistfully, *to love and be loved*. My colleagues' wants had proved to be as predictable as the public's perception of accountancy in general.

The weekend in question took place on Lise Michelson's narrowboat. Juxtaposing *tectonic* and *narrowboat* in the same sentence might at first glance seem odd, discordant even, but isn't that the way of it sometimes? The sunset that night, my last on the Anna Lee, had split the sky into blistering shards of blue and orange. An instinctive urge to record that exact moment prompted me to check my watch – 21:15pm, which was stranger still, as the need to know the time hadn't crossed my mind. As the water stirred beneath the boat's blackened hull and our hot chocolate cooled, I was acutely aware we might never see each other again. Fearful of an emotional outburst, I'd waffled on until my lungs scrambled for an in-breath. That was when, in a manner as straight as a crow's flight, Lise asked *why do you want numbers, April?* As I groped around for an intelligent reply, her attention was unwavering, as if she stood in the centre of time itself. Her questions didn't necessarily require answers, but at that point I wasn't to know, so this was mine:

I can count on numbers, Lise. Numbers mean certainty. One hundred minus eight will forever be ninety-two; the value of pi is always the same, no matter how big the circle; a prime number can only ever be divisible by itself and 1:

Numbers = Certainty = Security.

My magical mathematical formula had been cooked up as a way of steadying a seriously wobbly adolescence and had served me well ever since. I went on to add that my successful career in numbers *and* my sizeable, tight-knit family embodied the very essence of security – what else was there to want? But Lise hadn't meant that at all.

2

Fielding & Nair considered me a perfect fit for their ambitious accountancy business – well, more specifically, it was Gita Nair, renowned talent-sniffer and occasional poacher who had hunted my head. To deter her from swooping in, the competition had learned through bitter experience to hold tight to their bright sparks, but in my case Gita's plan was swiftly executed. Her invitation to join the management trainee programme at Leicester HQ was issued before my graduation cap had even landed on Loughborough University's tree-lined campus. Who wouldn't be flattered?

Work hard: play harder was encoded in the Hayle clan's DNA, and I was ready and willing to prove it. To reward F&N's faith, I passed every chartered accountancy exam with indecent speed before embarking on what Gita had guaranteed to be a stellar career. And what better way to enhance F&N's social culture status than to set up regular inter-office quizzes, an easy box tick as Uncle Max and I had been hosting them at our local pub for ages. As word of their popularity spread, our competitors wanted in, so we upped the ante with leagues and trophies, all of which proved that working hard and playing harder was a winning formula. On the personal front, it wasn't long before I'd saved a substantial deposit to secure number 44, a one-bedroom off-plan starter home on Leicester's premier Merryfield Estate. According to my dad, not only was it a sound investment, but my proximity to F&N's head office showed commitment and availability. So far, so predictable.

Fast forward eight years. My laser-focused approach had resulted in rapid promotion with a salary to match. F&N's new office, located in Loughborough's town centre, was the obvious next step in their strategy to dominate the Midlands, and guess who had been selected to head it up. Rumours of my imminent career-busting promotion spread like bird flu, and not everyone approved. For Maureen Umber, whose thirty-years-under-her-elasticated-belt entitled her precedence over a steam-roller upstart like me, the news was a crushing blow, but what could I do? To counter my first bad taste of hostility, I kept a low profile while privately relishing the prospect of becoming the youngest associate partner in F&N's forty-year biography.

π

While my dad expected nothing less, Mum's happiness rested upon her offspring's holistic welfare. Historically, my brother Bradley and I had sidestepped her quirky barefoot picnic / tree hugging outings in favour of Dad's 'thrill of winning' brainwash. If the activity in question was timed, we were up for it – cycling, swimming, ball sports – beating each other and our legion of cousins was far too exciting a prospect to pass up, and thus it had been ever since. Nevertheless, Mum's cautionary congratulations at my anticipated promotion were reassuring and I rolled my working sleeves up that little bit further.

There were, inevitably, consequences. My body and I had shared a chequered history, and it was becoming increasingly evident that my 'mind over matter' strategy was no longer viable. Persistently indignant shoulder inflammation was seriously denting both my sleep and enthusiasm, despite the killer combination of ice packs, analgesic rubs, and gut busting pain relievers. It was impossible to hide this sorry state of affairs from my mother. She was convinced that a restorative spell under her maternal eye would do me good and for once, I agreed.

After renting out number 44, I returned to Embla, back to my beloved bedroom, to home comforts, and to a potential romance with my brother's new running mate, Sebastian Espie. With Bradley and his wife living a few doors down, and regular rambunctious family gatherings at our local pub, The Red Balloon, as well as the myriad sporting events to dive into, it begged the question why I'd moved out in the first place. When it came to helping out I was no slouch: the plants never went thirsty, I was handy with a screwdriver, and above average in the culinary skills department although Mum, despite being super-busy herself, usually had something wholesome on the go. And so it went on – until the lights went out.

Despite months of meticulously planning for the new office and the roll-out of a slick PR campaign, a not-so-freak electrical storm knocked out the building's power supply and flooded the basement. The extensive damage and ensuing chaos delayed the launch. Although the data loss was temporary, it was no less alarming for that. It had taken several exhausting days for a team of us to restore the files before being confident of pronouncing the office match fit so I'd proved my worth a gazillion times over, but with the last dregs of my energy reserves beating a hasty retreat, the long weekend break with my sister-in-law couldn't have come at a better time.

π

'All set, April?'

I mentally ran through the checklist. Bag stowed, seatbelt fastened, water bottle at the ready. 'Yep, let's hit the road.'

Harriet drove sedately away from Embla and out through Westwytch village towards the A6 while I sank into the passenger seat's soft padding, my sigh a blend of relief and discomfort. We'd made it. As the car picked up speed, a leaflet fell from the dashboard and into my lap.

Angel Ninebarks – a truly creative space

Situated on the outskirts of the Monkton Estate, in its own extensive private grounds, Angel Ninebarks offers a unique environment in which to nurture mind, body, and spirit. Whether you embark on a creative workshop with our gifted tutors or recharge your energy with a treatment in one of the beautiful Arts and Crafts rooms, you won't be disappointed. The vegetarian/vegan meals are made with ingredients sourced from our kitchen garden or locally. Inspirational evening talks take place in the comfort of the library – all are welcome! Rooms are few: early booking is recommended.

The house had already lived up to its hype which was why Harriet and I couldn't wait to go back. The fact that Angel Ninebarks was only an hours' drive away was an added bonus. With luck, (and the stash of ibuprofen in my bag) all would be well.

'I am *sooo* looking forward to this, April. We've both been under pressure, but that electrical storm must have truly upset F&N's applecart. Such bad luck.'

'The shape of things to come, Harriet. Even our brand spanking carbon neutral building isn't immune to power outages and flash floods. Anyway, let's not relive that nightmare. I'm as relieved as you to escape, not least as Sebastian's training regime is reaching its peak. No prizes for guessing what he and my brother are doing this weekend.'

'Bradley's still sulking after I pulled out of the mixed triathlon, and I still haven't found the courage to tell him that my running days are over. You know how much I adore your brother, April, but this hamstring injury has kept me out of action for weeks, and my boss is making noises. I was fortunate to get extended sick leave this time.'

My ears pricked. Harriet and Bradley had fallen headlong for each other at our local running club. Together they'd racked up a series of impressive triathlon wins which cemented their well-matched relationship. There was no one happier about this turn of events than me. Sebastian Espie's arrival on the scene had ratcheted the pace up several gears, and what had been a serious hobby for my brother had subsequently become 'serious'. Their chat was saturated by what constituted the best nutrition, the latest equipment, and, inevitably, *Iron Man*, which was all well and good, but Harriet was ready to talk babies and Bradley had been ambivalent at best. Her decision to quit running may have been a protest.

'Bradley will come around. I'll ask Seb to back off. Don't get your hopes up, though, Harriet. Those boys have a one-track mind.'

Harriet slammed her foot on the brake. 'What an idiot! That van driver nearly ran us off the road.'

I winced, praying that the jolt hadn't set off my back. It was so unusual to see Harriet agitated. While she matched Bradley for determination and output, she possessed a sufficient wodge of empathy to temper what was occasionally considered by outsiders as aloofness. The fact that she'd lightened my brother's dark moods far outweighed her slightly annoying tendency to know what's best. The triathlons often took place in gorgeous locations, but with crowds of people to catch up with as well as stacks of activities on offer, there was scarcely an opportunity to admire the scenery, let alone exhale. Harriet's job was also at full-pelt. She needed this time-out as much as I did.

'Thanks so much for re-organising the break, Harriet. You must have worked a miracle to find us a room this late, *and* on a Bank Holiday. I was so disappointed when we had to cancel our Easter visit.'

'I was about to confirm a spa weekend when someone from Angel Ninebarks offered us a short-notice cancellation. I grabbed it without asking about the accommodation, so you'll have to forgive me if it's another four-share. Let's hope for quiet nights this time around. Who knew that such a placid woman would holler in her sleep like that. What was her name?'

'Prudence Boyce, book-binder; lives in Leek.' We laughed at my fine recall. 'Let's hope Pru is enjoying a staycation this weekend. Have you decided what activity to do?'

'Japanese woodblock printing. If we're not making a community piece, I'll give my efforts to Monica when we get back on Monday.'

'I forgot it's Mum's birthday! Oh well, she'll love anything with a Ninebarks emblem on it. She said you'd asked her to come with us this weekend.'

'I thought she might appreciate a return visit after so many years, but with the mounds of extra work coming her way, and your grandma's demands, Monica has barely a minute for herself. I'm not convinced that either Bradley or your dad appreciate just how much she holds the family together.'

π

Harriet's observations were spot on. While Grandma Radka's unrelenting requests were generally aimed at her four children, all of whom lived within a five-mile radius, several landed in my mother's capable lap. Without the maternal tie, it was easier to deal with an imperious mother-in-law like Raddy. I, however, was guilty as charged. Mum was no pushover, but she was the ultimate caregiver, the single exception being Sebastian, but that was his fault. He'd never recovered from that first disastrous dinner party encounter at Embla, the one where he was supposed to make a good impression.

Seb was unaware of Mum's ecological pedigree, and in an attempt to impress us with his professional credentials, he made a passionate, albeit long-winded case for 'clean food' as the basis for peak health and fitness. After two courses of his waffle, my mother left the table. We weren't sure if she planned to return, (this had been known), but come back she did, holding a wonky, mud-caked carrot. *Is this clean enough for you, Sebastian? Picked this morning from the allotment, while you were dreaming of being first past the friggin' post.* Sebastian had mustered a smile amidst the laughter but had been wary of her ever since.

When he took over the tenancy at number 44, speculation was rife. Bradley was unusually chipper, as if he'd engineered the love-match of the century, and while this wasn't true, I had no intention of curbing his enthusiasm. As was her custom, Mum asked me straight out if Seb and I were in love, and did we intend to live together – not an unreasonable question for an interested mother to ask her adored daughter – but with no affirmative answer available, and feeling slightly aggrieved by it all, I flounced over to number 44 for an entire week, even though Seb made it clear I had disturbed his finely-tuned routine.

Questions of that nature had long since dried up. Was it even worth reviewing our 'friends with benefits' status? Our hectic schedules had pretty much drowned out any benefits, while an evening with just the two of us was as rare as a great white thunderstorm – rarer still when Sebastian picked up his share of the tab. His busy personal training/sports massage client list never seemed to produce the equivalent in earnings, although there was way too much new sports gear for my forensic beak to account for. He flatly refused my offer to do his books, knowing it would have saved him money, but even so, I could hardly call the constabulary as much as it made me uneasy, so the riddle remained unsolved.

A tight pull across my shoulders derailed my train of thought. The car had just passed the signpost for our destination. We were almost there. 'Harriet, I've a suggestion: let's kick the boys, the triathlon and work into touch for the entire weekend.'

She tooted her horn, and the driver in front showed us the finger. Laughing hysterically, we gave him the peace sign and drove on.

3

The large cherrywood desk squatting at the foot of the impressive staircase hall was unattended. Harriet was about to go in search of assistance when out of nowhere, a young girl/woman scooted over, plonked down on the office chair and skidded to a halt in front of the computer.

'First timers?'

'No, actually, this is our third stay. We usually come at Easter. Long, boring story. I'm Harriet Hayle, and this is April.'

'I'm Tish Swanson: guest helper, part of the furniture.'

As she scanned the screen, seemingly unaware of our scrutiny, I smiled at her *Here Comes The* *** neon T-shirt (the 'sun' was a super-shiny currant bun). Tish's rebel hairstyle proved that half term had arrived. She was likely to be a staff member's offspring, earning holiday cash, so I gave her a mental thumbs up. As a rule, I got a buzz from chatting to strangers, finding out about their lives and whatnot, and there weren't many occasions when other people had to organise me, but fatigue was pressing on my shoulders like a bricklayer's hod, so I opted for the nearest chair to take the strain. My jaded gaze settled on Tish's bundle of kaleidoscopic wrist bands, the kind you get at festivals and fund-raising events. As she reached across the desk, my stomach backflipped at the sight of a latticework of silver scars covering the underside of her right wrist. A split-second later, she pulled down her sleeve and turned towards us with a grin that revealed a startling set of teeth.

'Room 6 – lucky you to bag the only twin with ensuite, *and* an up-close-and-personal sunset view. Have you booked your bits and bobs?'

'We've already chosen our workshops if that's what you mean. Is there a massage session available?' Harriet shifted impatiently from hip to hip. She pocketed the room key, although no one locked their doors here.

'Just the one left – Saturday, 4.30pm, in the drawing room. Guess you'll have to fight it out, in a non-fisticuff way, if you get my drift.'

'April's boyfriend is a sports masseur, so she's okay on that front. What about reflexology?'

'That'll work. I'll sign your sister up for a session with Iris Kyler on Saturday at 2pm, in the library.'

'Sister-in-law, actually.'

Harriet was getting twitchy at the over-familiarity, so I stepped in. 'Harriet is married to my brother, and he's as thick as thieves with my insignificant other. She deserves a massage, *and* a medal ...'

A burst of laughter from the kitchen drew our collective attention. There was a buzz about the house, unlike our previous visits when the silence smothered you like a pea souper. Maybe it was always like this in May. At any rate, I was mighty glad to be here. 'What's all the commotion?'

'Lise is back. Everyone's super excited to see her again, especially Elkie, and she is *never* ruffled.'

Tish rolled the chair away from the desk and stood, without further enlightening us as to who Lise and Elkie were. She was evidently desperate to return to the frolics.

Pointing to her right, 'Room 6 is at the end of the hallway. Lunch is in an hour, but feel free to make yourselves a cuppa. The volunteer rota is in the dining area, so don't forget to sign up. Anything else, give us a yell. Catch ya later!'

The byte-sized firework whizzed off into the kitchen. I heaved myself upright, picked up my holdall and followed Harriet's jaunty step past the chatter.

'Lady Luck is smiling, April – a twin room! We'll sleep well this weekend. Did you notice Tish's teeth? Not a decent peg in the bottom row.'

'Great smile, though, and I loved the treacle-toffee haystacks. I counted sixteen evenly spaced bunches. Can't be easy on your neck and shoulders, tying your hair up like that.'

Harriet grinned at my nerdy head count. Thankfully she didn't mention Tish's scars – it was a guessing game I had no intention of playing. As she pushed open the bedroom door, I bumped into her emergency stop. The spacious, high-ceilinged décor would lift even Bradley's sourpuss chops. Harriet stepped inside and ran her hand tenderly across the wallpaper.

'Yum, yum – pale peonies on silk. Could be seventeenth century, Cantonese. Oh, would you look at that April, hanging above those delightful antique bedsteads. It's a Dennington frieze, early twentieth century.'

While Harriet continued her stalk-eyed tour, I headed for the double doors and stepped out onto a mosaic patio. The sun's rays had drenched the walled herb garden and the warmth was glorious. On the south side of the circular pathway, I spied a gorgeous handmade bench, fit for a witch/wizard. Someone had parked an ancient wheel barrow containing a wooden trug beside it, as if they had just that minute downed tools for a break. The borders brimmed with all sorts of herbs and had attracted the attention of numerous conscientious insects. And in the centre stood a tree whose smooth red-copper bark shimmered in the sunlight and crowned in white blossom, like a hopeful bride. We had something similar in our garden. 'Hey, Harriet, check this out.' I turned to see her bum-bouncing on the bed.

'Crisp laundered sheets, hand-stitched eiderdowns over soft woollen blankets, and the desk has an inkwell! The ensuite is spotlessly utilitarian with bottles of yummy lotions. Room 6 is so unlike the rest of the house but equally as delightful.'

'What do you think it was used for?'

'An office, or a sewing room, perhaps. Oh, I know, let's ask the tooth fairy. Tish is part of the furniture, after all.'

'Not nice Harriet,' but I grinned all the same. It was so good to be here. This place perfectly suited our turbo-charged personalities. We'd been on several mini-breaks before, but generally by day two I'd have abandoned my fitness programme for daytime telly and butterscotch chocolate squares while Harriet star-jumped her way through a gazillion exercise classes before conking out. Angel Ninebarks was a much better fit – a healthy balance of creative stimulation, interesting conversation, and rest.

Little did we know what a treat was in store when we rocked up at the house three years ago. Harriet had unearthed Angel Ninebarks' existence whilst researching a work project and couldn't wait to tell me about it. Her Master's degree in Textile History had landed her the dream job as head buyer for Fitzmaurice, the Midlands equivalent of *Liberty of London*. To have the opportunity to stay in a house of this calibre was her version of heaven. Harriet was delighted to be my personal curator, not least as there was always something new to discover.

Angel Ninebarks was originally known as The Dower House, a Staffordshire red brick Arts and Crafts style property originally owned by Marguerite Monkton. To help with the upkeep, the arthritic dowager employed a local couple, the Heathcotes, to whom she became extremely fond. Frieda worked in the garden while Edmund maintained the house. Before Marguerite's eyesight failed, Frieda had planted a fusion of flowers and shrubs amongst which were rows of vivid Angel Ninebark bushes. Their orange-red leaves and ivory cup flowers had thrilled the old lady, and she'd often insist that the couple join her for afternoon tea by that very spot.

The Heathcote's tender ministrations to the dowager and her treasured house were not forgotten. After Marguerite's death, her only son and heir, (after protracted discussions with the family lawyers) honoured his mother's wish by allowing the Heathcotes first refusal to buy it. Somehow, Frieda and Edmund found the money. It wasn't long before a dedicated band of live-in staff and supporters had put together an innovative workshop programme at the renamed 'Angel Ninebarks'. That was fifty years ago.

π

The Arts and Crafts Movement had set about re-humanising the purpose of the worker and their work in an age where industrialisation had obliterated individual creativity and the countryside in favour of the factory. Angel Ninebarks had transitioned seamlessly into an innovative hub without losing its ambiance or diminishing its heritage. Many of the original fabrics, furniture, and decorative objects remained. When Harriet explained that every window had been designed to suit the individual needs of each room, hence the uneven mix of casements, sashes, and bulls eyes, the logic of it overrode my squeamish obsession for symmetry.

In the large, panelled dining room, three round mahogany eight-seater tables and a smaller 'quiet table' were furnished with Morris and Co. walnut and rush chairs. The lustrous laburnum wallpaper was designed by Agnes Garrett who, along with her cousin Rhoda, were the first known women interior designers. At the far end of the dining room was a well-stocked, open all hours tea/coffee/cake area. Vision-inducing works of art were everywhere. In the drawing room hung a bewitching tapestry of the Norse legend, *Midgard*, whose half-human/half-tree figures were entwined under the glow of a golden orb. My mother's name was listed alongside the other makers, proof that she'd had a life before Bradley and I came along. The tranquil library and living room provided further comfort for the current quota of fourteen guests and six staff when not doubling up as treatment space during the afternoons.

Adjacent to the house was an enormous eighteenth-century oak-beamed barn in which the handcraft tradition thrived. Every object had been photographed and catalogued in a series of exquisite albums with *The Angels of Ninebarks* embroidered on their duck egg satin covers. The pieces that weren't sold to raise funds to support the guilds were either used or displayed in the house and garden. Angel Ninebarks epitomised the movement's manifesto: simplicity, beauty, and utility.

π

As we unpacked our bags, scintillating smells were a reminder that lunch would soon be ready. Without warning, a flaming arrow shot agonisingly across my upper back. Maybe I should have accepted Sebastian's apology massage, even if only to smooth things over, but it was the last thing I wanted. As the family metronome, I was generally relied upon to calm everyone's pre-event nerves, organise schedules, and carry out bike maintenance, but Seb's over-inflated reaction to our re-scheduled weekend away had tipped me over the edge. With the office fiasco still raw, I suggested he stuff his sodding regime and get a life. The massage gesture was kindly meant, but there was a conversation waiting in the wings.

While Harriet finished her wash and brush up, I swallowed two capsules and reminded myself not to think about family or work. We were here, it was great, and there was nothing like a tasty home-cooked meal to lift a sagging body and a flagging spirit.

4

The dining room chatter was pleasantly mid-volume. During lunch, Harriet made breezy conversation while I wended my way through a delicious pepper and pesto tart followed by a slice of maple syrup cake, listening to my fellow diners' Ninebark stories. As most of them were regulars the mood was high, particularly for those lucky enough to have bagged a massage with the enigmatic Lise Michelson. By all accounts, she wasn't here the previous year and no one knew why.

The only biographical information available was this: Lise was Frieda and Edmund Heathcote's niece. She came to work at Angel Ninebarks in May, before taking to the waterways on her narrow boat until August, when she reunited with friends for a month-long restful interlude at the house. Lise had taught various crafts before, but some years ago had moved into massage therapy, a fusion of Ayurvedic and Swedish, sort of, if we knew what they meant. Having experienced this marvel before, a number of guests had booked months in advance, although apparently there was so much more to Lise than a forty-minute effleurage, but exactly what they meant no one could successfully articulate.

Our table was at the far end of the room, next to the tea bar. There was a direct line of sight between Lise's table and mine, but I'd resisted the temptation to look over. Somehow, though, I got the feeling we were aware of each other's whereabouts although it was more likely to be my febrile imagination, which I'll freely admit, was prone to flights of fancy. Whilst fetching a cup of tea, I caved in to curiosity and glanced across to see Tish's haystacks bobbing enthusiastically in the direction of a striking, choppy-white-haired woman wearing a bleached blue jersey smock, and whose presence filled the space around her. So, that was Lise.

As everyone else appeared to have dropped anchor for the duration, I began clearing the table. It took willpower to resist a second helping of pudding, but my decision had nothing to do with winning Seb's approval. Mercifully, his obsession with my fluctuating waistline was on the wane, as were the endless reports of his clients' success, shared in the vain hope I might follow suit. Although I no longer competed in the triathlon, I could cycle for miles and go the distance with Bradley in the pool, but that's as far as exercise went. From way back Mum had drilled me to listen to my body's needs, but the relentless demands required to pursue Gita Nair's cosmic trajectory had resulted in consequences for which I was now paying the price.

Relieved to be on the move, I carried a handful of plates into the kitchen. Harriet had volunteered for dinner prep whereas I'd plumped for washing up. Before filling the large stainless-steel sink with hot soapy water, I tidied and cleaned down the worktops, and stacked everything to be washed in order. First into the suds went an enormous pasta pan. Despite my reddening hands, the act of scouring and rinsing was incredibly satisfying. Daydreaming, I thought of Bradley, and how he used to say that washing-up gloves were for wimps. He'd clash and bash the saucepans like a demented percussionist while I dried and put everything away, and all the while we'd bump and elbow in a bid to see who'd crack first. Besting each other, even when washing dishes, had been our number one priority until he had his rugby accident, after which he was allowed to skulk in his bedroom and generally duck out of things.

Despite his bouts of gloom, I continued to idolise my big brother. The concussion may not have left any visible effects on Bradley's sixteen-year-old brain, but there was no doubt in my mind that his light had shone less brightly. Before that we were equally matched, academically and in sport, and destined for the university of our choice. When his school performances nose-dived, the counsellor suggested a series of sessions to treat the depression, although my dad refused to acknowledge the diagnosis. Bradley had bailed out of the therapy plan early, but still, he'd done okay, and after a bumpy start, was making a good effort at managing Uncle Max's health club out on the eco-park. Sebastian's arrival, however, had lit a fuse under my brother. To catch a glimpse of 'young Brad' was to be celebrated, especially by my father who was buoyed by his precious son's return to form.

$$\pi$$

My childhood reverie was interrupted by the offer of help. Lise had appeared and was holding a tea towel. From up close, it was difficult to guess her age, but when she smiled it was like the sun coming out. I smiled right back. 'Sorry about that. I was away with the fairies. I'm April, by the way. Lovely lunch, wasn't it?'

'A fine homecoming. You cut your food in exactly the same way as my brother.'

Lise had been watching me! Did she know I was just that moment thinking about Bradley? I rinsed the pan three times before passing it to her, all the while grappling for a coherent response. It was extraordinary. 'My brother barely chews his food. He's long past the age to listen to my mother, not that he's ever taken any notice. Brad still tries to do everything at the speed of light. It's a family trait.'

'Your father's influence, perhaps.'

Once again, I was caught off guard. Maybe it was my dad's influence. Whether competing in sporting events, organising family holiday contests, or excelling at work, few would disagree that Vaughan Hayle was a great motivator and brilliant strategist. He'd risen to head of operations at Carrow Corp, the multi-national consumer goods company, through sheer productivity, energy, and will. When required, he was charisma itself. Propped up by his younger siblings' esteem, my dad was universally admired, in particular by my aunts who often wondered (out loud) why he had married my mother, as if she'd had no say in the matter.

Dad's professional developments may have encompassed emotional intelligence and an enviable corporate vision, but when it came to Bradley and me, his expectations outweighed his affection by a country mile. And yet there was something about Vaughan Hayle that made us want to please him. On the surface, my aunts may have had a point with regards my parents' compatibility, but with my lousy relationship track record, I wasn't best equipped to comment. There were times however, when my dad looked at my mum in a way that forced me to look away, as if I were trespassing.

Lise stacked the last pan beside the oven before hanging up the tea towel. She thanked me for washing up, said it was nice to meet me, and left the kitchen, removing any possibility of a reply. As the water drained from the sink, I wondered what that was all about.

π

It was wonderful to be back in the barn. Sofie Warburg, our tutor for the weekend, had brought the history of stained glass up to date in a captivating way. Although influenced by the medium's medieval past, her designs were inspired by the early 20th century pioneering stained glass artists such as Margaret Rope and Mabel Esplin. Alongside depictions of the natural world, Sofie chose to feature the scores of unacknowledged craftswomen whose works she was committed to unearthing and restoring to glory.

Who knew there was so much to consider when it came to making glasswork. From a functional perspective, we were encouraged to examine how light passes through the glass, and how it impacts an atmosphere, or space. Environmentally, the use of recycled materials, silicone, and lead-free paint ensured sustainability. Personally, it was a different story. Sofie, frustratingly, had almost nothing to say about herself. Surely I wasn't the only one who was interested in the backstory of this diminutive, softly-spoken woman whose prodigious confidence and knowledge was carried so lightly. It was this nonchalance that set the Angel Ninebarks folk apart. Whether they were unwilling to share their histories, or were really not that bothered, it raised the question why I wanted or needed to know in the first place.

The current project, a modern interpretation of Edward Burne-Jones' *Pomona, Roman Goddess of Abundance*, was well underway. As was the custom, each group added to it until it was complete. Our task that afternoon was to focus on the bottom section of the panel by making templates of the foliage before tracing them onto pieces of glass. Once we'd recovered from the startling realisation that we were contributing to such a magnificent project, the group set to. Quietly and diligently, we followed Sofie's instruction until our hands found the skills to work independently. Then, in what seemed like a blink, tools were downed and cleaned, until the following morning.

π

Harriet sat at the desk, making notes. Her printmaking course confirmed that the eighth-century woodcutting tradition was thriving, and like ours, it perfectly fitted Angel Ninebarks' philosophy. Working on the far side of the barn, her group had been shown how to gouge various shapes and patterns from either wild cherry or Baltic birch plywood, before using non-toxic water-based inks to make the prints. There was no doubt that Harriet's 'woman sitting by a stream' would look fab.

Hunger and anticipation drove us to the dining room where we carried our soup bowls and plates of breads and spreads to the table, greeting our new acquaintances like old friends. Lise was nowhere in sight. This was curiously disappointing as I had felt drawn to her in a way which was impossible to explain. Whilst spreading a generous dollop of mushroom pâté onto a slice of spelt toast, I made the mistake of asking Tish where she was.

'Lise has taken Frieda back to Quietwater. They never stay on for supper. Lise and Elkie sleep on the Anna Lee. The trip is on the horizon, so there's a lot to get ready.'

Tish's assumption that we were familiar with the minutiae of Lise Michelson's life was beginning to grate, and I had no intention of asking anything further, despite a longing to know more. Having just burned the roof of my mouth, I belatedly blew the contents of my soup spoon while she nattered on.

'I've never been on board, but by all accounts the boat is super cool, and has all the latest eco-techno bits and bobs, which is no surprise is it, given the Angel Ninebarks' way of going about things.'

'And what about the Monkton Estate, Tish. Is there much co-operation between the owners and here?' asked Harriet.

'Yeah – loads. The Monktons have passed the day-to-day running over to their daughter, Cornelia. We call her Nelly. When I work for her on the estate, it doesn't feel like work, if you know what I mean. She's been to lots of our workshops and Frieda has put her right on the growing front. Within five years, Nelly aims to have a mini version of the Knepp Estate up and running, and I reckon she'll do it.'

Blushing furiously, Tish chomped down on a huge piece of bread as if going for gold, and I wondered if it hurt her to eat, given the current state of her dentistry. Was there something going on between her and Nelly? If there was, for some reason it made me feel unaccountably happy. Tish continued chatting, and then she put down her spoon and said, in all seriousness, 'I know where I'd rather be when it all goes tits up.'

I had to smile. Harriet's aversion to coarse language had been muffled by the friendly, laid back atmosphere. She was in the mood for conversation. 'So, Tish, let me get this right: the Anna- Lee is a canal boat of some description and is situated nearby. Is this where Lise lives?'

'Only when she's in England. Lise rustles up a crew and goes off on her narrowboat for the summer. Apparently she's been doing it for decades and knows the waterways like the back of her hands.' Tish crossed her fingers. 'With a bucket of luck I'll be invited one day, although Lise knows so many people it could take a while yet, but on her last trip, she took out a guest helper and his kids, so you never know.'

'How kind of her.' Harriet dabbed at her mouth with the napkin. 'I'm *sooo* looking forward to my massage tomorrow.'

'Seriously, Harriet, you won't be disappointed. There's a rumour Lise may give it up, which would be a total bummer, but no one can stop the clock, can they? Not that she's over the hill by any stretch, but there's only so much energy available for the likes of us. Lise spends most of her time with Frieda in the garden, although no one retires here. Edmund still runs the carpentry workshops and he's well over eighty – *and* he has his own teeth!'

We chuckled our way to the library where Iris Kyler, reflexologist, was about to begin her talk on the body's meridian systems. If we were still awake at the end of it, she promised an update on Angel Ninebarks' fiftieth anniversary celebrations, scheduled for the following May. With mugs of tea in hand, and the Roycroft lamps exuding a homely glow, Tish had bagged the seat next to me and throughout the talk, took it upon herself to interject in as quiet a voice as she could muster. I didn't mind in the least, but with the possibility of being tailgated, I was determined to conserve any resurgent energy for the next frantic session at work. Harriet, as was her custom, had fallen asleep, but no one seemed to mind. As soon as the talk ended, we bolted to the bedroom for the comfort of cool fresh bedsheets and a holler-free sleep.

5

Iris Kyler may have been the most gifted reflexologist in the universe, but as soon as my bum hit the recliner in the makeshift therapy room, *aka* library, there was no way of knowing. When she woke me up forty minutes later with a glass of warm lemon water, Iris suggested that I literally put my feet up until supper as, evidently, my mind-body-spirit were under par.

Back in room 6, the afternoon sun poured through the patio doors and onto the carpet. It was the perfect spot on which to lie down. My aching back immediately released into the thick rug, ready for a sunbeam marinade. Once again I dozed off – well, that was until a snuffling sound ended my afternoon delight. The source of the melody emanated from the herb bed. It was a dog. Having never had the pleasure of human's best friend for a pet, the subject of dog breeds wouldn't win me any quiz points, but my best guess was a German Shepherd. We eyed each other with mutual inquisitiveness. 'She' was a beauty: slender, mid-height, and her regal red/gold coat totally befitted her haughty air.

Lise was placing various cuttings in a trug, suspended from the crook of her arm. Effortlessly, she gathered the herby produce, and paused to inhale the fragrance. I was about to creep out of sight when they turned towards the patio doors and an inexplicable force propelled me into the garden. The dog's tail scarcely wagged, but she wasn't unfriendly, so I bent down to stroke her luxurious coat, desperately trying to hide my crimson cheeks. 'Hello again, Lise. I hope I'm not disturbing you.'

'It is me who is disturbing you. My apologies. This is Elkie.'

'So, this is Elkie! Tish mentioned her earlier. She's adorable. Is she yours?'

'Elkie belongs to herself, but she mostly lives with Frieda and Edmund at Quietwater Cottage.'

'A free spirit, then.' I straightened up and peered into the basket. 'Looks like you've been busy.'

'Remedies and poultices. England has a fantastic medicine cabinet if you know where to look. Are you familiar with lemon balm?'

Lise held out a bunch of fresh green leaves. The citrus scent tingled my nostrils. 'Hm, lovely. I think Mum has made tea with these.'

She nodded. 'The plant has healing properties. It eases anxiety and insomnia and is also said to enhance mood.'

'My brother could do with some of that.' We laughed, and her ocean eyes crinkled.

'I'll make a remedy for you.'

'Wow – thanks, Lise! That's really kind of you. Not sure Bradley will drink it, though.'

'But you can.' She turned to look at the sundial. 'It's almost time for my last body. Elkie, say goodbye to your new friend.'

'Will you join us for supper?'

'No, but I suspect many of you will need an early night.'

As the companions faded into the distance, I sat on the witch/wizard bench under the waning light and was bowled over by an urge to follow them. Everything felt so tranquil, including me. Reluctant to disturb this exceptional state of affairs, I stayed there for a long, long while. Tish was right about the sunset. Its awesome display kept me entertained until the cooling air sent me inside. Soon after, Harriet came crashing in – wide-eyed, oily, and uncustomarily incoherent.

'April, I've had *the* most amazing massage ever! I simply must lie down. Will you wake me in an hour?'

She collapsed on the bed, and there she remained until seven thirty the following morning, when I nudged her with a cup of tea. 'Harriet, the breakfast gong has been gonged.'

Her throaty groan was comical. My sister-in-law never slept in, and according to Brad, she'd even been up with the larks every day of their honeymoon. Harriet levered herself up and sipped the strong black liquid, her nose wrinkling. Wisps of tangerine hair plastered her forehead. I resisted the temptation to send my brother a photo of his gorgeous wife.

'What day is it?'

'Sunday.'

'I missed dinner prep, and the talk!'

'Never fear, Tish will fill you in.'

She put down the mug and fell back on the pillow. 'Oohhh, I feel as if I've been hit by a milk cart, but in a good way, if there is a good way, and if milk carts still exist. April, have I really been asleep for fourteen hours?'

'I didn't have the heart to wake you, but you'll be relieved to know you weren't the only one missing at supper. There'll be a chorus of hunger pangs this morning.'

'Now you mention it, I am famished. Hey, why don't you ask Lise to squeeze you in for a massage? I told her about your back condition, your job, the family – in fact, I was rabbiting so much, Lise asked me to stop talking! I've never met anyone as direct as her before, excluding us that is, but she wasn't remotely offensive. Anyway, I'm convinced a session with her will do you the world of ...'

'I'm fine, Harriet, honest. Why don't you have a refreshing shower, and I'll meet you in the dining room.'

Harriet sat up and swung her athletic legs out of the bed. She stretched and yawned and smiled her medal-winning smile, the one that had captured Bradleys hard heart.

'Aren't we lucky, April – we have our family, our careers, Angel Ninebarks, and I've almost finished an exquisite print for Monica's birthday.'

I left Harriet to her euphoria and went in search of porridge.

6

Our final session was almost over. As dismaying as this was, the window had come on a treat. Using a glass cutter, we'd scored and cut the coloured panes, and had ground down the edges before adding copper foil, ready for soldering. Sofie intended to hang the new panel in the hallway before the month end. To see it *in situ* when we returned the following year would really be something to look forward to. So many caring hands had contributed to its creation, and our names would be recorded for posterity in an *Angels of Ninebarks* album.

During our final tea break, in answer to someone else's question, Sofie explained that she was currently researching examples of Pre-Raphaelite stained-glass windows in and around Staffordshire, to include in her new book. As an academic *and* a craftswoman, was Sofie consciously bridging her left and right brain? That very subject had been raised over dinner the previous evening, prompting yet another riveting conversation which had got me thinking. What if the historic uncoupling of art and science had caused unintended consequences to our relationship with the world, and we were only just waking up to it? The consensus was that it didn't have to be either/or, but wasn't that the way most education systems functioned: to drill down into a student's so-called talent or aptitude, further narrowing the scope until forty or fifty years later, health and wealth permitting, the opportunity to use the other hemisphere might arise?

As we sat quietly together in the cathedral-esque barn with shafts of sunlight anointing our eager heads, my shoulders were at this point seriously unhappy. It was impossible to follow the soldering technique without flinching. Unsurprisingly, Sofie had noticed this, and suggested I finish up early, as my contributions were very much appreciated. This was typical of the way these fine Ninebark souls treated one another – an affectionate hand here, a listening ear there. Meandering back to the room, I wondered why my life didn't mirror their collaborative vibe. There was no rush, or competition; no need to plan ahead; mealtimes were for sharing and cementing friendships. Fielding & Nair were excellent employers, but they had one goal only, and as long as you shared it, you were cheered on. Until then, I'd never considered F&N as anything other than a forward-thinking company ...

That was it! Everything was future based: forecasts, accruals, revenue, gross margins, profits & losses. Commanding the accountancy landscape with their brand was the ultimate objective, but then what? *Hey, hang on a minute, April, don't you appreciate the certainty that comes from working with numbers? And what about the intended promotion, the one you've worked so hard for?*

It was far too beguiling to stay inside, and besides, those unbidden questions were twisting my melons as Uncle Max liked to say. I picked up a blanket, and stepped into the herb garden, hoping to 'bump' into Lise before we left. Yet again she had been commandeered over lunch, and with Harriet as a new acolyte, no less. I was beginning to feel as if Lauren Laverne had sent me to the desert island without the bloody discs! For the third time that weekend I had sat at the quiet table, alone. I may have cut my food into small squares, but I could match Bradley for speed eating. Not so that day. Instead, I decided to focus on the sensation of each mouthful, feeling the texture, enjoying the taste. It felt good 'not' to talk.

Mum would have approved of my mindful eating. No matter how rowdy Embla's dinner table, she was rarely agitated. *Quietly independent*, that's how my dad had once described her. It used to annoy me how Mum rarely joined in the family events, and that my dad had stood in her corner. *Your mum and me may have different perspectives, but we share the same core values, April. One day you'll understand.* Despite this incomprehensible attitude, I continued to trail my inimitable father everywhere, taking his word as gospel, although not everyone felt the same. One time, when we rocked up at our holiday lodge at Brightside Park, someone said, *it's time to take cover – the LoudHaylers have arrived.* I took it for granted that our fellow holidaymakers couldn't wait to reunite for another fortnight of Cornish fun with the Hayles, but that particular family had disappeared for the rest of the week.

π

I headed towards the spinney. How the others could stay inside chatting while the weather was so good was beyond me, but on the other hand, I had the whole garden to myself. During last year's Easter visit temperatures had registered record-breaking figures, and it was whilst walking towards the wooded area that I came across a hammock, suspended between two sycamores. Lying in it had been surprisingly good for my back, and I was in the market for a repeat experience. As I approached the spot, an invader had beaten me to it. There was no mistaking the hair.

Lise swung herself up. 'I'm cooked. It's your turn, April. The hammock will release your shoulder pain.'

How did Lise know my back was sore? *Harriet said she'd talked about you during her massage.*

'Sofie and Iris mentioned your difficulties. We take care of our people.'

'Yes, and you do it so well. It's been really tough at work of late, and there's a truckload of stuff going on elsewhere.' I sighed. 'The weekend is almost over and, well, I don't actually want to go home, which is shocking to even say it out loud as I never feel that way ...' I willed my mouth to stop talking about me. 'Have you had a good day, Lise?'

'Surprising, and tiring. Perhaps my massage days are coming to an end.'

'From what I've heard, Tish and Harriet won't be the only ones to be sorry about that.'

'But we must tend to ourselves.'

'Oh – yeah, of course. Not sure how good I am at that, though'

'You are here, and that is a start.'

Lise held out the hammock while I carefully lowered myself into position. The tenderness with which she wrapped the blanket over me sparked a brim-full of tears. It was mortifying. As I lay there, furiously blinking them away, the sun blazed a halo behind Lise's head (or had I imagined that?) She tucked a tissue into my hand.

'Let the pain out, April. You will feel better for it.'

She pulled the hammock towards her and released it into a gentle rocking motion, like my parents used to do at the swing park, and incredibly, I was a toddler again – red dress, white socks, black shoes and laughing wildly to go higher, higher. Now, the sway had the opposite effect by soothing my physical tension, and soon after, the emotional wave subsided. I stayed there for what seemed like an eternity until Elkie's nose nuzzled my hand. The sky was a deep cosmic blue, and the temperature had dropped by several degrees. Lise was sitting on a nearby bench. She poured a cup of steaming liquid from a flask and waited for me to stand before passing it over. The taste was bitter, but strangely pleasant. I drank it in a single gulp.

'Supper will soon be ready, and we are about to leave. There is a remedy for you, at the desk.'

'You're going! Harriet wanted to thank you for the massage.'

Lise took the cup and reached for my elbow. To say I was unsteady was the understatement of the year. As soon as the wobbling stopped, she released my arm. 'Thank you for being so kind, Lise.'

We stood there, and her head tilted towards a sound which sliced through the darkening sky.

'Ah, the tawny is home.'

She smiled as if a precious child had returned. Then she turned to me, her face obscured in the shadows.

'I have a narrowboat, moored at Quietwater. Tish may have mentioned it. On the last Friday of this month, the Anna Lee will set out on a four-day trip along the Shropshire Union Canal, before departing for the summer. There is a single lock on this particular stretch of water – an easy ride. Perhaps you'd like to join us. You can rest and gather your energy.'

I'm rarely lost for words. Never before had I been on or considered taking a trip on a narrow boat. Westwych lay only a few miles from Barrow upon Soar, and we'd cycled the towpaths before but had never walked them. The boats appeared to float by in an abstract way and at a frustratingly slow speed – maybe that was the point.

'I'll leave the details at the desk. Goodbye, April.'

After a brief hug, Lise disappeared into the garden with Elkie gliding beside her while I stood there, wondering whether to laugh or cry. Four days on a narrow boat! Peace, rest, *gather your energy* ... who had ever said that to me before? Mum! She was on the same wave length, and though it had been a while since I was the recipient of her attention, plenty of others were. She had left a career in Occupational Therapy to set up 'Homebodies,' with her friend Liz. Its primary purpose was to build self-sustaining creative networks for older people in addition to supporting those who wished to remain in their own homes, until the end. It wasn't unusual for Mum to be called out in the middle of the night, to hold the hand of her 'homebody' as they left this world; to comfort the families; assist with arrangements. Dad had abandoned his attempts to persuade her to employ more staff, although despite his outward show of frustration, he admired her commitment.

I pulled the blanket around my shoulders and walked back to the house. Mum would be thrilled to hear about Lise's invitation, of that I was certain. As for the boys ... The noise of a hairdryer filtered under the door of room 6. I paused outside. Should I tell Harriet about Lise's offer? *Does that mean you plan to go?* There was no denying the sizzle in my stomach. The trip required a single day's annual leave and I still had five owing from the previous year. Sebastian and Bradley might be put out, but they didn't exactly *need* me. But Lise had said 'we'. She must have meant Elkie, although according to Tish, lots of people travelled with her, so I was probably just another deck hand to help out. Did it matter? I was easy going and a tidy houseguest, and in any case, this wasn't my event to organise. All I had to do was turn up. Lise hadn't asked for an answer, so there was no pressure either way, only my fear of the unknown.

7

No sooner had I entered the dining room than Tish's rainbow bands waved me over.

'April, have you got a minute?'

'Let me fetch breakfast, and I'll join you.'

I felt so upbeat, I'd have cleaned every window in the house if asked. The previous nights' sleep had been the best in ages, and there was a glimpse of my energy returning. After having slept on it, the decision was made. I'd be a fool not to join Lise on the boat. I decided to tell Harriet before we left the house as that way we'd work out a strategy on the way home.

When I came back to the table, Tish's features were uncharacteristically solemn.

'April, I'm so sorry if my chatter drove you to the quiet table this weekend. You may have noticed that I get over-excited. Believe it or not, I used to be much noisier, but now ...'

Suddenly I understood. Beneath the effervescence was a sorrow that made my heart ache. I squeezed her hand.

'To be truthful, April, I don't know where I'd be without Angel Ninebarks. There's a good chance they'll ask me to join the staff as Iris is moving on, and I've been on the waiting list for ages. Ever since Frieda and Edmund took me under their wings, I've learned enough to contribute to the upkeep of the house, and to earn a living. As a staff member, there are so many benefits, *and* I'll be invited to join the August time-out. Can you imagine it, April – an entire month of total chill with a bunch of fab folks in this beautiful sanctuary.'

'It sounds heavenly. So, where is home?'

'A bedsit in town. I've a few jobs on the go and I sign up for guest helper as often as I can.' Tish pulled down her bottom lip. 'See these? I lost most of my teeth during a fight. Things got pretty bad for a while, until Ninebarks, that is. I've been saving like mad to have them fixed properly and I've almost got enough. It's been one disaster after another but coming here has restored my faith in humanity. Have you noticed how no one asks where you bought your threads?'

I nodded. Gossip was scarce, and mostly everyone listened without interrupting. Tish had spared me the worst of it. I felt grateful and awful all at once. 'You've found more than a home, Tish. In this environment, you can only thrive.'

'Lucky me, eh?' Look, here's my number if you'd like a coffee sometime.' She pushed a scrap of paper into my hand. 'Thanks for listening, April.'

'Hey, Tish, before you disappear, there's something I want to tell you. Actually, it's a bit embarrassing ...' With heat flushing my cheeks, there was nothing else to do but blurt it out. 'Lise has asked me to join her and Elkie for a weekend on the Anna Lee.'

'Really?'

She threw her wiry arms around my neck.

'You *have* to go! I'm *sooo* happy for you, April. You totally deserve it.'

'How can you say that Tish? You don't even know me.'

'I know a good'un when I see one. Make sure you keep in touch, April Hayle. I wanna hear all about it.'

Tish gently fist-pumped her chest before darting off to the kitchen. Porridge finished, I walked over to Harriet who was sitting on her own, spreading jam on a slice of toast in that decisive way of hers. I sat down. 'Sorry about that.'

'Your coffee's cold. What were you and Tish talking about?'

'This and that. She's had a rough time of it, but it looks as if things are turning around for her.' I grimaced at the cool liquid. 'I was just telling her how Lise has asked me to join her first boat trip out this season. It's at the end of May.'

'You?'

'Yes me, Harriet.'

'On her narrow boat?'

'Yup.'

'That's the same weekend as Bradley and Sebastian's event. How disappointing for you.'

'Why so? Surely the boys can manage without me for once in their lives.'

'But everyone is expecting you, particularly your dad.'

For the second time that morning, heat blasted my face, but this time it was in anger. Harriet's tight-lipped reaction was completely at odds with Tish's open-hearted response which had, as a matter of fact, blown me away as I'd only known her for five minutes.

Harriet rested her knife on the side of the plate. 'April, you're not seriously thinking of accepting Lise's offer. She's a stranger. For all you know, she could be ...'

'She could be what, Harriet? Why furrow your brow now? You've been singing her praises all weekend, along with the rest of the group.'

'Complimenting Lise Michelson's massage technique is hardly the same as showing concern for my sister-in-law's welfare.'

Family mediator I may have been, and outbursts were unusual, but my stubbornness was a trademark. What on earth did Harriet expect Lise to do to me? Did she think Angel Ninebarks was some kind of dating bar? Sensing I was ready to dig in, she realised the futility of continuing with her protest.

'April, I apologise. It's none of my business, so please forget I said anything about it. I'll talk to Bradley, and ...'

'No need, Harriet. I'll handle it.'

'And your dad?'

'He'll get over it. The last time I looked, Vaughan Hayle was just about eligible to join the grown-ups.' Our laughter contained more than a crumb of relief.

'As you say, April, the boys will cope. As a matter of fact, you do look tired, and despite trying to hide it, I can see your back is sore. By the way, Bradley has arranged for us to have dinner at Embla tonight. He's even organised a birthday cake, can you believe. We'll give Monica her present then. Sebastian will join us as soon as he's finished at the gym.' She checked her smart watch. 'Shall we go? I've stripped the beds, paid the balance, and the bags are in the car, which has now charged. I wanted to say goodbye to Lise, but ...'

'I'll thank her for you.'

Before joining Harriet outside, I stopped at the desk. Beside the computer was a package with my name on it. Inside it was a chestnut brown glass bottle, and a handwritten note:

Quietwater Bridge,
mid-morning

8

Geometrically speaking, our family is the equivalent of an equilateral triangle – impossible to present a best side to the world when every side is equally *ab fab*. Our coat of arms, should we have possessed one, would declare *Hayle – the family you simply can't live without*. Even our patois was steeped in combative sporting metaphor, much of which we'd invented to consolidate our uniqueness and further distance ourselves from the non-believers. Despite all that, while not quite capsizing us, it had taken a thirteen-year-old newcomer to challenge my unshakeable belief in the Good Ship Hayle.

Oleanna Irving arrived at Danesford Vale High School like a comet, showering everyone around her with stardust. Olly, one of her many monikers, was announced to our class by the head teacher, so we knew she was a person of importance. Her parents were artistic royalty. Nathalie Irving, (multi-award-winning theatre director), and Piers, (costume designer with an Oscar) had temporarily relocated from Islington to the area, having accepted a two-year contract with Mercia Arts, the jewel in Leicester's creative crown. They had rented an Edwardian villa with two pianos and was within walking distance to Danesford

Vale's unique media centre, the sole reason they chose the school. It was the perfect springboard from which Olly's future career was launched, and I was saved from disaster.

Until then, I'd been a popular and, according to my teachers, an exceptional student, but when a sudden growth spurt sent my spine spiralling into a twenty degree right-sided curve, the resulting scoliosis spelt disaster in untold ways. Dad had insisted on surgery; Mum said it wasn't bad enough to warrant such drastic action as she felt that my spine would improve with less invasive treatment. They left it to me to decide. The thought of having metal rods drilled into my skeleton freaked me out, so I was willing to submit to any and all treatment, with mixed results.

Cricket and hockey had to go, along with any hope of county selection. With that went my father's interest, or that's how it appeared, until I began to excel in mathematics, and cycling (my new upright bike was transformational). After Bradley's rugby concussion, my father had drifted like a ship without a rudder. He hadn't a clue how to cope with a depressed teenage son and, scarcely a year on, a terrified 'distorted' daughter, and left the restitution of his children's welfare largely to my mother.

While everyone else tip-toed around my strangely skewed appearance, Olly announced to her new classmates that she had come to drag us shirelings into her uptown cosmopolitan world, and appointed me, Crooked Polly, membership secretary of her new club, Square Hole (*round pegs, wonky tonks, and renegades welcome: zombies need not apply*). She made me laugh like no one else on earth. Saturday night sleepovers at hers were totally nuts. When not composing their own musicals, she and her siblings played a multitude of instruments, and were often dressed in *the* most outlandish costumes, while many of the house guests were famous for something or other. What Oleanna Irving didn't know about the arts wasn't worth knowing. Her musical limbs embraced everything from Italian opera to Eighties synth-pop bands such as Human League, Erasure, and Haircut 100. It became a weekly ritual: clear a space on her mucky bedroom floor and jerk about to *Favourite Shirts* on repeat until we felt sick.

Conversely, Olly couldn't stand it at Embla. The tournaments were too serious, and she had no desire to cheer on rugby or cycling teams with my pumped up cousins, although she and Mum got along famously. While Olly occasionally came for tea when no one was around, she stayed over for one night only. In a gesture designed to make her feel at home, Mum had organised a game of charades. Her team included Olly and Bradley. Not only had they won hands-down, but Olly had everyone, including my brother, in hysterics. My dad had given a good impression of enjoying the evening, but I sensed his discomfort at being side-lined while my new best friend held court in his living room.

Olly, however, neither wanted nor needed approval. Hers was a world of multiple identities, chosen to suit her environment, taste and humour. *Labels stuff us into ever smaller boxes, April, and I refuse to be pigeon-holed.* Oleanna, Olly, Lea, Leanna, and/or Olé taught me that I was free to be whoever I wanted to be and bugger what anyone else thought.

Later that same night, after yet another forensic examination of my weirdly errant spine, Olly announced that my parents were the most mis-matched couple in the ancestry of couples. She had crabbed around the bedroom, parodying a typical wildlife presenter's reverential tones. *The Hayles are pincer-like in their movements. The males, fully immature and exploding with testosterone, have only one purpose driving their undeveloped brains – to win at all costs. But inevitably the unit will splinter, a consequence of its own inability to adapt, and thus will become extinct by its own hand.* Oleanna's critical outsider's view of my family had shocked me to the core, and I never fully forgave her for it.

Before leaving Danesford Vale, her parting gift was a one-act musical revue called *Whose Shoes?* Inspired by the Kirsty McColl song *In These Shoes*, and with Olly as MC (who else?), it was set in a Baz Luhrmann-esque frontier town in which the barperson, played by my cousin Xander, wore platform boots and served long drinks to a rabble of top notchers including Dolores Huerta (activist), and Ellen Ochoa (astronaut), each wearing equally eye-watering footwear and singing songs of triumph against adversity. Nathalie and Piers' input made it an unforgettable show. With its Cuban-influenced musical score and phenomenal costumes, *Whose Shoes?* had subsequently acquired cult status and, inevitably, the film footage found its way to YouTube. By the time she left Danesford Vale, the legend of Oleanna Irving was born.

Fifteen years on and Olly had amassed armfuls of garlands as producer / director / actor / writer for her company, *GirlMeetsBoy*, which regularly rattled the show bizz industry. Barely a month went by when Olly wasn't in the media spotlight, particularly after her marriage to the controversial American actor, Dee Mulvaney. Although we were estranged, Olly had stayed in contact with my mum. I knew this because certain postcards and fliers pinned on the kitchen board could only have been sent by her.

π

Olly's prophetic words were very much on my mind when Harriet dropped me back home that afternoon. Embla was unusually quiet for a Bank Holiday Monday, as my uncles generally came over to watch whatever sporting event was on. I had stayed in my bedroom, undisturbed, to put together a present. It was shameful that Harriet had to remind me of my own mother's birthday, and while not intending to outshine her woodcut print, at least I'd have something original to give.

At the sound of cars pulling onto the drive, I was aware of a creeping nervousness. It made tactical sense not to announce the news of my trip over dinner as it was far better to talk to my family on an individual basis, but it was, nevertheless, bloody annoying. Surely another weekend away wouldn't cause that much of a crisis? With the present nicely packed in its box, I breathed out, and skipped downstairs. The babble of voices was reassuring, as was Mum's favourite Sandy Denny vinyl, crackling in the background.

As soon as I bounced into the kitchen, like a game of musical chairs, the chatter stopped. A shiver whipped along my spine. Harriet must have told the family about my boat trip! My mother will never know how important her hug was that day and had thanked me for the print, knowing it was made from Harriet's fair hand. Something was up, though. Mum was off kilter, although exactly how I couldn't say. As for the others, none of them would meet my eye.

'We're ready to eat, pet. Harriet's been telling us about your weekend,' said Mum, as she passed around the plates.

Bradley and Sebastian exchanged a glance while Harriet's feeble smile confirmed her guilt. Dad, as usual, gave nothing away. He was rarely effusive and almost never demonstrative unless it was a back-slapping occasion. At any rate, they'd had time to digest the shocking news that I wasn't available to serve their interests at the next triathlon. Any lingering doubt vaporised. I was sodding well going. 'Thanks for showing an interest, Mum. The weekend was fab, even better than our previous visits. Ninebarks has the right combination of rest and activity to ...'

'If you want my expert opinion, *professional* massage and an excellent fitness regime is the *only* way to ensure good health on a long-term basis,' said Sebastian, puffed up, and talking to no one in particular. 'April knows this, but she has consistently refused to take my advice on board. Instead of gobbling Jonty's chocolate cruffins three times a week, she'd be much better served by a lunch-time workout, or at the bare minimum, getting out on her bike. I've helped countless clients prevent burn out in this way.'

I stared at Sebastian. His sanctimonious declarations were becoming as predictable as death and text messages. Then, without warning, my mother stood and rested her hands on the table as if to steady herself, although she was perfectly calm.

'In any other circumstances, Sebastian, I would defer to your *expert opinion*, but we are discussing my precious daughter's welfare. You haven't been around long enough to know that April has relentlessly given every last drop of intellectual and physical energy to her studies, to her career, and to this family. A lunchtime bike ride – really? I doubt April even has time for lunch. If my girl has courage to face it, a burn out would be the making of her.'

My brother shifted on his seat bones, his jaw unable to decide whether to open or close while my father was as still as a runner on the starters blocks, except for a flicker of alarm that darted across his face. Smarting at the rebuke, Sebastian acted as though he'd been given a detention and fiddled with his cutlery, his dark eyes averted. Harriet literally forced an unopened champagne bottle on Bradley, desperate to reset the temperature. It was ridiculous.

My mother, as composed as could be, served herself a ladle of casserole before sitting down. I gave her the package.

'You've already given me a beautiful gift, April.'

'This is extra special.' It was meant to be for her sixtieth birthday, but in the quiet of the afternoon, something had prompted me to give it to Mum that night. Various people had sent photos and memorabilia that celebrated the notable events of her life to date: Glastonbury, where she met Dad; childhood snaps taken on various Cornish beaches; environmental campaigns. I'd even managed to obtain an old school photo, as she'd succeeded in wriggling out of the annual rigmarole. On the front cover, I had the lyrics to *Who Knows Where The Time Goes* inscribed on parchment by the art tutor we'd met at Ninebarks the previous year, which was where the inspiration for the book came from. Funny how at that precise moment,

Sandy Denny's haunting voice was singing it. The album had taken a year to collate. Although there were still gaps to fill, I'd gathered enough material to make it worthwhile, and as my mother turned the pages, her guileless eyes shining, I was so glad to have done it.

A 'pop' lightened the atmosphere. Glasses were filled, and chit chat bubbled around the table – recalibration over. While Mum took her precious birthday book into the living room, Dad's cool voice floated towards me.

'I thought the album was meant for next year, for your mum's special birthday. Didn't you say there were contributions outstanding?'

'Change of plan. Anyway, Dad, every birthday is special, isn't it. With luck she'll come with us to Ninebarks next year, eh Harriet?'

Harriet raised her glass and mouthed a 'sorry'. Bradley's sniffer dog nose must have wheedled my news out of her, so I didn't blame her in the least. My dad said nothing more, but he wasn't happy about the gift, and it unsettled me. When Mum returned, we got on with the business of eating as if nothing had happened.

9

Sebastian was edgy. I had hoped he'd go back to Merryfield as his clients were often booked in for early morning sessions, and I was too tired to argue. In fact, he rarely stayed over, but there he was, parked on the edge of my bed, black briefs and white T-shirt taut against fast-twitch hairless muscle and sinew. Seb pulled on each finger, making a sickening cracking noise which betrayed his anxiety.

'You're going, then.'

'Do you mean to ask if I've accepted an unbelievable invitation to stay on a narrow boat for four glorious days in splendid company, as it can only do me good?'

'There's no need to be sarcastic, April.'

'There's no need to be selfish, Sebastian.'

Stalemate. I slumped on my dressing table stool with the kind of gut-wrenching sensation that comes when something momentous is about to happen, and most of you wants it, and yet there is still an element of doubt. I could have backed down and blindly followed the flock, but my proverbial hooves started to burrow.

'Your mum was a bit off tonight.'

'I thought Mum summed it up nicely.'

Silence.

Sebastian reached for his socks. 'Look, April, I can't stay up all night waiting to find out what the hell happened to have made you totally disrupt our arrangements – again – when you know how important this triathlon is. Harriet was banging on about a woman who'd given her *the most fantastic massage ever*, and that everyone was raving about her, and that you'd caught her eye ...'

'For your information, Sebastian, I didn't have a massage, but that's not the point. Why can't you be happy for me? Do you really expect me to trail you and my brother around the circuit indefinitely, logging your times, fine-tuning your saddles, forever at your bloody beck and call? For goodness sake, I'm almost thirty. I need something new in my life.' I took a deep breath, and dived in. 'Our so-called relationship is so loose it needs more than a belt to tie it together. I think it's time to re-consider whatever it is we're supposed to be to each other.'

In an instant, Sebastian came towards me. Was that contrition, or did I detect something else? He offered his hand to pull me up. We faced each other, his chin habitually tilted up, but still half a head shorter than me. The urge to snort at his unflattering sock/boxer short ensemble took some effort to divert.

'I'm sorry, April. It's just that we ... I assumed you like things the way they are. Before I came on the scene, you were massively involved in the events, long after you stopped competing. I thought you enjoyed it.'

'I do, Seb, but I'm tired of organising accident insurance and day licenses. I need a break.'

The grandfather clock struck ten. We agreed it was best he went home and we'd catch up later in the week. As soon as his tail lights disappeared, I trotted upstairs and opened the window. Seb had ditched the natural deodorant I'd given him in favour of his previous brand and the chemical runoff had saturated the air, and my blouse. After a shower and clean pyjamas, I slid contentedly into bed. Embla was my haven. Her purple Swithland slate roof, sturdy stone walls, oak porch, worn herringbone floors (on which Bradley and I used to skid, our socks serving as skateboards) and large comfy rooms had constituted my safe and happy home. So many cherished childhood memories were made here and in Westwytch, and I could pretend that all was secure. But the reality was that changes had already crept in: Mum's 'bedroom' across the landing; our oldest friends' relocation to Aberdeenshire; the proposed housing estate earmarked at Charnwood Forest's ancient woodland, whipping up intense feelings and dividing opinions.

I turned off the lamp. So, Seb and I had reached a crossroads. That we hadn't wanted to spend the night together was confirmation this was the end for us, but not for my family. Bradley wouldn't be happy about our break up, but his friendship with Sebastian was solid. I couldn't help but wonder that half the reason I had drifted into this thing with Seb was to earn my brother's approval. It was a rare day that Bradley's disposition was sunny, even with Harriet onside, and he still wore that haunted look, as if expecting the worst.

When Sebastian first mentioned he was looking for lodgings, Bradley had gone overboard to help his newest and best buddy. Number 44, he said, was the perfect solution, or so he convinced me. *When your tenant moves out, Seb can move in. He'll look after it like his own. You'll have peace of mind, April. That alone must be worth a rent reduction.* Bradley's sweet talk was as impressive as my father's, and just as hard to refuse, and so Sebastian Espie moved into our lives. Competitions, quizzes, film nights, family holidays – there was scarcely an event he didn't attend. At the urging of inebriated uncles, Seb would strum a clutch of crowd pleasers on his guitar, and even Dad had sung along to *The Day We Took The Train.*

After one such night, Seb had sought me out. He was attentive: how did I cope with the scoliosis as a teenager; did I still have the x-rays for him to look at, if that were okay; would I like a complimentary massage, as he was certain of being able to help? Without fanfare or fuss, we had slipped into the stream, no longer spare parts after a night out, but as we had never enjoyed the fireworks so often exploding in those first months of a new romance, there was nothing to extinguish.

With Bradley's help, it wasn't long before Sebastian had overstepped my fairly relaxed boundaries. While Harriet and I were at Angel Ninebarks the previous year, the boys had taken it upon themselves to extend number 44's patio area to put up a sports massage shed. I was furious. Mum and I had spent weeks planting a wildlife friendly garden only to find that an entire border had been swallowed up, and my herb bed had been relocated to a dark corner of the shrinking plot. Fortunately, the ornamental fruit trees were intact. Bradley had been apologetic and had claimed it as his idea. The savings made in room hire would mean that Seb could increase his rent to me, which he had always intended to do. I'll admit it was awkward to take money from Sebastian, but I'd already reduced his erratic monthly payments. Bradley's faith in him, however, had remained undiminished, so I forgave the transgressions, and life went on, but not quite the same as before.

Previous relationships were never discussed. Bradley had warned me off. Seb was still reputedly cut up after being jilted by his fiancé three years earlier, so that was that. The only person I'd ever truly loved was Oleanna Irving, the fact of which would have remained entombed had Mum not accepted, on my behalf, Olly and Dee's wedding invitation at Abbey Road Studios. Emboldened by several Pina Colladas I had badgered the DJ to play *Together in Electric Dreams* as Olly would *have* to dance with me to *our* song. Fortunately, before I could unburden the weight of my unrequited love onto her, Mum had extricated me without causing further embarrassment. Those five years had whizzed by, and I'd long since given up wishing or hoping to see her again.

Meeting Lise Michelson had stirred a deep emotional well, but this wasn't the same *at all*. There was a mystery to her that had everyone bewitched. Sofie and Iris were like-minded souls, but without knowing how or why, I got a strong feeling that Lise's way of experiencing the world was unique, and that the boat trip might turn out to be the single most important event of my life. Taking into account Tish's comments, kindness alone would have prompted Lise's invitation. Anything else was a figment of Harriet's over-active imagination. It would have been useful to talk to Mum, but one of her dear old ladies had died, and that generally meant more work for her and Liz.

I rolled over again. Tension clung like ivy around my spine, so I breathed into it, willing it to ease itself out. Despite the atmosphere at dinner, Mum had been visibly moved by my birthday book. As soon as we disappeared, she'd have sat in the living room, specs at the ready, reverentially turning every page, savouring every detail of her happy life – at least I had believed it to have been so. Had Olly been on the right track, all those years ago? Were my parents mis-matched? Mum was an only child, raised in a quiet coastal community by older loving parents, now long gone, while my father's immediate family currently numbered thirty-nine. At Brightside Park, while the Hayles were busy pitting their wits at the pool or the beach, my mother would reunite with her friends. On her return, Dad would go immediately to her. If he'd won at something, she'd say, 'well done, Vaughny' and only then would he relax. Yes, my parents were different people, but they'd found a way to make it work.

The grandfather clock struck midnight. Its familiar chimes chided me it really was time for sleep. I thought of Sebastian lying spatchcocked, the duvet kicked off; of Angel Ninebarks and her inhabitants, tucked up in fresh white bedsheets and soft woollen blankets; of Lise and Elkie, snuggled up on the Anna Lee, dreaming of a peaceful harmonious earth. Then I slept like the dead.

10

Those three weeks cleaving my old life from the new hurtled by. It suited me fine. The staff had settled nicely into the Loughborough office, helped along with baskets of Jonty's tasty pastries, and even Maureen Umber had told a joke. Rumour had it that after a lifetime of living alone, she had finally found someone to love, (the bets were on a four-legger rather than two). Apart from the usual get togethers, the majority of which I had ducked out of, it was dinner and bed. Short of entering the triathlon myself, every single detail required for the meet had been well and truly nailed. Sebastian and Bradley were totally in the zone, and even if I had wanted to discuss our next move, Seb wouldn't have approved of this kind of conversation at such a vital point. Harriet's 'happy sailing' text was the only reference anyone made to my trip.

In spite of the frenetic pace, I had made it my number one mission to research the history and potential delights of narrow boating. As this was a brand new experience, looking a fool was not an option. Locating Quietwater Bridge took a while, and I was beginning to wonder if it existed at all until I found it in my recently acquired *Definitive Guide to Britain's Canals and Inland Waterways* book.

This is what it said:

> Bridge 10a, known colloquially as Quietwater Bridge. Folklore
> has it that in the 1850s, a local woman, suffering from
> an unspecified mental condition, was told in a dream to
> spend the night where the soft sandstone bridge meets the
> water. The following morning, she returned home, her soul
> quietened, and for some time after the spot became a place of
> pilgrimage.

Ignoring my internal cynic, if this were true, could
there have been a better sign. I was definitely in the
market for some serious R&R. The book recommended a
suitable parking spot, and with an early start, there'd be
loads of time for a recce, but when was 'mid-morning'? The
dictionary defined it as falling between sunrise and noon!
Without wanting to reveal the details of my forthcoming
weekend, I asked my colleagues. Believing it to be yet
another potential quiz question, they universally agreed
that mid-morning fell between 10am and 11am. Lise didn't
strike me as a woman who'd hang around indefinitely, and
as I aimed to arrive at Brewood (pronounced 'Brood') for
breakfast, there was no way I was missing this boat.

$$\pi$$

The towpath, although wide, was muddy. I hopped,
skipped, and jumped over the worst patches and was
grateful there was no one around to see me. Long stretches
of cavernous cuttings were steeped in huge mature trees,
the effect of which enclosed the canal, blocking out the
minimal daylight. A nameless stationary boat, painted as
black as coal, and whose darkened windows concealed

who knew what, spiked my pulse rate as I hurried by it. Having been born and raised in the Leicestershire countryside, recognising the difference between a robin and a raven wasn't too tricky for me – the latter's doomy croak was totally appropriate for this scene, reminiscent of those psychological horror films that Dad and Bradley occasionally stayed up late for, and I wished never to have witnessed, no matter that it had been many years ago, and from behind the safety of a large cushion.

In the distance loomed a lofty ornate bridge, complete with an elaborately curved balustrade. According to my guidebook, estate owner Sir Wil Monkton had commissioned its construction in 1785, after granting permission for the canal company to cross his land in exchange for a suitably imposing bridge. As soon as I reached it, a blue tit's trill chipped at the ominous atmosphere. The grassy towpath beyond looked considerably more welcoming and the sky was a brushstroke lighter. I checked the book. My destination was tantalisingly close.

After a good mile of high impact walking, a reddish-pink stone bridge came into view. Compared to the previous austere bridges, its storybook appearance looked out of place, but the towpath was all the more cheerful for it. I approached it slowly, partly to catch my breath, but also to quell the rising feeling of panic that had begun earlier that morning. The bridge number was obscured by a proliferation of ivy, so I ducked underneath to check the other side: 10a. I rested my rucksack under the arch and stretched my arms up and out. It was 9.58am, definitely within the mid-morning time range. The canal water scarcely moved, as if the world had stopped turning.

I waited and looked, looked and waited, my head bouncing like a tennis match spectator. On the opposite bank, a solitary sandstone cottage, whose front garden functioned as a jetty, was also deserted.

Instinctively I zipped up my jacket. This was a really bad idea. Even the brethren of ducks that floated by in a perfectly shaped V couldn't raise my plunging spirits. And then, as if I needed any further confirmation, a solitary glob of rain splashed onto my cheek – great for the mallards, but what on earth was I thinking? I could turn back, pick up the car and in less than an hour I'd be back in Embla's warm and welcoming hearth. It was still possible to make it to the event without being missed. Harriet wouldn't say a word – she'd be glad to see me. Who wouldn't have got carried away with the fantasy of a boat trip to paradise?

It was now 10.45am.

This is it, April. Count to ten and follow the first thought that comes into your head.

A faint chugging sound cut my count at eight. I turned to see a dog poised on the bow of an approaching narrow boat, its nose pointed skywards, sniffing the silently broody air. It was Elkie! The sleek navy/alabaster boat perfectly matched Lise's striped Breton top and was a heartening contrast against the damp funereal colour palette. She waved as if expecting me, and within minutes had skilfully slowed the boat to line up alongside the towpath. Elkie hopped off to officially welcome me. That dog must have heard my heart pounding when she pushed her cool nose to my flushed cheek and gave it a single lick (I'd soon discover that Elkie rarely paid anyone that sort of attention).

While our love-in was going full steam ahead, Lise had tied the ropes to two well-spaced bollards and as soon as the Anna Lee was secure, she walked towards me with her arms outstretched.

'Hello, April. It's good to see you. Elkie will show you where to put your rucksack, but she can't make coffee. Would you mind?'

'No – yes. Hello! Is it ...'

'Everything is out. No need to look so concerned. I'm easy to please. I'll join you in a moment.'

We laughed, and I knew it would be okay.

11

Elkie's tail, like a tour guide's umbrella, led me down three steps and into a surprisingly bright galley. Before I could get a good look around, she indicated where to leave my shoes, and ambled along a wooden-floored corridor before coming to a stop. I quickly followed on. The guest berth was separated from the front of the boat by an arched door. This had to be the bathroom. Feeling slightly foolish, I said to the waiting dog, 'Won't be a mo, Elkie,' before disappearing inside.

A freestanding bath! My amazed eyes swept the room. Across the bath lay a bamboo caddy with bath/body oils, soap and pumice, and a wrought iron towel rack was suspended above it. A cluster of ridiculously healthy potted plants in a wire stand stood beside the sink. Lise had created an exquisite bathroom in a teeny space. As I dried my hands on the thick striped towel, I imagined Harriet's reaction. *Geranium and rose lotion – yum, yum.*

When I came out Elkie was gone, so I sneaked a peek into the berth next door. Barring a single photo frame showing a black and white image of two children, the boy smaller than the girl, there was nothing to indicate that this was Lise's room. The bed was covered in a pale flint downy duvet, the sort that made you want to jump under and never get out again. A pewter jug filled with wild flowers stood underneath a stained-glass porthole window. The pattern depicted the Anna Lee, her captain and dog, and was without a doubt, one of Sofie Warburg's creations. Through the double doors that led onto the foredeck I spied yet more plants and two folding bicycles. Everything was spick and span.

On my way back to the kitchen I passed the shower room. *You used Lise's bathroom!* Oh, well, it was an honest mistake, and she probably wouldn't mind. And there, on the beech worktop, were two mugs, a cafetière, and a plate of biscuits, set out on a tray. Even the kettle had been filled. I switched it on and surveyed the room. Above the muted clay freestanding units dangled a trio of sparkling copper pans from a pot rack. A row of cooking utensils had been fastened to the wall above the oven, and the white-fish scale tiles and butler sink were pristine. Apart from the compact compost bin, everything else had been stowed.

After filling the cafetière, I moved to the saloon, pleased with my recollection of the boat's technical terms. The L-shaped seating bench was covered in a hardwearing grey hessian and would easily convert into a double bed. If there were a television, or computer, they must have been stored behind one of the neatly engineered cupboards. The hobbit-size wood burning stove was unlit, but the interior was warm. This was not what I was expecting at all. Of the dozens of interiors I'd seen online, none matched the Anna Lee for its stylishly understated über-cosy vibe. I could have whooped at my good fortune, and already, layers of accumulated stress began to melt.

Just then, Lise came down the stairs. She washed her hands before taking the tray over to the table. 'How do you like yours?'

'Black, thanks.' I sat down and was grateful to have my nerves cushioned by Elkie's presence nearby. Lise reached over to the shelf, took a biscuit from an enamel tin and passed it to me.

'Take care to use the right tin. Elkie's treats are not quite as tasty as ours.'

Lise's humour took me by surprise. I held out my hand to Elkie, and in a well-rehearsed action, she gently lifted the biscuit from it. 'How many is she allowed?'

'Elkie will tell you. Now, before we start our journey, you'll want to know what's in store. While I don't usually keep to a fixed itinerary, come Monday morning there will be a crew waiting. Twenty miles lie between us and them. For a mathematical mind such as yours, April, the calculation of our daily mileage rate should be straightforward.'

Before I could work out how Lise knew about my capacity for the numerical, she had spread a map over the table and indicated the various stages of our journey. Our leg was super leisurely: late starts, early stops, and what promised to be masses of restful gaps in between. Lise patiently answered every question – from how to use the on-board facilities, to my return journey to Brewood. As this had been pre-arranged, there was no need to book a taxi. In the spirit of such generosity, I apologised for using her bathroom. 'I must admit, Lise, a bath was the last thing I expected to see.'

'It comes in useful when we need to rescue injured wildlife.' She smiled at my incredulous expression. 'Our waste water, except the compost loo, is released into the canal which is why we use sustainable products but if you come into contact with the water, it is important to wash or shower. The waterways have been cleaned up, hence the increase in fish such as carp and bream, but with industrial and farm leaching to deal with, and the critical need to expand the use of these corridors for wildlife, there is a lot more work to be done.'

π

Midday came and went, and so with it the threat of a downpour although the gunmetal clouds stubbornly refused to budge. Lise started the engine and the Anna Lee purred into life. As we moved steadily along the water the trees thinned out, revealing the wider landscape. With the skipper's experienced hand on the tiller and keen eyes scanning the canal, I reminded myself to relax. We passed horses and sheep nibbling at swathes of meadow; ancient steeples piercing the dark sky; stationary boats with roofs stacked with paraphernalia and through whose windows I spied a dream catcher, underwear drying on a circular rack, and a much-loved Paddington Bear. Then, Lise motioned for me to take over.

'The maximum speed per hour of a narrow boat such as the Anna Lee is four miles: we are travelling on average, at two. If you can overcome the counter-intuition to steer as if you are driving a car, this will be easy. Remember that the reaction of the boat is much slower, so keep your gaze wide. Push the throttle forward, and you will move forward; the same for backwards. Put the throttle in the middle, and gradually, twenty tonnes of boat will stop. If a boat is coming towards you, try to keep to the right.'

She waited for a nod to indicate I'd understood which I had, in theory, although at that point I was still adjusting to the terrifying reality that I was steering the boat. To disguise my anxiety, I flailed around for a question. 'What are those long poles on the roof for?'

'The central channel of the canal is around four feet deep, but if water levels drop, or we hit a shallow stretch, the boat may run aground, so we use the wooden pole to push off. The extendable pole and net are used to fish out light rubbish such as plastic bottles. Now, you are currently holding the tiller with your dominant hand. If your shoulder aches, use the other hand. You don't yet have the action neurologically mapped, so this is the most efficient way.'

Lise placed a warm, open hand on mine.

'If you soften the palm, you will feel more by doing less.'

Immediately I relaxed my grip and my breath. Lise's instructions were so familiar as I'd learned similar techniques to help with my scoliosis way back when. With the exception of the occasional comment about the boat, or the flora and fauna, we cruised in companiable silence as the boat glided effortlessly, parting the dark water. The surroundings sprang into life, as if the land had been waiting for me to notice it. Lise returned the wave of the crew on Rocksteady. It was one of seven boats we passed that afternoon, each one with evocative names such as The Long Goodbye, Dusty, and Galadriel.

Before we reached the single lock on our journey, and all the while keeping a close eye on me, Lise brought up sandwiches and tea. I wolfed down several delicious squares of thick sourdough and rye bread, *smørrebrød*, which were topped with a selection of cheese, asparagus, and juicy pickles. If this were a taste of things to come, I had hit the jackpot. Snack finished, we reached Wheaton Aston. From the opposite direction we met a boat about to make its way through the lock, which apparently made the transition easier. I had hoped to have a go at lifting the paddles and opening the lock gates, but as it turned out my assistance wasn't required. The cheerful three-strong team from Two's A Crowd took both boats efficiently through the lock before we set off again with smiles and waves. According to Lise, one of the joys of narrow boating was the camaraderie, and willingness to help. The skill was to distinguish between the enthusiastic amateur and the expert boater to avoid mishap.

π

The first drops of rain fell. A damp chill had sunk through my fleece, making me shiver. Lise passed me a waterproof jacket.

'The weather is closing in. With the wind blowing the boat from the side, we are beginning to crab, can you see? Let's moor up for the night. With luck, the wind will be on our side, and the Anna Lee won't be rocked about.'

'I had no idea there was so much to consider. Will the storm affect us?'

'The roof is made from four millimetres of steel and is insulated. Last year, the Anna Lee was overhauled. She is water tight, and the vents should prevent steaming. Even so, it may be noisy, depending on how hard the rain is driven down from the heavens, but I like it.' Lise's smile was reassuring. 'Now, how are you, April?'

'Great, thanks. My shoulder is stiff, but that's no surprise, is it.'

'As it's going so well, you can moor up.'

My horrified expression clearly amused her, but I needn't have worried. When we approached our stopping point, Lise demonstrated the reverse gear change and talked me through the process of bringing the boat to a stop. Once on the towpath, she expertly secured the rope around the mooring posts, as well as banging in extra stakes for good measure while Elkie cat-walked the path. I let out a colossal sigh. It was such a relief to have reached this point in the day. Obviously Lise wasn't testing me, but to have avoided calamity made me want to punch the air, although I was under no illusion that the rest of the trip would run as smoothly.

I washed the cups while Lise busied herself with something out front. It felt like a kind of domestic bliss, like she and I had travelled together many times. Then, a wave of weariness buckled my knees. This generally happened at the start of a holiday and would pass soon enough, especially after a good night's sleep, but when Lise saw me slumped over the table, she suggested I rest before sharing a light meal. This would allow time for my food to digest sufficiently, should I want a massage later. *Should I want one?* – was she kidding!

π

Under soft pink lighting, we ate pumpkin salad served on plates of textured porcelain and drank lime and ginger cordial from smoked glass tumblers, while the rain battered the roof. How could it be that in just seven hours, I was wallowing in a sublime parallel universe. Then, a powerful image of Grandma Valerie's house appeared, the time when Mum and I had stayed at Brightside Park holiday lodge as Valerie was recovering from an operation. It had rained hard that day, too, and her living room was aglow with candles, and a crackling fire. We didn't know it then, but that was the last time we'd be together. Before leaving, Mum had said something odd: *leaving Cornwall was the second most sorrowful thing I've ever done.* I suddenly wondered what the worst thing had been.

'Would you like a cup of mint tea?'

'Sorry, Lise. Yes please. I've recently developed a habit for daydreaming. I was remembering my Cornish grandmother.'

Lise poured the tea while I bit into another of those tasty biscuits we'd had earlier – *vaniljekranse* – traditionally eaten at Christmas, much like Scottish shortbread, and just as delicious.

'Good memories?'

'Sad. Valerie was a gentle soul, always overjoyed to see Bradley and me, but we preferred the company of our cousins. I regret not getting to know her better. My grandma Radka, however, is the total opposite.'

'How so?'

'She's a *tour de force* – the only person who can ruffle my dad's feathers. My aunt Petra takes her to mass every week, but whenever Raddy wants to do something special, like go for afternoon tea, she asks my mum to accompany her, which really annoys Petra. All my aunts are wary of Mum as she doesn't fit into their idea of 'normal'.' I sipped my tea, acutely embarrassed to have been tittle-tattling. If I could keep my mouth shut for five minutes, Lise might talk about herself.

'My maternal grandparents lived in a fundamental religious community. My father's parents were innkeepers who drank the profits dry. They say that one good grandparent is worth four bad, so you are in luck, April.'

Our laughter covered my surprise, although why I should have been so surprised was a mystery as everyone came from somewhere, didn't they. But recalling what Tish and the other guests had said, for Lise Michelson to have shared even a snippet of her life with me was somehow significant, as though I was now the keeper of secrets, and if I were lucky, there would be more.

12

Add a cap of fragrant oil. It will nourish your skin and bones and will help during the massage. The twenty-minute soak in the tiny tub, exactly as Lise had suggested, had done the job. Whilst drying off, I was aware of yet another bout of nerves. It was ridiculous, and so out of character. Apparently, the adjustable saloon table had been used for massages many times before. Lise must have guessed that my back was troublesome, and of course I trusted her, but the butterflies were almost as disturbing as my sore wings.

As a diversion tactic, I calculated that there was still another 64 hours to go until Monday. Better still, there were 3,840 minutes, or 230,400 seconds. This was an old school trick often deployed to either delay the pain of the start of a new term or speed up the end of it, depending on the circumstances. Then I thought of Harriet. She'd be thrilled to hear that I was about share her massage experience. As I rummaged for my phone, I noticed a cotton waffle robe laid out on the bed, yet another of Lise's endlessly kind gestures. After stepping into a pair of regulation Sloggis, I pulled on the robe, flicked up the hood, and scrolled through the messages at lightning speed. Nothing was going to lure my attention away from this brilliant adventure. There were dozens of posts referring to the imminent triathlon, but nothing from Sebastian. I changed my mind about messaging Harriet, powered down the phone and closed the cabin door.

π

'We'll begin with you lying on your front. Tell me if at any point you feel discomfort or pain. I like to work in silence but the occasional snore is permitted.'

I climbed onto the converted table, and for the second time in three weeks, Lise covered me with a blanket, but this time I was smiling. The saloon had been transformed by the wood burner's golden glow and an infuser scented the air. Outside, the wind harried the leaves and blew the boat away from the bank, causing the mooring lines to creak and strain, the effect of which was similar to the hammock's rocking motion and it risked lulling me to sleep, as much as I was determined otherwise. Elkie was curled up in her basket nearby. Save for one other boat which was permanently moored several metres away, we were alone.

Lise's cool hands rested on the base of my neck and at the tail of my spine, for what seemed like an eternity. Confident there was no need to hold on to my body, it began to release, feeling incrementally heavier with every second. Lise's fingers and thumbs skilfully mapped out my spinal curvature, pausing at each facet joint as they communicated some kind of magic with the obstinate bony structure. A subtle tingling sensation pulsed along my spine and across my ribs. Bliss! When it was time to turn over, Lise moved her stool to the head of the table. From this seated position, she placed her hands on either side of my head and rested them there for a good long while. Then, she slid her forearms underneath my shoulder blades, and that's where they stayed until, beat by beat, my wings released into the cradle that her arms had created for them. Shortly after, I plunged into the void.

In the dream, I was soaring above the waterways, riding the thermals in a space with no horizon, while beneath my magnificent wings the Anna Lee eased along the black water. The landscape was literally alive, its vibrations rippling through my feathers, the only sound in an infinity pool of peace. I was no longer separate from my surroundings but was inside, above, below, feeling everything and nothing, and finally – exhilaration.

Bolt upright, I gasped for air, my chest exploding. It was morning; I was in bed; the Anna Lee was moving! Within minutes, teeth brushed, body dressed, I flew to the stern, the sun flashing, blinding.

'Good morning, April. No need to rush. Elkie and I have had a slow start.'

I stood beside Lise, rubbing my eyes. The world had been jet washed! Glints of light bounced off the water while luscious verdant greens throbbed under a vast, empty sky. Birds lingered in slow-mo, their sweet song pulsed in my ear drums as the lightest of breezes caressed my face. And there was Elkie, trotting like a towpath queen as the sun's rays glistened in her ritzy coat. Lise steered the boat into the bank to let her on. My heart was bursting, and my eyes were wet with happy tears as I gathered her up in my arms.

'Elkie approves of you.'

'We're a perfect match, Lise. Have you had breakfast yet?'

'Yes, thank you. There is fruit, muesli, and kefir. If you prefer to toast the sourdough, there is jam and honey. Coffee would be welcome when you've finished.'

Lise had laid it all out – again. I sat at the table, remembering not to shovel in the tasty granola but to *take my time and savour it*. No matter how often I had to remind myself, I was intent on enjoying, to the full, every single moment. In all likelihood, this would be my one and only stay on the Anna Lee, but surely I didn't need to cram it all in. Lise and Elkie's graceful, measured movements had already slowed my pace, but it was obvious that a single narrow boat trip and an annual three-nighter at Angel Ninebarks wasn't going to cut the mustard. For all the yakety-yak about lifestyle choices, I was beginning to wonder if my world view had been too narrow all along.

π

As morning slipped into afternoon, we stopped by a deep wooded cutting for lunch. My senses had remained sharp. Plaintive buzzard song floated above lichened-covered bridges which ran alongside thick borders of swaying nettles and purple loosestrife, all of which fed into my brain in a 3D loop. A pair of swans glided alongside the boat. Their stark ivory feathers, the texture of the finest tissue paper, made me want to reach out and stroke them. As for my back, apart from the occasional self-induced flare up, the worst thing about having a scoliosis was my anticipation of strangers' reactions. Unsurprisingly, I'd become an expert at disguising my shape, but this was a brand new day, and my wings were spreading.

I left my jacket onboard and sank into the fold up chair, soaking up the warmth. Meanwhile, Lise and Elkie had walked towards an old tree whose spindly branches reached out in every direction. Using my hand to shield the sun, I watched them in action. I could have sworn that Lise was talking to the tree. Then, she rested her hands on its trunk before leaving something by its roots. Conscious of prying, I took the lunch things down to the galley. Soon after, Lise came back and solved the puzzle.

'Over the years we've planted many trees, shrubs and herbs along the towpaths. It's good to say 'hello'.'

'How lovely! It must be thrilling to see how much they've grown, just like children.'

She nodded, and soon after we set off again. After a while, Lise's attention was drawn to a sweat-soaked runner (ears plugged, arms banded, and waist belted with kit) who pitched and rolled along the path. It was a look I knew well. The stark reminder was completely at odds with my current situation of cruising at a snail's pace which was now, without a doubt, my preferred choice. Just as I was about to comment, Lise said,

'The distance between the boat and the horizon remains the same, no matter how fast we travel. Speed isn't necessarily a barrier in order to pay attention, but a slower pace can be an advantage.'

Her perception stunned me. I didn't know it then, but Lise's observations would reappear to reorient me through what was to lie ahead. But before I could envisage what those rocky roads might be, she brought me back to earth with a bump and a smile.

'Now, you must take the opportunity to walk. If your attention wanders, Elkie will stop you from falling in.'

Lise's mischievous grin lit my heart. How could I refuse? 'I'd love to. Actually, I'm more than ready to stretch my legs, but this time I'll leave my step counter onboard. You'll pick us up at ...'

'Wood Eaton, before we go through the Cowley Tunnel.'

'Wow, a tunnel! That'll be exciting.'

'Hm. At only eighty-one yards long, it'll be over before you blink, but the impressive solid rock cutting will raise your pulse, that I can guarantee.'

I was still grinning as Elkie led me along the grassy path. We followed a pair of orange-tipped butterflies engaged in a mating ritual, or maybe they were siblings, teasing each other like Brad and I used to. Whatever they were doing, it was delightful. Lise had shown me a picture of willowherb and had given me a basket. A good patch of it grew in this particular area, as did many other edible herbs and plants, and with the changing climate, they might have made an early appearance. If I weren't sure what to pick, Elkie would act as official sniffer. Was there anything this wonderful dog couldn't do?

Strolling in the breeze felt *sooo* good. My breath was full and steady, and what I could only describe as jubilation charged through my veins. I was invincible! It was startling how, only a few hundred feet from so-called civilisation, these networks of canals, towpaths, and bridges existed in their own sub-terranean world. That afternoon, we passed only a handful of dog-walkers and a quartet of cyclists. The owner of Bedraggled insisted that the eel he'd caught that morning was 'this big' and had proudly taken out his phone to prove it really had weighed in at four pounds. He was travelling with his father and grandfather, three generations of life-long narrow boaters, and very happy to declare it so.

Elkie and I waited by the bridge. Reflections from the water flickered like diamonds on the echoey underside of the faded red brick, the effect of which was anesthetising. I thought of home, and heart. So, where was my heart? Elkie had captured it from that first moment, there was no other way to describe it. She was as fine a companion that anyone could have wished for. As for Lise, this was unknown territory. There was a magnetism, a sense of timelessness about her. I felt totally safe within her circumference and nothing unsettling or untoward could happen to me, or us, whilst she were nearby. If Lise Michelson had asked me to stay on the Anna Lee, I'd have given everything up to do it and the thought of it was terrifying.

13

After crossing the invisible watery border between Staffordshire and Shropshire, we moored up by Norbury Junction. It had been another terrific spell during which we encountered a gang of orange-stockinged mallards clambering unceremoniously onto the bank, and the splash of shimmering kingfisher blue, as the bird flashed passed the boat – twice. As for the human species, the most moving encounter of the day took place between Lise and a liveaboard called Siobhan Boyd, the skipper of Forever Young.

She met Lise at Angel Ninebarks and had been both guest helper and live-in staff. Siobhan had lost her family in a tragic accident. It was Lise's invitation to travel on the Anna Lee that had prompted the start of a new life for Siobhan on the inland waterways. Forever Young was temporarily moored beside High Bridge, an imposing Grade 11 listed affair built by Thomas Telford. It was rumoured that during the 19th century, after the death of a boatman, a ghostly creature had haunted this place ever since. Despite the sunshine, there was an undercurrent that made me shiver.

Siobhan and Lise had walked to the bridge. At this point I was becoming accustomed to Lise's way of doing things and wasn't surprised to see Siobhan's expression look infinitely brighter when they returned. We drank iced tea on Forever Young's foredeck, sitting among fragrant pots of exquisite lilac blue roses, her beloved husband's favourite flower. After an emotional farewell, we travelled quietly on.

Later that evening, I discovered that Lise had inherited her love of narrow boating from her uncle Edmund. Their family had come from a long line of boat people dating back to the industrial era, which was generally described as 'golden,' even though life was punishing, and the busy waterways were polluted beyond recognition. It was the vision of pioneers such as L.T.C. Rolt and other enthusiastic volunteers who, from the 1940s onwards, were instrumental in revitalising the dilapidated canal system and reinventing the inland waterways in a second 'golden era' for our enjoyment and leisure.

Listening to Lise's abridged biographical resumé, which was without embellishment or drama, was akin to hearing the story of someone else's life. But when she turned her attention to me, offering neither advice nor comment, there was nothing to match the feeling of being listened to. In the still evening, I became acutely aware of the content of my conversation, and how much of it came from my father, my teachers, and Gita Nair. What was my opinion? Until then, it wouldn't have occurred to me to find out. Lise gave me time and space to enquire into what 'paying attention' really meant. Without it, I would be forever held captive by everyone's else's views and beliefs.

Every now and again, Elkie would nudge Lise's knee. While stroking the dog's lovely face, she would murmur endearments that required no translation. It was humbling to witness the affection between them. Before turning in, I thanked Lise for inviting me and she said, *The invitation was the easy part, April. You made the courageous decision to come, and so I must thank you.*

π

Sunday, another day, but so distinct from the day before, even the hour before. Every bend, every bridge, every curve brought another view, a fresh impression, an unexpected perspective. I couldn't work it out. With every mile I became increasingly in tune with the canal-scape. The Anna Lee's temperate two-miles-per-hour tempo had aroused in me a state of utter docility. Life as I knew it was suspended, as if a circuit breaker had unplugged me from everything and everyone. Oddly, there was no hint of tension or ache across my back. As is often the case in chronic conditions, I'd become accustomed to the varying shades of discomfort, and so the absence of it required a considerable mental adjustment. Every now and again I'd check in with my body, and once reassured, my mind expanded again.

Lise and I discussed the boat: from construction to renovations, to its overwintering at Quietwater. She steered while I mooched; I took over while she jumped off to pick herbs, but never for long, and always with me in her sights. Whilst moored up, she'd catch up with friends. During the last stop that day, she had chatted at length to a liveaboard who was as dishevelled as his boat. So dilapidated were Babooshka's rusty hull and rotten windows, it was a struggle to imagine the boat being fit for purpose, but survive it had. Lise had given the man a basket of goodies and had received an awkward embrace in return. My understanding of her character was deepening. Whether it were trees, plants, dogs, or people, each received equal amounts of Lise Michelson's loving care and attention.

Through her field glasses, a hidden world was revealed to my amazed eyes: the grey heron poised by the bank, eyes lasered on dinner, and a sparrowhawk flying back to base with a snack quivering in its beak. After decades of travelling the canals, Lise knew every garden, woodland, and hedgerow from which she foraged. Their contents were becoming more familiar, and soon I could identify the likes of borage and wild garlic. This was some education!

π

Of course, my good thing had to end, and what an end it was. The last leg was through Woodseaves Cutting, with the mighty Wrekin rearing up to the South West. It was awesome, just how I imagined a *Lord of The Rings* film set would be. The essential technical knowhow required to create a canal through this unrelenting rocky topography, let alone the enormous effort involved in breaking through a hundred feet of it *by hand*, was incredible. We slunk past deserted towpaths, through sunken cuttings bordered by pre-historic ferns and creeper vegetation, and crawled under towering bridges, the effect of which made my skin prick. The canal was eye-wateringly narrow in places due to slips and avalanches which had resulted in mounds of enormous sandstone boulders that even Frodo Baggins would have baulked at.

Equilibrium restored, we reached Tyrely. It was five o'clock. While Lise set about putting the boat to bed for the night, she suggested I take a peek at the five lock flight, the first of which was situated just a hundred feet away. It was a gorgeous spot, with weather to match. The former lock-keepers' cottages were lovingly kept, and their fully restored heritage was proudly displayed on impressive plaques, fastened onto their exterior walls. Elkie and I followed the downward slope running adjacent to the locks, past enormous trees with magnificently exposed roots, past benches whose nameplates conjured up contented *gongoozlers*, (people who watch the narrow boats go by). And there, beside the twin blossoming cherry trees like debutantes in their 'coming out' season, Elkie and I sat, enviously studied the crew of the Not-So-Busy-Lizzy as they made their way through each of the five locks while their hypervigilant houseboat pug, Paisley, remained glued to the skipper. Job nicely done, I waved them on their travels, and walked back to the Anna Lee, ready to make supper.

There was no need to ask whose turn it was to prepare our meals, as Lise and I had fallen into a natural groove. My signature courgette and herb pasta was polished off with a glass of aromatic cordial, followed by one or two sweet orange chocolates, another of my 'thank you' offerings. I was disappointed not to have had the opportunity to treat Lise to a pub lunch, but as we stood on the stern under that momentous sunset, she said that my company was payment enough and had wisely steered our conversation away from the emotional and into the technical. Having spent three days on a moving home, the nature of which had grabbed my attention like nothing else in recent memory, my curiosity was happy to be satisfied.

Before turning in, Elkie and I sauntered along the towpath under a galaxy of dazzling stars. My eyes quickly acclimatised to the dark. Cornish night skies were equally as stunning, but there was always someone around to take my attention. Here, it had been possible to contemplate the heavens as never before. Silence underpinned the swish of my walking shoes as they brushed against the burgeoning paths, and the melancholy owl song. The Anna Lee's lights were a beacon, her presence a refuge. Tomorrow's departure had exposed an ache in me that was growing at an alarming rate.

π

Lise had made hot chocolate. We sat opposite each other, me talking, her listening, and the water moving imperceptibly beneath our feet. Later, while buttoning up my pyjamas, I replayed Lise's question: *why do you want numbers, April?* An ancient dream, submerged within my consciousness, bobbed to the surface. I could see them so clearly, my father and my uncles sitting at our kitchen table, discussing their children's career choices. In a sleight of hand, Xander had relinquished drama school for a degree in hospitality management while I had been steered away from engineering towards accountancy. *Come what may, April, people will always need an accountant.* The perfect course existed at Loughborough, my home town. No need to leave Embla. Fewer Debts. No brainer.

Sorrow overwhelmed me. For all my talk of certainty and security, and a life in which there was nothing I wanted, even as I had said it, already those fantasies were dissolving into the ether. That night, in the hush that settled over the Anna Lee, it hit me like a freight train. There was something else beyond the daily grind. There was a way to thrive that wasn't driven by societal or familial expectations. Many people, like those at Angel Ninebarks, proved it was possible to live within the shadow of the great machine and not be swallowed up by it. My true purpose, whatever that might turn out to be, was waiting for me and I wanted *that*. I'd had a taste, and this was a defining moment. Nothing would or could ever be the same again.

Before climbing into bed, I remembered the triathlon. After twenty-four hours of celebrating, recriminating, and 'what ifs', the Hayles would also be hitting the sack. I powered up the phone, convinced that nothing could possibly disturb this nascent inner quiet.

Hi April. Seb sustained a mild ankle injury, worse in the pride department.

Brad smashed his PB! H xxx

I scrolled through reams of race chat, captions, and photos: Bradley carried on my uncles' shoulders, celebrating his new personal best; Dad and Harriet high fiving. There were no images of Sebastian, and no message for me. I could have called him, but the truth was, I hadn't thought about him, or them, *at all*. Sebastian Espie belonged to a chapter of my life that required no re-reading. I slid the phone into my bag and turned off the light. Tomorrow would come soon enough.

14

I pulled back the curtains. Streaks of refracted light streamed through the porthole window opposite, creating a silhouette on the wall beside my bed. The arboreal image danced and jigged, the result from a passing narrow boat on its way down the flight. I opened the window. Cool morning air rushed in, accompanied by birdsong and breezy tree music. Immediately my spirits lifted. In just four days, I'd learnt so many new and interesting things: the technical and practical requirements to keep the Anna Lee safely afloat; the social aspects to narrowboat travel; the ability to calculate between two points exactly when we'd arrive at a particular destination. I'd even made up a formula to calculate distance ...

L (lock miles)=M (number of miles) + N (number of locks) over 2.

... which I'll admit, was super nerdy, but oh so satisfying. Paradoxically, life on board was spontaneous and flexible, and I liked that, too. If Lise wanted to stay on at a particular spot, arrangements were revised with no bother.

On a personal level, it was impossible to sum up my gratitude. The lengths to which Lise had gone in order to make my trip restful were incalculable. Not only had the massage been too wonderful for words, the food amazing, and the overall comfort off the scale, but rather than disturb me in the morning or at bedtime, she had climbed out of the foredeck and walked along the towpath to the stern, rather than walk through the interior gangway. Not that it would have mattered as Lise was so unobtrusive, there were times when I wondered if she had been on the boat at all.

Reluctantly, I hauled my protesting body out of the nest, washed and dressed, and packed up my meagre belongings which took all of two minutes. Then I cleaned the bathroom and berth, trying my best to ignore the reality that was nipping at my heels. Every passing second brought the finishing line closer, and as a consequence, the contraction across my shoulders mirrored this growing turmoil. Lise must have expected it. After an extra-affectionate 'good morning', we shared a royal breakfast of freshly baked cottage loaf, and *frittata*, (the eggs collected from another of her mystery suppliers earlier that morning), and of course, that superb coffee blend with an aroma that made my mouth salivate. We ate mostly in silence, although her perceptive eyes anchored mine, stripping out the stuff and nonsense.

'You've been a fine deckhand, April. Don't be surprised if your re-entry is a little bumpy, so take it slowly.'

She reached across the table and squeezed my hand. I was too choked to reply. Meanwhile, Elkie had rested her beautiful, knowing head on my leg, and I fought to keep it together, even though it wouldn't have mattered a jot if I had sobbed my sorry heart out. Lise's compassion was unlimited. At no point had there been tension, or judgement, or even a show of frustration at the incompetence of one or two boaters along the way. Her temperament was as calm as the canal water itself. I'd seen it at Angel Ninebarks, where guests and colleagues orbited her benevolent star, and during these last three days whilst travelling the waterways when she encountered not only her friends, but also with strangers. Now I understood why.

π

Elkie's bark alerted us to visitors. Lise stepped off the boat to greet the threesome, one of whom was Sofie Warburg. She was carrying what appeared to be a rolled up sleeping bag under one arm, and a holdall in the other.

'April! So nice to see you again. My, you look well. The Anna Lee has sprinkled her faery dust over you.'

Sofie put down her bag, reached out and touched my cheek. This unexpectedly intimate gesture completely threw me. Then the older man offered a hardworking hand to shake, or was it to steady me?

'Edmund Heathcote, at your service. I trust you've kept my niece out of trouble.'

I instantly recognised the co-founder of Angel Ninebarks from a photo that Tish had shown me in the library. Edmund Heathcote's gold sleeper earring glinted in the sun. He was what my mother would describe as gangly and his Celtic beard-bead was almost as impressive as the pony-tail which reached all the way down his back. There was more than a hint of the swashbuckler about Edmund Heathcote and it impressed me enormously. 'Lise let me steer, and I'm relieved to say we didn't have to call in the Canal and Rivers Trust to rescue us.'

Edmund's infectious chuckle skittled along the towpath, capturing the attention of the third traveller who had been, until that point, engulfed in Lise's capable arms. Sofie introduced him as Kristian.

'Are you another of Ninebarks' waifs and strays, April?'

I blushed at the comment. Kristian might have been Lise's twin but not quite as tall, and from what I could make out from under his zipped-up windcheater, considerably less robust.

'April's technical aptitude is impressive, brother. She could teach you a thing or two about the Anna Lee.'

He *was* Lise's brother! Then Kristian grinned at the admonishment, and instantly his studious expression softened.

'Praise indeed from the waterways guru. Well then, April, may I offer a warm welcome to the newly crowned queen of the bilge pump. Henceforth, I will defer to your expertise during our voyage'.

Kristian peered at me through his brown-framed specs as if scrutinising plant life. If I had to hazard a guess at a profession, it was either scientific/academic, or in fine-stitch embroidery. 'Sadly, this is the end of my amazing adventure. It's back to real life for me'.

'Now there's a statement ripe for deconstruction. You could get trapped onboard for weeks with Lise's friends on that subject alone, never to be seen or heard of again. It's just as well I'm here to rescue you,' said Edmund, who had traded his large canvas bag full of produce for Lise's basket, which was brimming with our collection of healing herbs.

'Clean linen, coffee, and pastries. Thank you for the fresh

supplies, Edmund. Stay for tea. I want to know how Frieda is, and of course, all the Ninebark news.'

'I'll make it, Lise. I've got to fetch my rucksack anyway.' I hopped back on the boat and into the galley, immensely glad for the temporary reprieve. While the newly-formed crew laughed and chatted above water level, I made a pot of tea. Seeing my tears fall onto the worktop was too stupid for words, so I pulled myself together, did a few rapid in and out breaths, and carried the tray back up to the stern. I listened intently to the spirited group as they discussed the next leg of their journey – who was joining *en route*, where they planned to stop, what they wanted to see. Leaving the 'Shroppie' to meander the Four Counties Ring sounded so appealing and I'll admit to feeling envious of what lie ahead for them.

The siblings were a riveting study. This was a different Lise: more animated, and her smile contained all the joy of reuniting with a precious loved one. Lise was a sturdy oak to Kristian's spindly silver birch. His long, slim fingers held his mug as if it might break, whereas Lise's capable hands effortlessly supported hers and yet their faces and expressions were carved from the same exquisite piece of marble – so mesmerising that I had to look away to stop from staring.

'April, was your trip everything you hoped it would be? To have experienced something like this must have opened doorways into your imagination – who knows where it might lead.'

Sofie's unbound workshop hair was a mass of garnet curls, a regal wrap majestically draped around her shoulders. There was no disguising her excitement at the imminent adventure, which only amplified my misery at having to leave. 'I had no idea that so much more could come from so much less, if you know what I mean, Sofie. I'll never forget it.'

'Your trip is but a memory, April. Dust and ashes. It would be best not to hold on to it.'

Lise shot back, 'Just like your piles of old books, Kristian – dust and ashes.'

Everyone laughed except me, the outsider who had no idea what the in-jokes were. But once again, the wise man threw me a lifebelt.

'Kristian and Sofie are scholars, April. They've dedicated decades to resurrecting the ghosts of the long dead. Sofie, at least, uses her mind and hands to create.'

Kristian's pale eyelashes blinked rapidly. The comment was lovingly said, but it had landed on a sore spot.

'Uncle Edmund sees through my disguise. And of course, my days would be better spent growing cabbages and making fluted dowels from reclaimed oak, but I fear my heart belongs to the cemetery.'

The light-hearted exchanges were almost enough to ease my increasingly wretched state. I was desperate to hear more but was acutely aware that the spectre of time had reappeared to take control of my life, to push and pull me here, there, and everywhere, if I let it. It really was time to go. Kristian was right, though – the trip was already a memory, and I hadn't taken a single photo.

'Our route is not so far from your home. We can always use an extra pair of intelligent hands.'

'I can come back, Lise?'

Everyone laughed at that, but it was kindly meant.

'My sister never says anything she doesn't mean.'

Kristian's earnest expression threw me into Lise's earth-mother hug. Then, Elkie nudged my leg so I bent down and gave her a final cuddle before stepping dazed and confused onto the towpath. As the crew retreated into the boat, Edmund swung my rucksack over his shoulder and we walked up the side of the bridge, out of the cocoon and towards his car. I turned to take a last look at the Anna Lee. Standing at the entrance to the hatch was Kristian, his hand raised in farewell.

Second Quarter

15

On the wall in Mum's garden office, surrounded by nature images and iconic spiritual symbols, is a spectacularly colourful painting of the *corpus callosum* (the thick band of nerve fibres which act as a bridge for the left and right hemispheres of the brain). Circling the 'bridge' are a clutch of quotes from the likes of Carl Sagan, Mary Lucy Cartwright and William Blake – science and art – just as it should be. As if on cue, when I was desperate for a few motes of wisdom to help navigate my 'bumpy' return to Embla, I recalled the quote from Blake: *'Hindsight is a wonderful thing, but foresight is better, especially when it comes to saving life, or some pain.'*

The more I peered at my family through this freshly scoured lens, the clearer it was that a dismantling of sorts had already begun. During the previous year's summer holiday at Brightside Park, Dad had glibly noted the increasingly low turnout, and had been uncustomarily despondent. Mum had pointed out that as a number of cousins were now raising infants, inevitably our high-octane holidays would end, or at the very least mutate into something less frenetic. Dad's reaction was typical: sell the lodge and move on, but Mum was having none of it. Her father had co-built the seasonal holiday park and had gifted her a lodge which had served as our treasured holiday home ever since. Dad's siblings had followed suit, ensuring regular reunions and tighter family ties throughout the generations. As Mum had family and friends in the area, she occasionally went to Brightside Park on her own, so that conversation was going nowhere.

This year was to be our last big gathering. I'd forgotten that arrangements had been made for a pre-holiday meet at Embla rather than at our local pub, The Red Balloon, as the Bank Holiday non-regulars usually filled it to the rafters. But even if I had possessed Blake's gift of foresight, returning home after four days of heaven to face a group of people whose mode for living was diametrically opposite to the Ninebarkers, and who'd treat me like the invisible woman, or worse, was always going to be painful. Maybe I was exaggerating, but now that I'd had a glimpse of a 'me' that might never have seen the light of day, was it any wonder I was reluctant to go back?

π

When Edmund dropped me off at Brewood that day, I sat in my car for ages, unable to move. During the journey from Tyrley, he had generously filled a number of biographical gaps which had further inflated my infatuation with the mysterious Quietwater community, and the Michelson siblings. The delightful waterside cottage, a stone's throw from where I had waited for the Anna Lee just days before, belonged to him and Frieda. That was Quietwater Cottage. The canal guide's 'miracle bridge' story was true: Lilly Tams was Edmund Heathcote's six times' great grandmother and was born to a Staffordshire boat family. Lilly had traded tradition for a peripatetic life on land and had drifted from place to place, her mental health becoming increasingly fragile along the way. When she met length-man Jim Forrister, whose job was to oversee that particular section of the canal, it was in his cottage by the bridge that, after the incident, Lilly lived out her days peacefully. After discovering the family link, Edmund saved Quietwater Cottage from demolition, and immediately began its renovation. With Frieda by his side, they had notched up fifty quietly loving years in it. They never intended to live in the old dowager's house. *It was far too grand for us. Far better to share our good fortune with others.*

While Edmund occasionally took the Anna Lee out, Lise was her official skipper. Refits and maintenance were carried out by another branch of the Heathcote family, a father and daughter team, living and working at Fereday Boat Yard, five miles west. When not in England, Lise's whereabouts were generally a mystery, although she kept in contact with Frieda, and her parents who lived in Denmark. Kristian's sporadic visits were divided between the Anna Lee, and Quietwater Cottage.

I told Edmund that Tish had given me her phone number and he said, *Dear Tish, always on the lookout. She'll be a good friend. Don't wait until next year to visit, April. If it gets too choppy, you may need a sanctuary. But remember, it's often more painful for those who may feel you are leaving them behind.*

I started the car and opted for the picturesque route back to Westwytch. Passing a country inn, I stopped for lunch, and sat at yet another picnic bench, this time with no calming water or wooded banks for company. The pub's sizeable crowd were making the most of the long weekend, and it hadn't mattered at all that I was alone. Finishing this thing with Sebastian was long overdue and was now at the top of my priority list. Once again, I'd be footloose, but this time, it would be a liberation. With Embla just over the horizon, I'd formulated a plan. As there'd be zero space to park on the drive, I'd leave my car in the village, and come in through the side gate beside Mum's office, where, with a bit of luck I could whip upstairs without being seen.

π

'April, you're home!'

I put a finger to my lips. Harriet tiptoed up the stairs behind me, and into my bedroom. My over-enthusiastic hug surprised her. 'Sorry for the cloak and dagger, Harriet. I need a minute before seeing the family. Hey, you look flushed.'

'It's a scrum down there. Bradley has actually drunk two ciders, but under the circumstances, he's entitled to celebrate his success, and it is *soooo* good to see him upbeat.'

'How's Sebastian?'

Harriet frowned. 'He's staying at ours. Bradley insisted on putting the fold up bed downstairs, at least until Seb's off the crutches ...'

'Seb's on crutches! I thought it was a mild sprain.'

'April, the ex-ray was clear. The doctor classed the injury as a grade one, and a few weeks at the most should do the trick, but Seb's the expert. Bradley will drive him to and from work so he can continue with his personal training clients, but the massages will have to wait.'

'What sort of mood is he in?'

Harriet wrinkled her nose.

'Be honest, Harriet. I don't want to make things worse than they already are.'

'Let's just say I've seen a different side to your boyfriend this weekend. Are you two having problems?'

'Why d'you ask?'

'A hunch.' She sat on the edge of my bed. 'I may as well tell you that the entire event came unstuck from the beginning. I don't know what sort of weather you had, but it rained non-stop in Warwickshire. Your uncle Max and Vikki's van broke down, so the bikes and tri-suits were late arriving. No prizes for guessing how Sebastian reacted to that. Mid-way through the race, he got tangled up with another rider and they crashed into a rail. Thankfully both received no more than bruises and sprains, but when Vikki offered to call you, apparently Sebastian bit her head off.'

That wasn't a good move. My aunt was a champion tongue-lasher, and she wouldn't have been happy to be on the receiving end. 'Is Vikki here? I'll go down and apologise.'

'She couldn't come, but Max is busy smoothing things over. He feels responsible for getting the weekend off to a bad start.' Harriet sighed. 'Anyway, enough of the psychodrama. Tell me everything.'

I sat on the faded blue velvet stool, reflecting on Harriet's summary. Sebastian was milking it, and Bradley would be too blind to see it, but that was their business. Did it matter that Seb was staying in Westwytch? He wasn't likely to pop in for a cup of tea with my mum. 'How to describe those four days, Harriet: wonderful, magical, unbelievable. You'd have loved the Anna Lee.'

'Did you take any photos?'

'Didn't even think of it. I only found out about Seb's injury last night. I knew that if it were serious, you'd call. Anyway, you were right about Lise's massage technique. I couldn't believe it when she offered me a session, which, by the way, knocked me out for hours, but since then I've felt amazing.'

Harriet's 'pipping the leader at the post' grin was a tonic. Maybe it wouldn't be so bumpy after all.

'I told you she has magic hands. It's been weeks and I can still feel the effects. If only Lise were available on a regular basis.' She laughed. 'I had visions of you jumping overboard after the first morning. I mean, two miles an hour for someone as zip-wired as you, April. Thank goodness it didn't turn into your worst nightmare.'

'Whose worst nightmare? Oh, you're back.'

Bradley's lopsided smile evaporated, and my heart sank. He was ruddy-cheeked, and wearing a baseball cap backwards, all highly irregular.

'Seb's in the living room, resting up. He's been through hell, and you didn't even have the decency to call him. Everyone's rallied round ...'

'Take it easy, Brad. It's not exactly April's fault, is it? Seb will be up and about by Tuesday.' Harriet's smile was almost, but not quite, convincing. 'Shall we go down? I was about to make tea, but you know how everyone prefers yours.'

'Sure.' Recalling Edmund's wise words, and the potential for my family to feel awkward or disjointed, I was determined not to get sucked into their theatricals. 'Hey, congratulations on your personal best, Brad. You must have smashed it in the transitions.'

'Oh – yeah, thanks. It was pretty amazing, wasn't it Harriet? Fastest ever 1500 swim, and T2 changeover was supersonic.'

I followed Bradley's tipsy tweet into a packed living room, which smelt like a department store's perfume counter. My 'who wants tea' shout was greeted with the same response as always, as if I'd never been away. Sebastian was enthroned in Dad's sacred armchair, his booted right foot resting on the footstall and an ice pack at the ready. I resisted the urge to laugh, kissed his royal cheek, and made suitably sorry noises about the injury. After that I spent several minutes batting off Xander and Declan's banter, before escaping to the relative quiet of the kitchen. It was good to see my cousin's new partner hold his own with my lot. It helped that Declan held the 25 mile club TT's fastest average speed, and he was The Red Balloon's restaurant manager.

Insanely relieved to get that initial scene over, I began slicing through Mum's triple-layered carrot cake. Just then, my father sauntered in. He was carrying a trayful of empty glasses.

'You're back, then.'

'Hello, Dad. It's good to see you too. I had a great time, thanks. Where's Mum?'

Never one to rise to any bait, my sarcasm flew over his hair gel. The Hayle clan still felt the need to outdo each other on the grooming front, that was guaranteed.

'She's at Millie Gladwell's house. The family arrived yesterday to confirm the funeral arrangements.'

Of course! Why didn't I go there before coming home? Millie Gladwell had been the most endearing of Mum's homebodies. When Fielding and Nair's annual charity project included her bungalow in the *Redecorate Robertson Row* project, she had cheerfully provided refreshments throughout the day. Her bread pudding was legendary. 'Mum must be taking it hard. Millie was as good as a mother to her.'

'It's your mother's way to get over-involved.'

Yeah, in the same way that you and the precious family are over-involved. I filled the teapot, my hackles up. Dad hovered nearby, obviously with something to say. *Please don't let him start on about Seb. I don't think I can take another bashing.*

'Bradley did well. It's great to see him find his form. He feels guilty about the accident, so he's overdoing the Nurse Nightingale bit. Your mum thinks Sebastian is playing on the injury. She offered him an Arnica remedy but he wasn't keen.'

'What's your opinion?'

'About Sebastian's injury?'

My father stood for a while, thinking, mulling, chewing it over. He did that a lot, and it had never bothered me before, but now it was bloody infuriating.

'He's not faking it. I didn't realise until this weekend how much our family mean to Seb. I wonder if Bradley would have done so well without him onside'. He wiped the tray with the cloth and stacked it with plates and cutlery. 'Despite being laid up, Seb has suggested a terrific idea to reinvigorate the holiday this year: a surf and turf event, with league table, and medals, and even a sand-castle competition for the nippers.'

For the first time in days, my shoulders contracted. 'That'll give him something to do while he's nursing his injury.'

Ignoring my comment, my father continued to wax on as if Sebastian sodding Espie were wholly responsible for my brother's improved psychological wellbeing. What about Harriet and me! It was more than annoying. This was typical of my father's personality – the holiday 'problem' was now strategically solved and his vision could be actualised. I tucked a bunch of folded napkins under the forks, wishing he'd buzz off.

' ... Russ is all for it, although your aunt Chrissie's pulling a face. She wants to go abroad this year and had her eye on Portugal. Still, my spoilt little brother usually gets his own way. Russ never wants to be left out of anything, does he? To quote his well-worn cliché, *when all's said and done, blood is thicker than water.*' He picked up the re-stocked tray. 'Right, best get back to the fray. Harriet's offered to help us clear up before your mother gets home. In Brad's current state, he's about as useful as a chocolate teapot, bless him. Never could hold his drink.'

My father laughed at the thought of his 'blessed' son, and exited the kitchen with the laden tray, leaving me to digest his proclamations. He wasn't interested in hearing about my trip, and neither was Bradley – not even a pretence at being interested, *and* I was expected to clear up their bloody mess! Had they deliberately colluded to make me feel insignificant as retribution for feeling betrayed, or was I over-reacting? It was impossible to keep cool, which was the biggest surprise of all. In fact, the strength of my anger was worrying, especially after feeling so chilled.

Having prided myself on owning a steady and balanced personality, to experience the other extreme was not a state I wanted to wallow in. Lise and Edmund had been so right to put me on alert.

As for Sebastian, he was clearly loving his moment in the spotlight. I wasn't at all surprised that he hadn't asked me about the boat trip. It just proved we had nothing left to say, and it meant that letting him go would be so much easier. With a bit of luck, they'd all buzz off home, and I'll have a good catch up with Mum over dinner. She at least would want to know the ins and outs of my weekend, and for once, I'd be overjoyed to share them with her.

16

The town centre was oppressive in the June heat. Pedestrianisation was all well and good, but how could acres of concrete absorb the increasing amounts of rain? Even F&N had raised the issue with the council after the flash flood's devastating effects on the new office. Perhaps this time the planners would get their act together and get planting. Loughborough's overheated shoppers and their dogs would definitely appreciate the much-needed shade.

At Jonty's Café, I sat at a table furthest from the window and ordered a *Frappuccino*, just the thing to cheer me up before driving to number 44. It had been four weeks since the boat trip, and I was having trouble keeping up appearances. Everything felt anaemic. My work/life routine was the equivalent of wading through treacle and my mind had taken to drifting back to the waterways, usually somewhere between Quietwater Bridge and Tyrley. Reliving those magical moments with Lise and Elkie, (and curiously, the quietly serious face of her brother), was fast becoming hard-wired. This hadn't gone unnoticed. When Gita Nair arrived onsite for the monthly update, she asked to see me. Her unfaltering interest in my career was flattering, but her disappointment was the last thing I wanted to take on. The upshot of our 'chat' was to discover if her protégé continued to be the excellent prospect she had so confidently predicted.

My apparent downturn had been attributed to the death of a close family friend. While this was stretching the truth somewhat, I reiterated my commitment, and explained that a chronic, childhood spinal condition had flared up, and was affecting my sleep, blah, blah. My medical history wasn't a secret, but Gita was no fool. No one could have sustained such a pace without a fallout somewhere along the line, and that might have been why my promotion wasn't mentioned, which was, interestingly, a relief. She suggested I finish up the remainder of last year's holiday by taking a couple of long weekends. It was an inspired idea, one that I immediately implemented.

π

There was no news from Lise – obviously. I was the last person she'd have been thinking of whereas the Anna Lee's new crew had been very much on my mind. I wondered how Kristian and Sofie had changed the dynamic. Did they wander the towpaths under celestial skies, with Elkie leading the way: were they getting it on in the same berth that I had slept in? *And what if they were?* I had pinned the canal map to my bedroom wall in an attempt to follow the boat's progress, based on their conversations that last day. By now, even with several long stops, they must have reached the Caldon Canal. Lise's invitation to re-join her onboard may have been genuine, but I just couldn't bring myself to turn up. Such an unscripted move had the whiff of desperation about it, and it wasn't my style. As there was no obvious way of contacting her, apart from speaking to Edmund, I resorted to Plan B.

With Sebastian and Bradley now fully re-engaged in their training schedule, I used the 'busy workload' chestnut to absent myself in order to drive to the nearest canal for a top-up whenever I could. It was easy to get away. With lunch or an evening snack tucked into my backpack, I went in search of the local towpaths. These were considerably busier this now being the summer season, and yet there were long periods when I didn't see a soul. When a narrow boat floated by, I always waved, and almost always received a wave in return, and when I encountered another human on foot, often we'd stop for a chat. It never failed to amaze me how a person will tell you their entire life story in exchange for admiring their dog.

Those short intakes of nirvana had become more than a pilgrimage. As soon as I entered the aqueous labyrinth, my stresses and strains were superimposed by uplifting sensations, just like those I had experienced on the Anna Lee. Under the circumstances, it was enough. Amazingly, my spine had remained pain-free despite the tension at home, but the most shocking discovery of all was that I really liked being alone.

π

The cool coffee was a tonic. A cyclist rolled on by, prompting me to think about Sebastian, and the evening ahead. When had we ever sat in a café, chatting away the morning? Harriet had been lumbered with him for an entire week. I got the feeling that she was glad to be shot of her husband's best mate. I visualised the scene ahead. Having carefully prepared my pre-dinner speech, and using the friendliest voice possible, I'd suggest that Seb and I release each other from the 'bond' and stay friends. Our financial arrangements would remain as they were until he was on his feet, (I was considering moving back to number 44 within six months) and my family would continue to welcome him as before. We'd clink glasses of filtered water, talk triathlon over a basic protein salad, and endure a brief hug before I left him to his early night.

π

My mother and I were passing ships. The opportunity to talk to her about my trip never materialised as when she came back from Millie Gladwell's house that night, she had declined dinner, and gone straight to bed. I rarely saw her at breakfast as she was generally the first one up and out, and as I usually worked late, apart from weekends, we only ever shared an evening meal when we made a date. But there was no mistaking the peculiar atmosphere at Embla. Even Dad was treading lightly. To my surprise, he'd delegated a European business trip to a colleague in order to help clear Millie's bungalow. The 'family' consisted of an elderly sister and a grizzled gum-chewing niece who had flown in from Malaga, both incapable of opening an envelope. Mum's prolonged emotional reaction to Millie's death had made her extra-sensitive, but as Harriet astutely pointed out, there had been other losses that year and when taken together, they must have shaken her up.

With regards Brightside Park, I had no idea if my mum planned to join us, but even if she were, there was no way she'd bother attending the next get-together, scheduled at The Red Balloon for the following week. The events/social programme for 'Brightside Unleashed', (Sebastian's super-duper name for it), had to be rubber-stamped, and it promised to be a raucous evening. Max was determined to make up for the Warwickshire fiasco and had arranged with Declan to lay on a good spread. He also intended to foot the bar bill. This generous act would bestow universal forgiveness for his perceived misdeed. Despite feeling discombobulated, I intended to be there.

Jonty's mop swish snapped me back to the evening ahead. I finished up my drink, thanked him for the coffee, and was once again smothered by the stifling air. I walked to the car, aware that every second brought me closer to releasing the burden of being with Sebastian, and it couldn't come soon enough. At least my breakfast meet with Tish was something to look forward to. She'd immediately followed up my text message with a phone call, during which we'd nattered on like old pals. When she suggested getting together, I was more than relieved. Remembering what Edmund had said about needing good friends, there was no one better suited to hear every detail of my voyage on the Anna Lee than Tish Swanson.

17

'Forget your key?'

No smile, no kiss.

'Yeah, sorry – mad rush this morning.' The spare house keys were, as always, in my bag, but it would have been wrong to let myself in knowing that in no time at all, I'd be on my way to Embla, untied and floating free. I followed Sebastian's closely shorn head along the hallway. He was wearing a shirt and had gone to town on the aftershave, but my alarm bells really clanged when I entered the kitchen. The table had been laid with wine glasses and a vase of white chrysanthemums, *and* there wasn't a single item of training gear in sight.

'Join me in a glass.'

'You don't drink, Seb.'

'I feel like celebrating.'

Please don't let him have come to the wrong conclusion about us. He passed me a glass of chilled Rosé and sat opposite. I prayed that the beads of sweat glistening on his top lip were the result of the scorching day, and not his nerves. Seb didn't do nerves well. Pulling himself upright, his chest rose and fell in time with his breath, unconsciously counting the beats per minute. Before I had a chance to open my mouth, there it was, the long determined sigh, which signalled the start of a speech.

'Since my injury, I've been having a serious think about things – training, work, home life – call it a review, if you like. A bit like those meetings you have in F&N, but this one with me as both boss and employee,' he announced, chuckling at his observations. 'Coming to Leicester has turned out to be a good move in lots of ways and, well, anyway what I'd really like, April, is for us to move up a gear.'

My baffled expression threw him.

'What I mean to say is I've realised how important you are, not just to me but also to the family. Everyone missed you in Warwickshire. Xander says you've always been the lucky mascot, so it wasn't surprising that the event went pear-shaped. Mind you, even if you had been there, Max would still have screwed up the ...'

He droned on, while I battled an escalating resentment. *The family.* Seb was telling me that *the family* – my family – think I'm important! I cut him off. 'It's good to know I'm not just someone who's handy with a toolkit.'

'Look, I didn't mean it to come out like that, but ever since you went away on those weekends, we've drifted apart. I'm not blaming you, April. My schedule is as mental as yours, and as I said, I'm willing to review it. We can do stuff, go out once a week, just you and me.'

Sebastian put down his glass and pulled on his fingers, making that awful popping noise. Despite feeling aggrieved, I was genuinely sorry for what I was about to say. 'I had no idea you felt this way, Seb, and I'm flattered, but the thing is, I feel exactly the opposite. To say that we've drifted apart is stretching it. Neither of us have cared enough to talk about our relationship if you can even call it that.'

Silence.

'Be honest Seb, the casualness of it suited us. It was convenient to hook up, two sad stragglers at the end of the night, no longer needing to go home alone. I can't remember the last time we had sex, let alone go out to a restaurant without the rest of the family in tow. We'd be much better off as friends, like we were before.'

Sebastian blinked away a flash of anger. He wasn't going to take this well after all.

'I read that all wrong, didn't I? So, you're calling it off – that's fine, April, if it's really what you want, but in my opinion, you're making a serious error. Still, this won't be the first time I've been dumped, will it?'

'I don't know Sebastian. We've never talked about your ex-fiancé. In fact, Bradley knows you better than I do, so what does that say about us? I've never insisted on hearing your backstory, but you must admit, it's a bit weird to say nothing at all. Who knows what you might be hiding.'

'That's what comes of having a suspicious mind, April.' His eyes narrowed. 'I s'pose you want me to move out.'

'Of course not! This is your home, at least for the next six months. I've been thinking about leaving Embla and will probably move back. Anyway, you'd struggle to meet the rent without the reduction and you're not the sort to take advantage, are you, Seb?'

He was wrong-footed and changed his tone.

'I was about to increase the rent, but then this bloody accident happened and it's put me behind. I've only just caught up with the personal training sessions. While I was laid up, I had to call every client to keep them on board. You have no idea how hard it is to be self-employed, April – people letting me down, changing their appointments, chasing payments ...'

'Please don't insult my intelligence, Sebastian. I spent two years working in our forensic accounting department. If I had wanted to dig into your finances, I'd have done it when you first came here.' I omitted to say that I had thoroughly checked his credit ratings profile as Bradley's impassioned reference for his new best mate was hardly reassuring.

We sat for a while, staring at each other. The heat was stifling, and I was desperate to get out. It was time to finish what I'd come to say. 'Look, Seb, if you're concerned about my family, I can assure you they like you, and won't treat you any differently.'

'Is that meant to make me feel better?'

'It's the truth.' As I got up to go, Seb put his hand on my arm.

'You're seeing someone else.'

'Excuse me?'

'That woman you met at Ninebarks – the one Harriet was banging on about. That's why you've been acting up since you came back from the boat trip. You've been waiting for the right moment to make me redundant, and now that you've found a replacement, I'm out on my ear.'

Spite is an ugly, distorted thing, and I was shocked to see such a transformation on Sebastian's face. 'That's an interesting theory, but you don't fool me. If you had genuinely cared for me, you'd want to know how the boat trip went. In fact, you'd have encouraged me to go, and I would have gladly told you all about it. But guess what, Seb – here I am in the dock, the accused, as if *I've* done something wrong! I'm sorry you're upset, but that's it – we're done.'

Sebastian followed me along the hallway, and for an awful moment I thought he was going to stop me leaving. I quickly exited the house while he stood at the door, barely able to contain his fury.

'Bradley said you were an iceberg. He said you use people to suit your own needs, but I didn't believe him. Either you're an expert liar, April, or I'm just plain bloody stupid.'

Bradley had said that? Surely that wasn't how my brother saw me. Anger burned my tongue, but I refused to be contaminated by those vindictive words. 'You're not stupid, Sebastian. Secretive, certainly; self-centred, definitely. You and Bradley make a great team.'

Under Sebastian's blazing stare I got into the car as calmly as was humanly possible, and with trembling hands, started the engine. By the time Embla's reassuring presence came into view, my breath was steady and my shoulders had dropped. It was over.

18

'I reckon you've been totally bitten and smitten by the Anna Lee. You look really good on it, April.'

I refilled Tish's cup. We'd been in the Top Dog Café in Brewood all morning, and had breakfast, croissants, stroked every dog, and dissected every single millisecond of my narrowboat trip. 'Thanks so much for listening, Tish. I expected to have this conversation with my mum, but as predicted by Lise and Edmund, my re-entry has been more than bumpy.'

'Most people who walk through Angel Ninebarks' door don't realise they're carrying a bundle. Things often feel as if they're getting heavier before they get light, if you know what I mean.'

'I know exactly what you mean. It's a sort of limbo-land. I don't want my life to be the same as it was before, but I don't know what to do next, outside of trekking the waterways with my telescope, hoping for a sighting of the Anna Lee.'

Tish spluttered on her coffee. 'It's that bad?'

'I'm joking about the boat, but not about the towpaths. I've stumbled upon a whole new world and it was right under my nose, Tish. Even though Harriet and I had been to Angel Ninebarks before, it's only now that I've figured out there's more to life than office politics and triathlon times. Trouble is, everyone else thinks I've lost the plot.'

'April, you need grounding. Why don't you join us for next weekend's workshop? It's a two-nighter, one small group, and light duties. The course is Hedgerow Medicine. Ruth Mackey knows how to have fun, and you said you wanted to do something worthwhile with your annual leave, so there you go.'

'What a fab idea. I'm definitely allowed?'

"Course you are. Didn't Edmund suggest you stay connected with the community? Well, April, now's your chance.'

Tish's grin was hard to resist. 'Thank you. It's exactly what I need. It'll give me breathing space from my family, and Sebastian. We've been on the road to nowhere for months, and he wasn't too happy when I broke it off.'

'That's the massage guy?'

'Yep. I finally jettisoned the family favourite and predict a plummet in ratings when they find out. The most shocking thing was that Seb was ready to commit.'

'What went wrong?'

'Nothing went 'wrong' as such. We sort of drifted into it, and my family acted like I'd picked a winner. Sadly, their opinions have been far too important for far too long. Seb's a popular guy, but there were so many times when it didn't feel right ...'

Tish's concerned expression brought me to a halt. I didn't want to ruin our lovely morning, but it felt good to talk to someone outside the family. I started to tell her how the Hayles had welcomed Sebastian into the fold despite knowing so little about him, but the words hovered, sounding flaky at best. 'Ignore me, Tish. I've just spent four days with Lise Michelson, and all I know about her is that she had dodgy grandparents.'

'Now that's what I call gold dust! But seriously, April, you don't strike me as someone who doesn't know a gut feeling when she feels it. It takes courage to go against the tribe. The risk is being exiled – an outsider, and I'm an expert at knowing what that's like.'

'I've never thought of it that way. How ironic would it be if Sebastian Espie took my place in the family.'

'Don't be daft. I can't imagine for a minute that your family would swap a total fab for a total drab.'

'Ha! Actually, I'm not without an ally. My mum's bullshit detector sussed him out from the start. He's always been nervous around her and tends to stick to Dad and Bradley. It's shameful to admit that I've only recently acknowledged my mum as an individual in her own right. Not only are her actions motivated by the wish to be of service, but she's maintained her independence from the inhabitants of Planet Hayle, which is no mean feat. Harriet and I want her to come with us to Ninebarks next year. It's about time I got to know her.'

'Your ma sounds amazing. Now that I've been asked to join the staff, I'll get to meet her.'

'You've been accepted, Tish? Congratulations!' A nearby cockerpoo jumped up to join our hug, which prompted another chat with his embarrassed owner. 'This definitely calls for a celebration. It's a pity Angel Ninebarks doesn't sell fizz, but my guess is you don't drink anyway. We'll find a way to celebrate next week.'

'This is the start of a whole new life, April. I'll have a home, and people who'll appreciate me for who I am, and not judge me for how I look. Oh, I nearly forgot to give you this.' She pulled a magazine from her bag. 'It's called *Mycelium* but it isn't all about mushrooms. It's our network magazine and it links the global community. You wouldn't believe the amount of brilliant initiatives going on, and so many other bits and bobs besides.'

'Thanks Tish. I can't wait to read it.'

'Check out the pages in the back. That's how I found my bedsit.'

It was all in the timing. There was every chance that the key to my next move might be in this magazine. Number 44 was an option, but the only reason for telling Sebastian I wanted to move back in was to get him to move out. I was looking for a new direction altogether.

Tish and I exchanged excited goodbyes. It was one of those special mornings where a new friendship is made, and on my part needed more than ever. During our chat it transpired that we were almost the same age, and yet Tish's world view was so different. Places like Angel Ninebarks were more than simply refuges for the marginalised or the lost. They proved it was possible to live peacefully *and* work creatively without causing havoc to humanity, and the planet. But even if the opportunity arose, would Angel Ninebarks be a good match for me? Thankfully, I didn't have to make that decision yet. Hanging around with these insightful, open-hearted people was enough to keep me afloat.

19

The most surprising thing to discover about lying was how easy I found it. Wasn't there a saying that desperate times required desperate measures? At that point, justifying my behaviour hadn't occurred to me, let alone to stop and consider the consequences or trajectory of my duplicitous actions, but the outcome would probably have been the same, whether I'd lied or not.

When I told Harriet that Sebastian and I had parted company, far from being happy for me, or offering support, she said it would make her life more than awkward. Obviously, she'd have preferred me to stay with Seb as now he'd cling ever more tightly to Bradley, the consequence being that Harriet's motherhood plans would drop off the radar, but that wasn't my problem. I may have overreacted to my sister-in-law's antagonistic response, but never before had I felt so alone and misunderstood. There was only one person who would be remotely interested to hear about Tish's guest-helper invitation.

Mum was, at long last, alone in the office. Thursday was Liz's day off, so I grabbed the opportunity to sound her out.

'Hi Mum. I brought you a fresh cup of tea. How's it going?'

'Thanks, pet. Now that Millie's funeral is over, we've finally caught up on the paperwork. I had to force Liz to stay home today, but she agrees we can't carry on like this. With social services under increasing pressure, people like us are stretched to the limit.'

'Why don't you take on more staff?'

'You sound like your father. Taking on more staff is as fruitless as building more roads to ease the traffic when the solution is to provide an affordable and efficient rail system the first place. It's not friggin' rocket science, is it April? Until our support networks become the norm, the more we do, the less the powers that be will do. Half day?'

'Gita suggested I take last years' leave before the end of summer. F&N think I'm going off the boil, which I suppose, in a way I am.' I swung on the seat of Liz's office chair like an anxious child. My mother didn't follow up on my comment which was frustrating as I was ready to hear some good sense. Now that I wanted her, she didn't appear to want me. 'Mum, I'm going back to Angel Ninebarks tomorrow as a guest helper. It's only for two nights, but if anyone misses me, which is unlikely, can you say I'm on a course. Sebastian mustn't know.'

'I thought you'd finished with Sebastian.'

'I have, but he ... Let's just say he wasn't best pleased when I ended it. The less he knows about my business the better.'

'It's a bit late in the day for that, April. You of all people must have seen Sebastian's plimsoles permanently parked under our kitchen table. Do you intend to go to Brightside Park?'

'Why shouldn't I? Mr Smartarse may have organised it, but I'm still a part of this family. Are you going?'

'Probably, but I could do with a longer break. Liz has already booked her holiday, so mine will have to wait. Connie wants me to stay with her for a week. Your dad won't be happy. He's never liked her.'

'Why not?'

'She frightens him. But Connie's my oldest and best friend, and if he took the trouble, he'd find that she's the kindest soul he's ever likely to meet.'

I felt awful. Mum was having a tough time, and even someone as capable as her needed respite. Connie O'Hara gave the impression of being scary, but when Bradley and I stayed with her for a weekend to give my parents a break, we had bundles of fun. 'I've an idea, Mum. Why don't we spend a few days together, y'know, after everyone else has gone? We could see Connie ... '

If the office phone hadn't rung, I swear my mother was about to cry. Something was going on, and it made me nervous. The call was taking forever, so I got up to go. Then, Mum put down the phone, and turned to me with a face I didn't recognise.

'April, why do you need to lie?'

'Sorry?'

'I'm asking why you need to lie. While you're away this weekend, think about the consequences that lying will bring about. I can predict the outcome if you can't.'

'But you don't even like Sebastian.'

'It's not about Sebastian. Now that he's lost his meal ticket, he won't stick around much longer. This is about you.'

The phone rang again. I thought my mother would leave it, but she didn't, so I stomped out of the office and back to the house, smarting at the scolding. What was *that* about? Why wasn't she champing at the bit at my suggestion to spend time together, bearing in mind it was her most frequent lament. Knowing how my mother felt about Sebastian, she should have been thrilled that I'd broken it off. And so what if I lied. If the Hayles hadn't been so myopic, of course I'd have told them.

As for my colleagues, no one wanted to hear about my new adventures. They were more interested in why I hadn't been promoted yet, although not one of them had asked me outright. It was my own fault, of course, as I'd never taken the time to properly befriend anyone. Apart from the quizzes and special occasions, socialising with my colleagues wasn't high on my agenda, although if Maureen invited me to her weekly pub lunch outing, in the state of mind I was in, I'd have been only too happy to accept.

I flew up the stairs to pack, pulling out clothes, banging drawers and doors, chucking the hangers around like confetti. My fledgling inner calm had taken flight into the grim atmosphere. Roll on tomorrow when I'd be away from this miserable house, and its unpredictable inhabitants and back at Angel Ninebarks, with people that understood me.

20

What a welcoming sight! Tish was waiting at the desk to greet me, wearing a cherry red *Rebel Yell* T-shirt and her characteristic grin. I followed her up the grand staircase to the top of the house, and into an enormous room under the eaves. The guest-helper accommodation consisted of four single beds, each one dressed with uniquely designed bed linen, and separated by sumptuous Japanese silk screens, creating a private, cosy space for the duration. My fellow volunteer, Josefina, another first timer, was just as eager to be on the staff and like me, raring to go.

Shadowing Tish was a blast. We soon got the hang of the booking system, house-cleaning requirements, and post-workshop barn clear-up. Ruth invited us to join the group activity, as this was part of the deal, and who were we to argue? Foraging around the estate's hedgerows yielded a generous bounty while adding to my growing knowledge of plant food and medicine. Conversation ranged from how to make nettle tinctures and plantain salves to the madness of removing words such as acorn, bluebell, and wren from the dictionary. When asked about the guest-helper programme, Josefina and I were only too pleased to share our enthusiasm with the workshop attendees.

Volunteer numbers were increasing, which was good news for the future of Angel Ninebarks, and a sign of changing times. Although the duties were light, the weekend was tiring as we'd kept late hours, talking way into the night, but the best moment of all was seeing Sofie's stained-glass window in the hallway. It was too beautiful for words.

In the past, people had upped and left when they discovered that life at Angel Ninebarks wasn't the utopia they imagined it to be. Tish's acceptance onto the staff was dependent upon a three-month try-out. After that, she was committed to stay for a minimum of two years, with regular reviews on both sides. In contrast to her former bedsit, the ensuite bedroom was spacious and comfortable. Although cooking was mostly shared, it was equipped with kitchenette and telly and was so much more than she had hoped for. House and garden duties were arranged via a rota, and according to experience. Anyone could learn any skill, provided there was time to do so. A decent living wage was paid, but as accommodation, food, and tuition was found, there was nothing much to spend money on.

Angel Ninebarks' sound business model was a balm to my figure-hugging brain. Marguerite Monkton had left a sizeable endowment, while the global Ninebarks family kept the goodwill flowing (tutors voluntarily donated a percentage of their earnings from in-house workshops). The guilds attracted sponsorship, and grants, and were often highlighted as exceptional experiential learning models. Once Tish had a suitable skill to share she'd be paid for her workshops, and subsequently increase her savings. If or when she left the house, it was important to be able to manage financially on the outside, but the option was available to join other like-minded groups.

It may have sounded strange, but I was glad Lise wasn't at the house. As much as I longed to see her and Elkie again, my sole purpose was to understand the Ninebarks philosophy and working arrangements before considering an application to live there. To see Edmund Heathcote again, though, was a huge boost. Being hugged so warmly by this benign father-figure couldn't have come at a better time.

With the exception of my mum, Uncle Max was the most openly affectionate of all the Hayles. He and I regularly messaged each other with new quiz questions and suchlike. It was Max's suggestion that Bradley manage his new gym, over on the business park. My brother was encouraged from the beginning to make the decisions, but Max was always on hand to help his antsy nephew. He must have suspected I'd been fibbing about work, but mindful of undermining his venerated older brother, Max had wisely suggested I call him when ready to pick up where we left off.

Under the circumstances, latching onto Edmund was predictable, particularly as he was also Lise and Kristian's uncle. He had joined us in the dining room for our last breakfast during which he enquired after the well-being of each guest and helper in a sort of post-event debrief. As soon as we'd finished, Edmund asked to speak to me in the library.

'Nothing to worry about, my dear. I thought it might be easier to relay this information to you in private.'

'Has something happened to Lise or Elkie?'

'You may rest assured that all is well on the Anna Lee. I've something for you. It came through the post yesterday.'

He gave me the envelope before turning to leave.

'Please stay while I open it, Edmund.' We sat together on the long chaise and with as much composure as I could muster, I slid a single square of notepaper out of the envelope. It was the same paper as before, when those four words changed the direction of my life forever. I read and re-read the note:

Etruria Basin,
mid-morning

Edmund roared with laughter. 'Lise is a one-off. Why use a hundred words when four will do. Two invitations, eh? You must have seriously impressed my niece, April.'

'This is definitely for me?'

'Yes, my dear. Two weeks' on Friday. It's the extra limb on the Four Counties Ring. The Caldon Canal is remarkably unspoilt and a feast for the senses. It was restored in 1974 – hard to believe it was the most polluted on the canal system, although there are still surprises lurking beneath that mysterious water. On one occasion, we rescued a brassiere from the propeller, and that particular riddle tickled us for days.'

'Crikey, I hadn't even considered such a thing. My first trip went like clockwork.'

'Give it time. Narrowboaters are by their nature generous storytellers, and the towpath telegraph does a great job of keeping the boaters informed. If you know one end of a spanner from another, they're generally willing to help.

Boating can be an expensive business, even when you are handy.'

A member of staff called out for Edmund, which was a real shame as I could have listened to him all day.

'Time to go. Frieda needs to prepare for her appointment with the orthopaedic surgeon tomorrow. She's finally agreed to have her hip replaced.'

'She'll be up and about in no time. My grandma has had both hips done and there's no stopping her now.'

'A cruise along the Caldon Canal and through the Churnett Valley would slow even the feistiest grandma down. It's about a seventeen mile run, in a roundabout route – a weekend at the very least will cover it. From there, the Anna Lee will make her way back to Quietwater, in good time for the August break. Lise doesn't suffer with 'itchy tiller'.'

'Ooh, that sounds uncomfortable. What is it?'

'The need to get going, to see what's around the next bend, to notch up the lock count, that sort of thing. As you know, Lise likes to meander, and though Sofie and Kristian will have sights to see, they are at least familiar with the concept of going with the flow. Give me a shout if there's anything else I can help you with, April. I hope you can join them.'

'Edmund, just try and stop me.'

π

I sat in the library, staring at the precious missive. Another trip! Once again, Lise had come up trumps. My heart was racing at such a rate, I felt like sprinting around the garden, whooping for joy at the prospect of another adventure on the Anna Lee. Did I mind that Sofie and Kristian were still on board? Surely they wouldn't be bonking all night long whilst we were moored up in such quiet surroundings. I laughed to myself – no, they definitely wouldn't do that.

I froze. *Oh, no, not again. It's the bloody Brightside Unleashed week!* There was no way I could get out of it. If I didn't show, that really would be it, as far as my family were concerned. I'd already volunteered as scorekeeper *and* I'd agreed to play beach volleyball, having been sweet-talked into it by Xander and Eva. Distraught, I tucked the note into my pocket and exited the house via the orangery to avoid being noticed. Instinctively, I made for the witch/wizard bench and there I slumped, my thoughts trapezing with no happy outcome either way. To say I was utterly miserable was the biggest understatement of the millennium.

Then, Tish appeared, all haystacks and grins. 'There you are! We thought you'd ducked out of final duties ... April, what's wrong?'

As ridiculous as it was, I cried like a babe in her arms.

'Don't apologise, April. Tears are supposed to be shed, or you'll suffer the consequences and believe me, I know all about that. Now, why don't I nip off and make a pot of tea and when I get back, let's see if we can sort this muddle out.'

And that's what we did. On that fine Sunday morning, sitting together in Angel Ninebark's lush herb garden, Tish and I concluded that there was no reason why I couldn't do both. After joining the Anna Lee for three days, I'd organise a taxi to take me back to my car at Etruria Basin and drive directly to Cornwall, in plenty of time for the first round of events. Tish reminded me that a third of my precious life was already over, and if I passed this by, an invitation from Lise might never come again. She was so right about that.

Thankfully she hadn't asked whether I intended to tell my family about the change of plan. Once I'd had time to mull it over, I was confident of knowing what to do. Then, Mum's warning flapped before my eyes like a race track's red debris flag. *Think about the consequences that lying will bring about. I can predict the outcome if you can't.* Based on my family's previous reactions, there was a strong possibility they wouldn't handle it well, in which case I'd keep the news to myself. Yes, it was lying by omission, but was it really so awful? As for the outcome, at that moment I couldn't have cared less. Tish had helped me to find a solution, and I'd earned the right to be excited.

21

The Red Balloon was rowdy and hot, but I felt cool and carefree. The evening was almost over, and spirits were high. Having artfully dropped into various conversations the headline of my delayed arrival, as it was assumed to be work-related, there was neither comment nor protest. Sebastian must have decided to postpone our break-up announcement as that wasn't mentioned either. He was on top form. After officiating over the details of his world class programme, he'd joked his way through the evening, bigging up the holiday as the best ever, (like he'd been around for thirty years to know) and predictably had bashed out the Hayle's top ten anthems to whip up anticipation.

After a couple of generous Spritz cocktails, I felt more chilled than I'd done in months. With no obvious risk of discovery, I'd bounced back to the habitual version of myself – joshing with my cousins, getting ribbed by my uncles, being sweet to my aunts. The weather was humid, so I premiered my new floral sleeveless top – the habit to cover up had of late felt less important. When it came to personal grooming and wardrobe, Eva never missed a trick, and as I predicted, she was about to give me the once-over. As Max and Vikki's youngest, and the last born cousin, everyone treated her as the baby even though she was twenty-two. To our universal relief, Eva had inherited her father's charming manner. It was common knowledge that when Sebastian first arrived on the scene she had fancied him, but when he and I got together, she couldn't have been happier for me.

'Hey, April, you're looking mighty fine. I'm loving your tunic, *and* the wavy hair-do. Aren't you lucky to have inherited your mum's sangria tones. It's good to see you show off your fine self. Must be Seb's influence.'

'Thanks, Eva. I feel great, and yes, Seb has had an impact, but not in the way you think.'

'What d'you mean?'

'We've split up, but you might want to keep that to yourself for a while, y'know, with the holiday coming up. We don't want to spoil it.'

Her thick-lashed eyes widened. 'Oh no! I'm really sorry, April. Are you heart-broken?'

'No, it's all good. We weren't exactly marriage material, were we?'

'Guess not. As long as you're okay, though.'

'Honestly I'm fine, but thanks for asking.' It suddenly occurred to me that Sebastian might take advantage of my darling cousin. Instantly, my protective shield was primed. 'Look, Eva, if Seb asks you out, just be careful, will you?'

'Me? I don't think he'd be that cheeky. It'll take Seb ages to get over a front pager like you. Anyway, gotta shoot. Mum wants to get back for the new series of *Peaky Blinders*. See you at Brightside!'

Overflowing with affection, I hugged Eva tightly before watching her tinted locks follow my speedy aunt out of the pub. I finished my drink and was about to say my goodbyes when Sebastian approached.

'Hello April. Great night, wasn't it?'

'Yes, it was. How are you?'

'Can't wait to unleash. Everything okay with you and Eva?'

This annoyed me. He'd obviously been watching us. 'Why shouldn't it be?'

'I wondered if you told her about us.'

'As a matter of fact, I have. Is that a problem?'

A pause. 'Of course not. I've always liked your cousin. Eva will make a great partner for the body boarding tournament.' He sipped his filtered water, flinty eyes glued to mine. 'Actually, I was going to break it to everyone next week. I haven't even told Bradley. Been putting a brave face on it.'

I ignored his sad act but was nevertheless surprised to hear that Harriet hadn't told my brother. 'Harriet and Mum already know about us, so that means Bradley and Dad will be in the loop. They'll be keeping it quiet, until you're feeling better, that is.' A cloud of fury swept his face. He'd been overtaken, and Sebastian was not a good loser. 'You didn't ask me *not* to tell anyone, did you Seb? Anyway, with regards the lodge, Harriet will share with me, so you can bunk in with Bradley. We wouldn't want you to feel embarrassed or left out.'

'My accommodation and travel is already sorted April, so don't bother yourself on that score. Anyway, enough about me. How was your 'working weekend'? F&N must be paying you a massive wad in overtime with all this extra effort to bring in new business.'

He knows.

'That must have been why your car was parked up at Angel Ninebarks. Have you brainwashed them into hiring your excellent chartered accountancy skills, April?'

Anger and shame blistered my cheeks. Sebastian had followed me there! My instinct was to run out of the pub, to get home, to think about what to do next, but something inside me reared up, forcing me to face him. Harriet had said she'd seen another side to Sebastian, and if I were in any doubt of his true colours, they were now on full display, to me at any rate. But he wouldn't dare cause a scene on his big night in front of my family. 'Here's a suggestion, Seb. When you make your tearful speech next week, don't forget to mention you've been stalking me. Better still, Max and Russ are over at the bar. I'm sure my uncles would want to know that their niece has finally lost her marbles and has joined a cult.'

Sebastian knocked back his drink and placed the glass on the table, just so. 'It'll keep. Goodnight, April.'

π

Back in the safety of my bedroom, I paced the floor. How quickly had Mum's words come back to bite. Sebastian had followed me to Angel Ninebarks! What to do? Should I tell Dad? I could scoot over to Bradley's house. He and Harriet would still be up, and they'd have to be on my side – but against who or what, exactly? Hadn't I decided that they weren't mature enough to let me have other interests? Talking to Harriet was pointless. She had her own concerns, and besides, she looked totally miserable at the pub and had left early. As predicted, Bradley and Sebastian had been in serious discussion about *Ironman* for next year's big project.

It occurred to me that as an outsider, Harriet, like my mother, had maintained a helicopter view of the Hayles. Maybe that was why they got along so well. Harriet had learned to play the family game, but was currently experiencing the downside, just as Mum had done. The difference was that my sister-in-law didn't have the benefit of her own support group. She and Bradley shared the same friends, mostly from the running club, and the demands of her job left no time or energy for book groups or knitting circles. While she was waiting around for my brother to decide whether or not he wanted to be a father, Harriet would be better served by following my lead and find new interests outside the family.

With the alarm bells subsiding, I changed into fresh pyjamas and brushed my teeth. Studying my reflection as uncritically as was possible, Eva's generous comments floated across the mirror ... *you're looking mighty fine.* The grey circles under my eyes had lifted, and my cheeks actually had what might be called colour. Yes, I was looking better, healthier. Feeling brighter by the second, I decided to play forward the next few days as a way of working out what to do. Would it really matter if my family knew I was about to embark on another narrowboat trip? When I arrived at Brightside Park, I'd be as enthusiastic as the next person. The most important thing was to be 'seen' to be in the gang.

As for Sebastian, I couldn't believe that anyone would make a fuss over our break up. He risked staining his reputation if he admitted to checking up on me. My guess was that he'd play for sympathy without casting me as the villain. What other choice was there? We needed to call a truce. I'd soon be a footnote in Sebastian Espie's life, but right now he was too angry and immature to do the right thing. I sent a text message to thank him for organising what was going to be a great event and wished him a safe journey. After packing two bags, one for the boat and one for Brightside Park, I climbed into bed, quietly excited.

22

Déjà Vu. Etruria Basin, mid-morning.

I was here and there she was, the fabulous Anna Lee, moored up just yards away. A nervous exhilaration pumped through my bloodstream so I deliberately slowed pace and breath on my approach. Standing beside Lise on the stern was a straw-hatted man wearing rolled up shirt sleeves and whose dark clip braces were fastened onto canvas boat trousers. It was Kristian. His outstretched hand helped me onto the boat.

'You can join us after all. Good morning, April.'

That welcoming smile floodlit the overcast morning and instantly calmed me down. Was this the same uptight guy I'd met in May? It must have been the Anna Lee effect. Then Elkie appeared from below, and immediately nuzzled my hand. Whilst cuddling the gorgeous dog I felt the siblings' arctic eyes lasering my back. When I stood, Lise held out her arms and in I fell.

'April, it's so good to see you! And good timing as Kristian is about to make coffee. After a short break, we'll set off. We've taken on water, and supplies. Sofie and Emmanuel have gone in search of ecclesiastical windows and will be back soon. As we are a full crew, it may be a little cosy on board.'

'Lise, I'm so grateful to be here, I'd sleep on the roof. And as Sofie is still with you, I can congratulate her on the stained-glass panel. It's hanging in the hallway and looks fantastic.'

'Ah, yes, you were at Ninebarks as a guest helper. How are the trees?'

We laughed, and those previous turbulent weeks vanished. I was so ready to set off on another tremendous adventure: no Sebastian, no Planet Hayle, no F&N.

Kristian had disappeared down the steps with my holdall. Questions as to where I was going to sleep, how had the trip been so far, who was Emmanuel, levitated like dust motes in the sultry air. Lise was as usual, ahead of the game.

'Thank you for bringing your sleeping bag, April. That was thoughtful. Emmanuel is a family friend and is extremely useful to have on board for many reasons. His enthusiasm may be a little overwhelming, so you have my permission to escape when necessary. As for the sleeping arrangements, you'll have the same berth, as a single occupant. We don't have a rota, so if there is anything specific you'd like to do, please speak out.'

'Sure. You may have guessed I'm not backward at coming forward, Lise.'

'An essential characteristic for a good crew. Sofie and Kristian will cook dinner tonight. It will give you time to readjust.'

Before I could thank her, Kristian's head reappeared at the hatch. 'You'll need a strong stomach, I fear. Coffee is ready.'

We retreated below to a basket of freshly baked pastries and the almost familiar wonderfully aromatic brew. I sat down with a mile-wide grin. To be back on the Anna Lee was the only place in the world I wanted to be.

π

We passed through eight locks that day. Lise had steered while Kristian and I walked on ahead on paddle duty. Watching a lock crew in action on YouTube wasn't nearly as interesting as doing it myself. The theory of emptying and filling the lock hadn't been difficult to grasp but I wasn't sure how my back would react. Whether Kristian was aware of this was impossible to say, but as we worked together, the entire process ran as smooth as could be. He was stronger than he looked and helped me more than once with truculent paddles. It was hugely satisfying to feel the heavy oak gates move as my body weight leaned against them; to hear the water seep, or on occasion gush through the gates, and to marvel at the click-click of the windlass as it wound the thickly greased paddles.

Our conversation was in the main what I'd call techno-historical. We agreed that for a lone boater, it must require immense patience and skill to carry out the various tasks needed to steer *and* lock, and yet we'd already passed two solo travellers that afternoon. Elkie had her own agenda. She'd perch in precarious positions overlooking the various locks, the effect of which made my hair stand on end. But by the end of my trip, her high-wire stunts would no longer cause alarm, and the canal terminology of cill markers, staircase locks, and winding holes would become friendly, familiar language.

After a short stop during which Lise practically climbed into the weed hatch to untie what appeared to be a pair of long johns from the propellor, we followed Elkie along the towpath cossetted by wooded valleys and hills. According to Kristian, before the railways arrived, the inland waterways had proved to be much more profitable than the roads – a single horse at a steady pace could pull at least thirty times as much on a barge than on a cart. When I asked about the rubbing strips attached to the sides of the bridges, he explained that they had been fitted to prevent the horses' thick tow ropes from damaging the bridge bricks. Kristian seemed bemused by my volley of technical questions until I confessed that way back when, I'd dreamed of being an engineer.

'Then the riddle is solved. But as an accountant, how do you express that side of your nature?'

I smiled at the question. It could have come from Lise. 'My family are cyclists. I'm often asked to fix saddles and such-like, and as my dad isn't wildly practical, I generally deal with the house stuff.'

'You live with your parents. Are they elderly?'

How to answer that? Was Kristian implying I was too old to live at home? 'Not unless you count sixty as elderly. I have a house, but for the moment I choose to live at Embla.'

'I apologise, April. We're an odd lot, so you must forgive us if we occasionally cause offense with our spirit of enquiry. By the way, do you know the meaning of Embla? In Norse mythology, in the story of *Midgard*, Embla, and her husband Ask, were the first humans. The gods, of which Odin was one, created them from pieces of driftwood.'

'Wow! So that's what the tapestry in the house means. I wonder if my mum knows that? I seem to remember her being interested in that sort of thing, but she's too busy caregiving to do much for herself.'

'Are you one of her recipients?'

'Occasionally.' I changed the subject, still feeling aggrieved at my mother's gloomy predictions. 'Where do you call home?'

'Copenhagen. My apartment is situated beside the Christianshaven Canal, within cycling distance of the university. My neighbours and I share a cat, or should I say, she shares us. Thomasine is a beautiful old-style Siamese. Unlike Elkie, she is the epitome of what you'd call a *scaredy cat* and doesn't like her routine disturbed. We make a fine pair.'

His sense of humour was unexpected. We laughed, and he said, 'So you see, April, there is a good reason why I don't go out as often as I might. You, on the other hand, have an enviable freedom. To be able to join us at short notice is impressive. Your employer and your family must be exceptionally understanding.'

Blood hurtled into my cheeks, unmasking my shame. As much as I didn't want to talk about the Hayles, I *had* to tell Lise's brother the truth. 'Actually, the only people who know of my whereabouts are Edmund, and Tish Swanson, who you may know from Angel Ninebarks. I'm scheduled to meet my family in Cornwall on Sunday for a massive contest, thinly disguised as a holiday.'

'Where do they think you are?'

'In the office. Workaholism and competitiveness are genetic dispositions in my family. Until recently, I never considered them to be so insular, but when my recent stay at Angel Ninebarks clashed with a triathlon whose competitors included family members, the overall reaction was, erm, unexpected. My sister-in-law was the only one to have asked me about it.'

Kristian was quietly absorbing this. His pace slowed to a stop, and he turned to face me, his eyes sorrowful.

'No one will win this competition, April. May the losers have the wherewithal to be gracious.'

As Kristian's words sank into my consciousness, I concluded that there would be no more lies. I'd find the courage to walk in my own shoes, to uncover a 'me' independent of the Hayles, whether they liked it or not.

Just then, Elkie trotted off to greet Sofie and a man who I assumed to be Emmanuel. After scooping her up, he made such a fuss that I found myself chuckling. Sofie reached us first. Her embrace was warmth itself.

'April! So glad you could come. You saw Pomona?'

'She's stunning, Sofie. You must be thrilled with the panel.'

'And so must you. Your handiwork helped to make it what it is.'

The crazy dog lover bounced over with Elkie hopping at his heels. I'd never seen her so playful.

'Meet Emmanuel Marcellin. He has a passion for all creatures, great and small. We can say *au revoir* to a peaceful voyage,' said Sofie, laughing.

'*Non*, I promise to behave.' The stocky, wild-haired man's grin was infectious. 'Pleased to meet you, April. I hear you are something of a nuts-and-bolts enthusiast.'

Emmanuel's titanic hand swallowed mine. 'I've been known to carry a spanner on occasion, but from the looks of things, I should have brought my pistol. Will I have to challenge you to a duel for Elkie's affections, *Monsieur Marcellin?*"

A mighty Gaelic bellow thundered along the canal, catching the rest of us in its wake. Emmanuel was the sort of person who instantly made you feel good. We were in for a terrific weekend.

π

The *badinage* continued over our towpath picnic, but later that day when Emmanuel and I shared the stern, I saw another aspect to his personality. He was acutely aware of the earth and everything on and in it. Unsurprisingly, his expertise in environmental science was in fierce demand. Fortunately I didn't have to dig too far to declare my eco-credentials, albeit vicarious. 'My brother and I learned about sustainability through a sort of maternal osmosis. There were no factory-made sandwiches or cans of fizz in our packed lunch tins, as much as we might have craved them. My mother has been a Greenpeace member for decades. In fact, she was volunteering at Glastonbury Festival when she met my dad.'

'*Quelle romance!* Two eco-warriors falling in love under magnificent Somerset skies.'

'If only. My dad and his brothers went to the festival to see a band called The Mighty Lemon Drops. That's the family joke – Dad went to Glasto for a blast of Indie and brought home a hippie.' I leant over to net a rogue plastic bottle before expertly and with satisfaction, dropping it into the rubbish bag.

'I sense that all is not quite well at home.'

Just like Kristian, Emmanuel had his finger on the Hayle pulse. I slid the pole back on the roof. 'My mum and her friend run a not-for-profit business which, amongst other things supports independent living for older people. My dad is a senior honcho at Carrow Corp. He says my mother is his conscience.'

'Truly? Carrow has an abominable track record. Your father will need much more than your mother's conscience to atone for his career in *that* business.'

'What do you mean?'

'You don't know? Multi-nationals such as Carrow aren't famous for their altruism, that's for sure. They serve their own selfish needs at the expense of others and use our precious planet's resources as a commodity, purely for profit. Your mother may be *engagé*, but your father ... you know April, the number is up. The new laws will dictate the new behaviour, like it or not. In the meantime it is we who will do the clean-up ...' He paused, mid-rant. 'Please forgive me. *C'est l' ésprit revolutionnaire*. A thousand thanks for Lise, and the Heathcotes. I still have the fire, but they help me to redirect it in creative ways: more evolution than revolution.'

We were back on an even keel, but Emmanuel's comments were disturbing so I made a mental note to look into Carrow's environmental credentials once home. Despite that, I'd sniffed a golden opportunity to find out more about these intriguing people and Emmanuel was willing to talk. 'How did you discover Angel Ninebarks?'

'A chance meeting, or perhaps not, depending on one's outlook. My father was horologist, and *maman* a fine artist.

They worked together in their atelier, in Normandy. It was beautiful while it lasted. When she died, my father sent his rebellious teenage son to school in Paris. That is where I met Sofie.'

To accommodate an oncoming vessel, Emmanuel skilfully slowed the Anna Lee through a narrow stretch while Snow Angel, a shiny stainless steel tug approached. A scruffy two-tone terrier, decked out in a pink polka dot neck scarf had staked its lookout position on the roof, the sight of which sparked an hilarious exchange with the crew as we passed.

'Impressive, *non*?'

'The boat, or the dog?'

'Both! Where was I? Ah, yes, after our studies, Sofie went to Copenhagen, to sit at the feet of Kristian Michelson, the esteemed historian, but he would hate me to say that. Do you know the Danish free thinkers? *Non*, okay, well, that is his profession, and of course, the writer Jens Peter Jacobsen. Anyway, from there we came to Angel Ninebarks.'

'You lived there?'

'But of course, for three incredible years. I am also specialist in the field of mycology and gave many workshops. The subject is becoming increasingly widespread, and rightly so. It was there, at Angel Ninebarks that we met Lise. It was as if I was once again embraced by my mother's loving arms.' He wiped his eyes with the back of his shirt sleeve. 'Of course Lise isn't a 'mother' in that sense, but there is in her a unique quality I've never encountered in anyone else.'

'I totally agree. You can imagine how I felt to be invited for another trip.'

'Ah, but that is because you are ready. It is so important to have the right people by one's side during the big life changes. I come back to the Motherhouse to rest otherwise who can say where I would be today ... Le Bastille perhaps?'

We travelled on in silence, but it wasn't in the least awkward. So much of what Manny had said had resonated, and although his remarks about my dad and Carrow Corp's ethics had shocked me, the scales were falling fast from my eyes. As we approached the next bridge, I spotted Elkie. 'Hey, the others are waiting for a pick up. Shall I put the kettle on?'

'Why not, April. I adore the English afternoon tea, but you know that on the Anna Lee, we too have our traditions.'

Emmanuel pulled a hip flask from the inside of his gilet, and I laughed out loud. 'I like the cut of your jib, Emmanuel.'

'Ha! Please, call me Manny. Fruity cake, a cup of Earl Grey, and a soupçon of brandy – this is what you call the life!'

23

The Caldon Canal was every bit as picturesque as Edmund said it would be. We had entered another world entirely, shielded from pockets of industry and housing estates by densely wooded hills and abundant valleys. Our mooring was in an enchanting spot, a few miles from an ancient woodland known as Hollinhay Wood. The late afternoon sun had cast caramel shadows over the land beyond the canal, the effect of which made me feel like crying.

I set about laying the table. Kristian and Sofie, so easy in each other's company, prepared dinner using the contents from a basket full of mushrooms that Manny had foraged from the woods earlier that day. Lise was visiting the liveaboard on Pinwheel, one of the permanent moorings nearby. The boat was immaculate. According to Sofie, the artwork had been hand-painted in the traditional style of the 'roses and castles' folk art which was probably invented by the boatmen's wives to brighten the cabin's ten by six foot interior which would have housed the entire family. My fascinating education was continuing apace, but the most revealing fact to emerge was that Sofie and Kristian weren't a couple after all. When Manny reappeared pink-faced from his shower, he wrapped his arms around Sofie's waist in a way that only a lover would do.

Travelling on the Anna Lee with this crew was totally different to my first trip. Over *Hen of the Woods pilaf*, the ebullient conversation encompassed topics ranging from the Ninebarks' anniversary guest list to the difference between existing and living. My opinion was sought, but mostly I wanted to listen. Lise had maintained her customary good-natured silence, but every now and then she'd skilfully steer the dialogue to calmer waters. Sofie and Kristian's reflective manner was the antitheses to Manny's fiery disposition but the mutual respect and admiration ran deep.

To my amazement, Manny was the editor of *Mycelium*, the magazine whose contents I had recently devoured. There were groups of people across the globe, either sharing houses along the lines of Angel Ninebarks or living in separate dwellings, but each committed to leaving a super-light footprint. When I asked him about the magazine's inception, Manny picked a mushroom from the basket and held it up.

'Mycelium is *the* root system: it reaches out underground, into soil, wood, and plant. On its return, nutrients and water are given to the mushroom. You may have heard of the *wood wide web*. It is, one might say a symbiotic relationship, as it facilitates the exchange of the good stuff from all over the forest and does so without fuss.' He kissed the mushroom before putting it down. 'From that very first day at Angel Ninebarks, it seemed to me that the house is also a life support system. It connects us in subtle, profound ways. So of course, the magazine became *Mycelium*.'

'Excellently summarised, Manny. And now we have a new addition to our ecosystem. I propose a toast: to April, fellow fungi. May she bloom and grow,' said Sofie.

I gulped the last of my wine, although secretly pleased to hear such an open-hearted comment. If anyone had noticed my beetroot blush, no comment was made, unlike my merciless family who spared no one's embarrassment. It was incredibly easy to feel inspired by these lovely people, the effect of which had sprouted the germ of an idea whilst walking the towpath earlier. Sofie must have guessed I had something to say and smiled encouragingly.

'These mind-bending mushrooms have got my grey matter in a spin, so please forgive me if this sounds far out, but I'll say it anyway. Sofie, while you and Kristian are out bridge hopping, researching your own specialist subjects, there must have been a number of industrious amateurs living and working along the waterways who would greatly benefit from their day in the sun. Why not excavate their stories? A collaboration between you and Kristian would make for an exciting read.'

Sofie made a kind of whistle, one that signified pleasure. 'Our baby fungi makes an interesting point. I've had many interesting encounters on my side of the bridge, Kristian, and have heard fascinating accounts from several of the locals willing to share their history with me. We already know so much about the Arts and Crafts glitterati – perhaps there is something here.'

'Indeed. If it hasn't yet been undertaken, it would certainly be a subject worth consideration. You and I could pool our resources ...'

Feeling mightily pleased, (and having been submerged by a huge yawn), I left them to it.

π

At some point during the night, a pitiful cry woke me up. Was it an owl, or a fox hunting dinner? Whatever it was, it had given me the shivers and it had taken an age to get back to sleep. When I awoke the next morning, the memory of it lingered until lovely Lise came by with a mug of tea and a biscuit, waving away the ghosts. As the Anna Lee was staying put for a while, there was no need for me to be up just yet. It was Saturday: day two. The morning sun was toasty warm on my sleeping bag and stomach-rumbling breakfast smells floated along the gangway. After drinking the delicious tea, I stretched luxuriously, revelled in a soapy shower and dressed leisurely. Over berry pancakes and local maps, we discussed the day. I say 'we' – it was thrilling to be considered one of the crew whose ideas and suggestions were incorporated into the schedule.

'Sofie and Manny are cycling to Leek and will stay overnight. Kristian and I will meet friends near Longsdon. You are welcome to join us unless you have other plans,' said Lise.

'I'd be delighted to stay behind. I'll make dinner, something with mushrooms. Will Elkie keep me company?'

Right on cue, the dog put her paw on my leg and in the next moment the boat lurched, prompting the cups and pots to clash and clatter. In a flash, Manny had jumped up to the window to gesticulate at the skipper of the guilty fibreglass cruiser. At the sight of my alarm, he sat down.

'Please excuse the outburst, but these stupid people are travelling too fast. You can see from the wash, it is breaking. In the places where there is no concrete piling, the towpath becomes eroded by this crazy driving. The skill is to cruise along without causing a ripple.'

Lise pointed to the map. 'If you are still in one piece, April, and would like to walk here is a picturesque trail around Hollinhay Wood. It's a steady climb to Ladderedge, downhill through the country park and back via Stanbridge Farm. Five miles in total. For your level of fitness, it will be easy. Here is the hatch key and my phone number, just in case.'

'Thanks so much, Lise. This will be a real treat.'

'My enthusiasm has overwhelmed our guest. Perhaps tomorrow we will read Proust under candlelight,' said Manny, sheepishly.

He tousled my hair, and cleared the table like a pro, his mischievous eyes twinkling. Until then, Kristian had been quiet, but not sullen. Like Lise, he possessed an enviable tranquillity. He passed me a slim book, *Letters to a Young Poet*, by someone called Rainer Marie Rilke.

'If the silence is too much …'

And in the next breath, he was gone.

24

Four hours had passed, and it had felt like twenty-four, but in a good way. After waving off my hosts, to begin with I didn't know what to do. Can you imagine what it felt like to actually get what you'd always wanted even though, until that moment, you hadn't known what it was because you thought you already had it? Yeah, it sounds confusing, but that's exactly how it was. I'd never paused to consider whether I actually enjoyed accountancy. Being good at something didn't necessarily mean getting pleasure from doing it. The clear, structured path I'd followed had brought financial success and a certain prestige, all of which had engendered a feeling of security. Whether I was happy or not hadn't occurred to me until recently. But on that awesome day, when I had the great good fortune to be the Anna Lee's skipper, *and* have Elkie for a companion, the elation far outweighed all previous experiences combined.

Our intended walk to Hollinhay Wood very nearly became a casualty of a bunch of friendly towpath encounters, the first of which were a couple who enquired about the boat. You can imagine how proud I was to announce the Anna Lee's sustainability pedigree alongside my crew credentials. Then came the solo boater, recently split from her partner of fifteen years. He'd taken the meaning of 'permanent mooring' literally and had refused to move Vagabond from its resting place at the marina. Newly liberated, the intrepid skipper was now single-handedly making her way along the inland waterways and had never been happier.

When we finally reached the ancient woodland, a frisky spaniel attempted to catch Elkie's attention while his owner was only too pleased to recount Merlin's most recent and hilarious antics. Ignoring the canine interloper, Elkie stoically allowed the human to rumple her coat before shaking the excitable duo off in order to resume our stroll. Lise had suggested I look out for wood sorrel and if appropriate to pick a handful, which I had. On the way back to the boat I nabbed a bunch of knapweed, chuffed at my budding foraging skills.

π

Holding a glass of lime cordial in one hand and Kristian's slim volume in the other, I headed for the foredeck, *aka* cratch, (under which items such as wood, tools and engine oil are stored). Until then, I hadn't sat in the space outside Lise's berth but was now itching to enjoy this new view. The deck seating was comfortably cushioned and was the perfect spot from which to watch passers-by whilst enjoying shade and shelter. With Elkie's bed nearby, there we roosted, undisturbed. Dozing off was inevitable and *sooo* luxurious, as not so far away the world was going about its feverish Saturday afternoon business.

Half-an-hour later, refreshed and ready to embark on a read, I opened the book. It was a relief to find a biographical summary along with a description of how the letters from the 'young poet', sent between 1903 and 1908, came about. People from the world over had written to Rainer Marie Rilke, celebrated poet/novelist, and many had asked him for advice, Franz Kappus being one of them. That both men had been students at the same Austro-Hungarian military school, albeit at different times, connected them in a deeper way. While the subject matter was unfamiliar, several passages immediately struck a chord: the importance of solitude (in nature, and with animals); not to 'torment' loved ones with the newfound joy that comes from being alone; to move out of self-imposed ideas of security in order to be ready for anything. Animated by these wise words I went inside to fetch my notebook, hopeful to have the opportunity to discuss my thoughts with Kristian later on.

Task finished, I rested my feet on the cushion and closed my eyes, absorbing this new information. The wash from a passing boat push/pulled the water in time with my breath – hypnotic, soothing. Then a single bark flicked open my eyes. Elkie stood on the gunwale, her plumy tail wafting like a bedsheet on a breezy day. Kristian ambled towards us and was carrying a basket. He didn't appear to be in a hurry, so I exhaled my panic and as I stood, the book fell to the floor.

'Forgive me for disturbing your Elysian idyl, April. You were napping, I think.'

Flustered, I picked up the book. 'Not at all – I mean, yes, but I don't mind. Did you forget something?'

'Lise has gone on to visit someone with whom I have no connection. She will be back this evening.' He looked at his watch. 'It's a little early for tea, but I'm in the mood for breaking the rules. Will you join me?'

'I'd love to. What would you like?'

He lifted the basket. '*Mentha gracilis* – ginger mint. And wild strawberries. A feast.'

We rendezvoused in the galley. Trying my best to ignore the endorphin effect, I rinsed the fruit while Kristian rummaged about for crockery. How did I feel about his premature return? *He's broken your spell, spoiled your quiet afternoon, April. Aren't you just a teeny bit annoyed?* Within minutes we were back on the deck with our bounty. Kristian had unearthed an exquisite tea set, so appropriate for his slender hands. While he poured the amber liquid, I visualised a high-ceilinged sunlit room with burgeoning bookcases surrounding the eager students who drink tea while listening to Kristian's riveting tutorial. Was that a fair picture of his university life? How much teaching did he do? With luck I'd find out. Before I could ask, he passed me a cup and saucer and glanced at the book.

'You read the *Letters*. The markers are encouraging. It is a pity you aren't one of my students.'

'I'd never heard of Rilke before today but now I am hooked.' My cheeks must have matched the colour of the strawberries.

'It's not quite your field of expertise.'

'No, it's a world away from numbers, although humans share the same basic concerns whether poet or accountant, don't they?' Feeling emboldened by Kristian's nod, I put down my cup and picked up the book, turning to the first scrap of paper. 'So much of it seemed to be written for me. Oh, I'm sorry Kristian, I didn't mean to ruin your holiday with shop talk.'

'On the contrary, I'd be delighted to hear your observations. I'll remove my mortar board and promise not to interrupt with crass words of advice.' He rested his straw boater on the bench beside him.

'But that's what Rilke says!' I flipped to the appropriate page. 'He recommends that Kappus shouldn't listen to anyone's advice, and then he does the exact opposite and piles on the criticism. But he saves the day by admiring the young poet's sonnet and recommends that Kappus look within himself to find inspiration.' I turned to another section, now on a roll. 'The passages which describe the importance of inner solitude got me thinking. Rilke says that if we can face the suffering that inevitably arises when we are first alone, far better to remain with it than to exchange it for the banal. 'Without silence, we will never know the unknown'. That totally gonged with me, although don't ask me to explain how or why. It was intuitive, I guess.'

Kristian's expression was gentle, friendly, and went some way to easing my embarrassment at the realisation that I'd probably dumped a bucketload of tosh in his lap.

'Distraction is, for the majority of us, unconscious and habitual. Why sit quietly and face your own drama when you can follow someone else's on a screen, or in a book? But I think it has always been so.' He paused for a while and then, 'Rilke is a matter for the heart, April. It takes courage to step outside of our conditioned existence, but only by doing so can we understand his meaning. I say this with humility, as I profess to 'teach' Rilke, and yet I am his eternal subject. Your sensitivity does you credit.'

'Did you just give me a compliment?' It was a joy to hear Kristian laugh, all the more so as it took him by surprise. 'Thank you for lending me the book. I'll order a copy when I get back.'

'Please, keep it as a gift from a grateful scholar. I have a novel that may interest you, another slim affair but weighty with meaning. The author of *Niels Lyhne* is Jens Peter Jacobsen. He was a naturalist, artist, and poet.'

'Rilke mentions Jacobsen in the book!' I scrabbled for the page. 'Here, in the second letter, he recommends that Kappus immerse himself in Jacobsen's novels as *'the love will be repaid a thousand, thousand times'.* '

'A wonderful recommendation. Rilke has never been out of fashion whereas sadly, outside of Denmark, Jacobsen has endured many years in obscurity. Recently however, perhaps as a sign of the times, he is enjoying a deserved comeback.'

We sat without speaking for some time, and when the teapot was empty and the afternoon light was deep and golden, I took the tray inside, leaving Kristian to his contemplation. He was unlike anyone I'd ever met, but that was good. Who needed more of the same? Somehow, he had blurred the boundary between teacher and student – we were simply two friends, talking about a favourite writer.

Before starting dinner, I almost asked him to join Elkie and me on the towpath, but quickly dismissed the idea. Kristian possessed an intense sense of privacy, like a door barely ajar, so I left him alone and went for a brisk walk to the bridge in an effort to burn off my sizzling energy.

Kristian had dinner underway. Elkie's bowl had been filled, and the table was laid, with wine glasses. Manny was the only crew member who appeared to drink and had opened a bottle of wine the previous night, whereas I had decided to steer clear of alcohol for the duration. But the thought of supping on a full-bodied Burgundy was incredibly tempting, especially as it appeared that Kristian and I were eating alone, and a drink would steady my nerves.

After a quick shower, I brushed out my hair, pulled on clean jeans, and buttoned up my floral tunic. I'll admit to taking more care than was usual even though Kristian didn't seem the type to notice such things. The only jewellery I possessed was a twenty-first birthday watch from Bradley which I never took off, and my grandma Valerie's aquamarine and diamond ring, which I'd left behind for fear of ripping off a finger whilst locking. My sorry excuse for a makeup bag was also at home, which brought to mind Grandma Radka, who was constantly disapproving. *One day it will be too late to wear powder, April. You will look like a circus clown.*

As I applied a coating of lip salve, I thought about Cornwall. By now, the Brightsiders would be enjoying a boisterous dinner. If Sebastian had announced our break-up, I couldn't have cared less. During that first trip with Lise I had fantasised that, if she had asked, I would have left everything and everyone behind to go with her. This was, of course, ridiculous. Lise Michelson was definitely not on the lookout for disciples, but it was interesting to catch myself in the act of projecting my ideals onto her, fashioning her into an idol, and inevitably to criticize her if she didn't live up to my expectations. My mother had pointed out this tendency after I had fallen out with Olly, and on other occasions, too. Mum said it was a habit worth watching. As much as I hadn't wanted to hear it, she was right. The reality was that like everyone else I had to earn a living, but at least I was beginning to get an idea of what I didn't want, and that was a start. Being around socially engaged people was super stimulating, but to live at Angel Ninebarks was not for me. Sharing a house or a boat with someone as stoked as Manny would drive me nuts. I wonder if Kristian felt the same?

I rested my knife and fork together in the centre of the plate, savouring the tastes and flavours of dinner. Lise was right about her brother – he cut his food in exactly the same way as me. 'The roasted veg parcel was delicious, Kristian.'

'I have a confession – Lise had pre-prepared it, but the sautéed spinach was mine, and the strawberry pudding is to thank you for your company this afternoon.'

'Hey, you're easy to please. I'm sure I did all the talking. No wonder you needed a rest afterwards.'

'No, that was sheer indulgence on my part.'

He raised his glass, half-teasing. Kristian Michelson was fabulous company. He was casually dressed in a collarless shirt and faded jeans, and his feet were disconcertingly bare. He smelled of bergamot and orange, that same shower scent we all used on the boat. Obviously we weren't on a date, but I found myself comparing him to Sebastian, and was relieved to find they had so little in common. Kristian's calm and modest manner was all the more striking because it was so unusual to be in the company of someone who, on the face of it, had nothing to prove.

The evening turned out to be full of surprises. I hadn't expected music let alone to listen to an eclectic play list. Some of the songs were familiar while others were sung in a variety of languages, and every one a perfect complement for the dusky evening. 'Nice tunes, Kristian. I had you pegged as a classical music lover.'

'You are right, but my first choice is Keith Jarret.'

He smiled at my bafflement.

'He's an American jazz pianist and composer and is popular with us Danes. What you are listening to now is a compilation, courtesy of Manny. This was played during my father's funeral, last year.'

'I'm sorry to hear that. Were you close?'

Kristian was quiet for a moment. I wondered if he were weighing up whether or not to talk about it, and I suddenly wished never to have asked. He emptied the last of the wine into my glass, got up to refresh the jug of lemon water, and placed on the table two ramekins. The puddings were topped with sprigs of ginger mint.

'If you're not too weary, April, I will tell you about my father, but first let's finish our meal, and then we'll take Elkie for a last walk.'

25

Elkie must have sensed the importance of Kristian's imminent disclosure, as after making a pretence at sniffing the paths, she trotted back inside and went straight to her bed. We sat as before, the night enfolding us in its cryptic cloak. He didn't keep me waiting.

'Jerry Cresswell was a small music business cog with big aspirations. He started out as a roadie, and later worked as a sound engineer, and erstwhile producer. There were rumours of a Danish folk singer whose voice, it was said, came from the heavens. Her name was Katrine Michelson. This was the late sixties, around the time of The Band and Joni Mitchell, hence Manny's compilation.

'After hearing Katrine's voice on a recording, Jerry was compelled to go to Copenhagen. He became her manager and soon after, her lover. Within a year, Lise was born. Convinced that success awaited them in Los Angeles, Jerry persuaded my mother to go. After a single critically acclaimed but non-commercial first album and several disappointments, Katrine was desperate to return with Lise to Denmark. My father, however, had become subsumed by the emerging hard core drug scene, much more profoundly than my mother had. So, after making furtive arrangements she took Lise home, and seven months later she gave birth to me.'

I pulled a blanket around my shoulders while Elkie rose from her bed to curl up at Kristian's feet.

'When my father discovered that not only had he another child, but Katrine had re-joined her parents' religious community, he came to Denmark for us. What he didn't know was that his wife had subsequently suffered from a breakdown, and her parents were raising his children. With little resistance from them, Jerry brought us to England. His parents' London pub proved to be unsuitable so we were left at Quietwater, to live with Katrine's sister Frieda, and her husband Edmund, while he went back to Denmark to nurse our mother.'

'So that's how you're connected! Lise told me that she had four grandparents, none of whom were any good.'

'We were fortunate to have been cared for by a wonderful aunt and uncle who provided stability at a critical time.'

'What happened to your mum and dad?'

'Would you like to hear a happy ending?'

'Yes please!' Kristian's laugh was music to my sad ears.

'Eventually, we re-joined my parents in Denmark, and slowly our family unwrinkled. At fifteen, Lise began what you might call a nomadic existence, perhaps in search of her own truth. Who could blame her? She had borne witness to the worst of extremes: a counter-culture commune; a religious sect; mental illness. Lise had effectively been not only my sister, but my mother and guardian. It was time for her to simply be 'Lise'.'

'Did she have an education?'

'That depends on how you define education, April. Everything Lise has learned has been through necessity. She has worked as a translator, calligrapher, herbalist, masseur. Any residual conditioning or memory of the past has, for the most part, been erased. It is this that makes her unique. I, however, chose another route entirely. Academia has provided a security that was, or at least I felt was lacking. But of late, it has occurred to me that I've relied upon the certainty of dead friends for too long. Lise leaves the creaky old door open so that I may escape into the living, breathing air.'

I sighed, a long, amazed, sigh. 'You must be *sooo* looking forward to the Ninebarks retreat. I can't imagine what it'd be like to totally chill for an entire month.'

'As I have never attended one, I can only guess.'

'I assumed you and Lise did this regularly.'

'I have stayed at the house, of course, but a long break in those circumstances has never tempted me. And you, April? In this new quest for solitude, perhaps a spell at Angel Ninebarks would suit you well.'

'It sounds appealing, but I'd struggle with the silent periods, not to mention sharing the same space with people whose habits might be as annoying as mine. I have lived on my own but that didn't work out. It might be different now. Have you lived alone for long?'

Kristian smiled at the assumption, but the Burgundy had given me courage to take a chance.

'My constitution wasn't quite what my former partner believed it to be. You see, for many years I have suffered with nightmares – not every night of course, as that would drive me insane. Nevertheless there are episodes and this has proved a challenge. For the moment it is easier to live alone.'

'But surely there must be someone to help. What about Lise? She of all people could cure you. My back has felt amazing since her treatment.'

'It's not a question of cure, April. The nightmares will pass, it's just that I don't know when.'

'Considering the circumstances of your childhood, why wouldn't you suffer? Do you blame your parents?'

'Lise and I have moved past that. We accept that they didn't, or couldn't raise us appropriately, but the latter years have been good ones. Katrine and Jerry founded a Ninebarks equivalent in Skagen, with the emphasis on music, rather than Arts and Crafts, but the philosophy is the same. The people there will take good care of my mother, although like Frieda, she is fiercely independent. Lise and I visit when we can.'

I squeezed Kristian's cool hand. 'Thank you for sharing that with me. No one really knows how other people suffer, or what their motivations are, do they?'

'There are those who lie or hide their past simply because it is too painful to recall, but only the individual can decide for how long they will carry the burden, or unconsciously inflict it on those closest to them through their choices. Taking responsibility for oneself rather than blaming the other is easier said than done but Lise reminds me that it is possible – essential – to break free from these self-imposed chains.'

I thought of Sebastian and his secrets, and wondered if I'd been too hasty in condemning him, but if he wasn't prepared to share his past, how did he expect any relationship to work? There was one last question I really wanted to ask but Kristian had looked shattered, and it was late. What I said was this:

'You are so lucky to have Lise for your guardian angel.'

'Yes. Her whereabouts may often be unknown, but in my time of need Lise is always there, as she was last night when the nightmares came. What I do know is that wherever she is, the land is being healed. Are you familiar with your local history?'

I shook my head.

'In the ninth and tenth centuries, a number of prominent English towns, Leicester being one, were controlled by the Danish Viking Empire. It was known as Danelaw. Ethelfleda was King Alfred the Great's daughter. She protected Staffordshire from the marauding Danes – a rare flame of light in an age of dark. Ethelfleda became queen, or Lady of the Mercians. I'm surprised she isn't venerated here.'

'We've only just started to sift the historical wheat from the chaff. Obviously there are humans who are still incredibly violent, but back then it must have been terrifying.'

'Which is why Lise visits specific sites to plant either a tree, or a specific shrub or flower, by way of reparation. Much like the healers who travel the Michael and Mary ley lines, it is an ancient tradition and sorely needed. But you know April, the Danes were gentle people, too. A recent excavation in a Mesolithic cemetery in Vedbæk revealed a young mother of some status buried with a baby on a swan's wing.'

In the silence that followed, my habit to fill it with talk had temporarily taken leave. It was a landmark moment.

'My sister appears to be in perpetual movement, but when she lands she is as solid as the mountain. It is tempting to see Lise as the ultimate outsider, wisely peering in at our customs and behaviours, but I suspect she doesn't think that way. Perhaps it is her nature to be detached, or she has simply chosen to liberate herself from the conditioning and culture she was forced to endure. Whatever it is, April, I am fortunate to have been born as Lise's brother.'

Kristian stood, and I felt the sadness of a magical evening reaching its end. Then he smiled as if a tremendous event had taken place, and he was delighted to have shared it with someone. I was so glad it was me.

π

Sleep was a long time coming. My mind had whirled like a dervish: creating, conjuring, imagining. As I'd suspected, Lise rejected any attribution of insight or wisdom – hers was a humble existence which ironically, made her a target for needy people like me. As for Kristian, he was *the* most interesting guy I'd ever met. From a purely physical perspective, I hadn't expected to feel so intensely attracted to him, although I had no idea if he felt the same. My quest to unlock the enigma of these unique siblings was a step closer to being fulfilled, but in the process of doing so, it felt as if my moorings had slipped.

26

The Sunday morning breeze gently rocked the boat. The Anna Lee was due to travel through flint mill and limekiln territory towards Cheddleton, on the other branch of the canal towards the bewitching Cherry-Eye Bridge, (so-called due to the bloodshot colour of the ironstone workers' eyes). My original intention was to leave after breakfast but as Kristian hadn't mentioned my confession, and neither had the others enquired into my schedule, I calculated that even by staying until the following morning, it was feasible to reach Cornwall in good time.

Lise was eating breakfast. She poured me a mug of coffee while Elkie gave me a customary lick. I tried not to go overboard with the affection as the thought of leaving the dog behind was already having an impact. Apparently, Kristian had taken off earlier that morning to meet with someone or other and the crew had arranged to reunite later that afternoon. Lise must have sensed my disappointment.

'Good morning, April. We are as before, the three of us. Kristian had a pleasant evening. He complimented your attentiveness. I was concerned that his premature arrival might have spoiled your wish for a quiet day.'

'Not at all, Lise. I had several glorious hours before Kristian came back, *and* I read his Rilke book.'

'Hm. My brother, the eternal scholar. The writer has interesting observations on solitude.'

'You've read it?'

Lise threw back her head and laughed. 'Don't be so shocked, April. My little brother believes me to be without erudition, and who am I to correct his eminence.'

Was this the moment to ask her about something Kristian had said that first time we met? Catching Lise alone had been tricky, so I jumped in. 'Do you remember when Kristian said it was a waste of time clinging to the memory of my trip?'

'*It's already dust and ashes.*'

'Yes! What did he mean by that?'

'When we re-run or cling to past experiences, it is impossible to enjoy the present. We may compare a spectacular sunrise to the previous morning, or hope for better the following day, but what if it doesn't arrive? Often we are disappointed, or worse. It's the same with relationships. A best friend's comment made many years ago may still upset or disturb us. Memory *is* the past, and it influences our every thought and action.'

'But if it were possible to live without the past driving us, that really would mean a fresh start every time we saw someone or returned to a familiar place. It's an awesome idea, but much easier said than done.'

'It's not an intellectual concept, April. This is quite different from absorbing a mathematical formula or scientific theory. Technical knowledge to build bridges and to cure disease is necessary, but it is the psychological memory that causes mischief. It is through the process of self-knowledge that the nature of the mind is revealed and this requires tremendous energy and commitment. Who is prepared for that?'

I digested this awhile, and then asked, 'Kristian appears to know the nature of his mind but why does he cling to dead poets?'

'For the same reason you cling to numbers, April – the illusion of security. Now, Elkie is ready to stretch her legs. Why don't you do the same?'

π

Out on the towpath, I rewound our conversation. Could Lise have been referring to Olly's comments about my family all those years ago? I was responsible for the friendship cooling off for no other reason than being upset at a perceived criticism, proving that those fifteen resentful years had caused considerable mischief to my mind and probably my body. But how was it even possible to live from moment to moment, without the memory barging in? Following a single train of thought while it pedalled furiously around my neural pathways set me on edge. During a mini-break, Harriet and I joined a meditation session in a bid to calm our crazy minds. Counting each breath from one to ten and back again sounded easy enough. Everyone laughed when I told them how I'd raced ahead to get to ten, and I wasn't the only one.

The relationship between Lise and Kristian was in a different league. In fact, I hadn't encountered judgement or unwarranted criticism from any of the crew. Excluding

Mum, sarcasm ran like a mud slide in my family. Yes, we celebrated our successes, the proof being a cupboard full of trophies, but the losses (read: weaknesses) were never discussed without some kind of barb, and inevitably they'd be compared to what had or should have happened. It was just as Lise suggested, the past and future forever encroaching on the present.

By the time we stopped at Cherry-Eye Bridge, I'd spent much of the day thinking on such things, and my brain cells were ready to detonate. Manny and Sofie were the first to return. They greeted me like a cherished friend: how was my day; what had I seen along the way? One of their stops was Cheddleton, to the parish church of St Edward the Confessor where they had searched out Edward Burne-Jones' *Three Angels Window*. William Morris, Dante Gabriel Rossetti, and Ford Maddox Browne had designed the other windows – so much talent under one ecclesial roof. Sofie's portrayal of the 12th century sandstone building and memorial gardens situated adjacent to the church, conjured up a heavenly tableau in which she and Manny had eaten their picnic before going on their way to Leek.

When Kristian came down the steps into the galley, he seemed lighter, no doubt having divested himself of a heavy load. Lise may have left the trauma behind, but I doubted her brother was as skilful in that respect. Why else would Kristian still endure nightmares and shut himself off from society at large? Those ghoulish cries on Friday night were his after all, as he had sought solace from his sister.

Lise had prepared a risotto. During dinner, Manny announced that after the August break, he and Sofie were to nestle in Normandy. As much as they liked travelling in their camper van it would be good to sink some roots. 'Being back on the Anna Lee reminds me it is time to step off the wheel, and besides, my father needs help around the place. Whether Sofie and I can enjoy the same harmony as my parents once did who knows, but I am willing to experiment.'

Sofie patted her lover's arm. 'Mushrooms and paintbrushes could make for an interesting combination, but we will return next Spring, for the Ninebark celebrations. Will you join us, Kristian?'

'If I can find the courage to be among a crowd, perhaps I will.'

They looked at me. I shrugged and turned back to look at the maps which once again covered the table. The following day's itinerary took the crew along the Churnett Valley, and I wouldn't get to see it. My heart sank at the prospect.

'April, as the morning promises to be fine, would you like to paint with me? I know a perfect spot for water-colouring, and the meadowsweet is delightful,' said Sofie.

Tomorrow. Monday. I *had* to leave in the morning. There was no way I could justify another day, and neither could I lie to these beautiful people. 'There is nothing I would like more Sofie, but I must drive to Cornwall tomorrow to join my family, and I've already outstayed my welcome.'

'How nice for them but incredibly sad for us. At what time will you leave? Perhaps we can have a celebratory breakfast.'

'Yes! Sofie and I will make *oeufs en cocotte*,' said Manny, his great hands clashing like symbols.

I couldn't bring myself to look at Lise but her heatwave of compassion almost knocked me over.

'I wonder if your family can spare you for one more day, April. It would be a pity to miss this opportunity, and Sofie as you know is a talented artist,' said Kristian.

'Why thank you, *eminent scholar*. You are right on both counts.'

Their spirited banter diffused my tension. Should I stay? Could I stay? I hardly knew what to do for the best. The fact that they wanted my company was *sooo* flattering, and when would I ever get this chance again. 'I'm sure the tribe can do without me for one more day. May I accept your fabulous offer, Sofie?' And that was that. I hadn't lied.

π

Tucked up in my sleeping bag, I was ready to make a start on *Niels Lyhne*. Kristian had given it to me after dinner. He was interested to hear my opinion. *My opinion* – for an instant I wondered if he were mocking me, but no, he was sincere and his eyes looked a teeny bit less sad. Before turning in, we'd taken our customary walk. On the moonlit path, Lise and Kristian had stopped to listen to the softly sighing wind. Then, Manny struck up his version of *Moondance*, swirling and twirling Sofie whose laughter made my heart ache. Was there someone who might love me without expectation or need?

I pushed the self-pity aside and read the novel's jacket cover, despite my eyelids objecting. There was so little time left to share anything of meaning, and I was desperate to tell Kristian I had started his book as come tomorrow, he'd soon forget about me. Thankfully, no one had asked about the Brightside Park event. The less I said, the easier it was to believe that once at the lodge I'd blend in with the crowd – but not now. I couldn't face it. Neither could I stay on the Anna Lee any longer, but that was okay. Two extra days onboard were enough. When I got home, Embla would be deserted, and I'd have space and time to think.

The interior door eased open. Sofie was dressed in pyjamas and was carrying her sleeping bag, about to bunk down in Lise's berth as Kristian had done. They hadn't asked me to share, for which I was both grateful and embarrassed.

'Ah, you are awake, April. May I sit?'

I bent my knees to make room. Sofie's presence on the bed felt birdlike, weightless. Her soulful eyes lit up the darkness.

'Did you feel pressured to stay? We can be very persuasive, but you must do what is best for you.'

My shoulders instantly relaxed. 'I've decided not to go to Cornwall, Sofie. Feeling as I do, the commotion would be too much. But it's more than that ...'

'They don't know you are here.'

'No.'

Remembering what Lise and Tish had said about letting the pain out, I did just that. My tears carried within them the culmination of buried disappointments, hurts, anxieties, and who knew what else. Was this the start of my crash and burn? Sofie held me tight.

'For a heart to soften, you must allow grief to touch you or you'll remain sedated. It is a risk worth taking.'

She poured a glass of water and passed me another handful of tissues.

'When I came to Angel Ninebarks, my family didn't understand it at all. They said I had two choices, which really meant I had none. Even if I didn't want to follow their footsteps into the family business, it was my duty, they said. In twenty years, only one sister is in contact with me, but you know, I would choose my heart, every time.'

She kissed my head, picked up her sleeping bag and walked to the door.

'April, no one can advise you. Whatever you do, someone will be hurt, but that is for them to contemplate. You have made good friends, and you are widening your horizons which is to be celebrated. Goodnight, my love.'

I slid under my sleeping bag and wept once again – for my family, for the lies that I had told, and for myself.

27

I had made a decision. Those final twenty-four hours would be memorable, for all the right reasons. After sending my mum a text message to say that my back was too painful to make the long drive, and would she send my apologies, I switched the phone to silent, put out breakfast and went walking with Elkie. Whatever happened, no one could deny me this unique experience.

Sofie and I spent a glorious morning nestled beside the hedgerow in our fold-up chairs. On the table between us was a jam jar filled with water, paper towels, a variety of brushes and two palettes. She made no reference to the previous night other than a gentle arm squeeze. Then we set to work. Sofie prepared the paper with a light wash after which she layered the colours from light to dark, indicating where I might add the darker tones. The only thing to remember, she said, was *not to try to get it right*. After watching her make a sketch, Sofie left me to experiment. To begin with, the pale pink blossom swaying on stalks of dark green/silver leaves was impossible to capture, but I persisted, and was so grateful for the personal tutoring. It was my first attempt at painting since childhood and I loved it.

At midday, we packed up our things and headed back to the Anna Lee, carrying a basket of meadowsweet for Lise. After lunch, everyone took turns to steer and walk. Feeling sapped of energy, I sat on a bench, gongoozling. It was fascinating to study the crew as they telepathically opened and closed gates and paddles. The general air of tranquillity went some way to tempering the emotional spouts that were threatening to erupt, but as quickly as I put them out, they'd re-appear far too frequently for comfort.

That evening, with Manny's music list humming in the background, we played an hilarious version of the sticky head game. The crew sang the chorus to *The Weight*, substituting 'Manny' for 'Fanny', which made Manny roar each time. The song's message – to put your troubles onto another's willing shoulders – perfectly summed up the crew. How ignorant of me to have assumed that my new friends were too serious to enjoy themselves. The songs and the games were their way of keeping things light-hearted, and it had worked, at least for that night.

π

We gathered on the towpath to say our farewells. Sofie and Manny's invitation to visit them in Normandy was the first thing to send me rolling downhill. Then, Lise gave me a new remedy to help keep me balanced, as would my renewed links with Angel Ninebarks. When she said we'd see each other again, I believed her. Elkie and Kristian had stayed behind. During our final stroll, he talked about college life, I sketched out a typical working week, and finally we came to the subject of relationships. I asked him if Lise had ever been in love. It was an impertinent question, but my curiosity was like an itch I couldn't scratch.

'To believe oneself in love with my sister isn't surprising. As for Lise's direct experience, it is not my tale to tell. You must remember, April, I saw so little of her for so long. Whoever she may or may not have loved, she is beyond that now.'

What did that mean? Had Lise's heart been broken? Was she still suffering? I wanted to dig deeper, but the clock was ticking and I was beginning to unravel. 'Was Sofie and Manny's invitation to visit them genuine?'

'April, are you so unused to the hand of friendship when it is offered?' Kristian held out a folded piece of paper. 'Here is mine, too. Lise, as you know is not one for keeping a regular correspondence, but as that is my speciality, it would be an honour to add you to my address book.'

'As pen pals, you mean?'

His sad smile almost broke my heart.

'I'm not quite as antiquated as you believe. While I lament the lost custom of letter writing, my usual form of corresponding is via email.'

I tucked the notepaper into my jeans pocket. A sudden urge to confess my budding feelings for him overtook all reason. It was a now or never moment. 'Kristian, you may be surprised to know that the feelings I have for Lise aren't the same as those I have for you.'

Kristian drew me to him and rested a hand on my head as if he were consoling a child. No kiss. No fond farewell. I breathed in his lovely, lonely soul, then I picked up my holdall and left.

Third Quarter

28

The big takeaway from my second journey on the Anna Lee was this: I must learn to live on my own terms. No doubt my actions would be condemned as selfish or worse, but the only way to survive such an acutely unsettling phase was to create a buffer zone around me while I attempted to work it out.

As soon as I walked through Embla's familiar oak door, I called Mum. Her 'straight off the bat' question was not what I was expecting.

'Is your back really sore April, or is this another lie?'

'Go easy on me Mum, please.' I breathed out, trying to get a grip on my turbulent state. After all, it wasn't her fault and she was the only one who had a handle on what was happening to me. 'I've literally just got back from a trip on the Anna Lee and you're the first person I've called. I've tried to talk to you about it, but you've been busy.'

A long pause. 'Sorry pet. Yes, I've been busy but I'm here now. Why don't you tell me what's going on.'

In brief, I explained how I hadn't expected to hear from Lise again, let alone receive another invitation to join the crew, so I couldn't pass that up; driving to Cornwall to join a crowd which included Sebastian Espie, regardless of the consequences, was out of the question. 'You of all people will understand that.'

'Thank you for being truthful, April. As a matter of fact, I do understand. This is the last place you should be.'

My stomach clenched. 'Why? What's happened?'

'Your father and I have had words – more than words if truth be told, but let's just say that your ex was making mischief, and I put a stop to it.'

In an instant, the magic vanished. Wasn't that bloody typical. I could imagine the family's reaction, especially Aunt Vikki's, criticizing my no-show to anyone within shouting distance. 'You may as well tell me what Sebastian said.'

'He told Bradley that not only had you dumped him, but you'd given him his marching orders from number 44. Your brother didn't know because he and Harriet aren't speaking. Sebastian also said that the reason you weren't here was because you'd gone off with a woman from Angel Ninebarks.'

Bradley had two responses. He'd have been livid, so no prizes for guessing what happened next. 'I guess everyone knows, then.'

'As a matter of fact they don't. I told Bradley not to interfere. As far as everyone else is concerned, you are feeling poorly and have agreed to my suggestion to stay home and rest.'

'You did that for me, Mum?'

'April, I would walk through fire for you.'

That's when the floodgates opened. My mother made me promise to call her in half an hour or she would drive home immediately. After a strong sugary coffee and a cold flannel,

I called her back. My father was 'extremely disappointed' with me and had apologised to Sebastian. Mum was furious and was all set to leave, but then my dad said that if I weren't in danger or dire need, would she stay until the end of the week. I assured her there was no need to come home and promised to check in every day. Thankfully, Mum had severely edited the content of their conversation. The less I heard about my fork-tongued father the better.

π

My moods swung like the grandfather clock's pendulum on speed until I was too exhausted to care – that was until my brilliant mother came up with a plan, which was this: as the family were due home on Saturday, I'd drive to Brightside Park that same day, and spend a week at the lodge, alone. There was no danger of us crossing paths. Acutely aware that a single week wouldn't be long enough to sort myself out, I called Gita Nair. My request for a two-week unpaid leave of absence left her temporarily mute, but at least this time I had told the truth about the family fracture. She reminded me to consider the company's comprehensive health scheme should I need to call the helpline, and in a voice which barely disguised her regret, suggested we keep in touch.

Calling Tish was not an option. The retreat was about to begin, and I couldn't burden her with my woes. That's not to say that Mum wasn't helpful – in fact, she'd been a lifeline, but this only added to my growing sense of guilt. How could I have side-lined her for so long? She'd always been there, waiting in the wings to be of service to her ungrateful kids, and what had we done? Bradley and I were like bladderwrack, clinging to Vaughan bloody Hayle for dear life because *the only way was the Hayle way*. What about the Trembath way? Homebodies had provided an essential outlet through which my mother expressed her true nature. She was one of the few people I knew who loved what she did, whether it was work, with her friends, at the allotment. It was meaningful; it made a difference. Wasn't that what was meant by living authentically? I had chosen to believe that my dad was the rock that supported the Hayle's stability – to have seen it Mum's way had felt too wobbly, too insecure, but in reality it was the opposite. She was the fulcrum on which the family levered itself whereas my father was the outsider: remote; undemonstrative; the ultimate selfish git.

And what of Kristian Michelson? I unfolded his note. His handwriting, possibly written with a fountain pen, was compact and precise, like mine. He'd be in Copenhagen by now, back to his glacial white walls, warm wooden floors, and the comforting canal nearby. Would Thomasine have played it cool, or would she have weaved herself luxuriously around his slim bare ankles as he sat at his desk, surrounded by mountains of books? Or would he be at the university, surrounded by groups of adoring students? I resisted the urge to send him an email for fear of being too quick off the mark, and at any rate, I didn't exactly know what to write. Reading *Niels Lyhne* was a legitimate way in, but as I hadn't had the wherewithal to start the novel, aside from sharing the Hayles' latest drama, there wasn't much else to say.

Of course that didn't stop me fantasising about us in a variety of scenarios: pen pals, long-distance friends

... lovers? Now home, the latter didn't seem remotely possible, and as usual my feverish imagination had gone full throttle, so I let it run on unchecked, knowing that eventually, it would run out of tarmac.

π

Despite feeling troubled, there was still no sign of a burnout. Remarkably, my back was holding its own. Lise's massage and her remedy, just like the previous one was doing something, but taking unpaid leave was by my standards a crisis, as was the current antagonism between me and certain family members. A long-term estrangement from Harriet or Uncle Max was unlikely, but as for my dad and my brother, I simply couldn't see a bridge between us. Unless they underwent a massive personality transformation or I became enlightened, we were destined to remain on opposite sides of the bank.

Attempting to sit with the turmoil any longer was pointless, so I made myself busy. Nothing had changed at Embla, but it no longer felt the same. After giving the house a thorough clean and watering the plants, I went across to Mum's office to do the same there. Homebodies was tucked away in its own garden-within-a-garden, and with direct access from a side gate, you might never have guessed it were there at all. Mum had cleverly designed the area in such a way that our lives could go on without mutual disturbance. As I pushed on the handle, the door swung open (Mum never locked it, much to my dad's frustration). I left the watering can on the desk and looked around. Mum was often in here when she wasn't working, as it doubled up as a place to hang out with her friends. I say hang out – they probably discussed the same topics as those at Angel Ninebarks. I'd been invited to join the group on various occasions but had never been tempted, although now I couldn't think why not.

The room was divided into an office area on one side and a circle of comfy chairs on the other surrounding a colourful rug. On top of the table in the centre was a singing bowl, and a single tea light. Facing the door, the corpus callosum painting was still there amongst harvest moons and waterfalls and cards from grateful families. Underneath the picture gallery ran a long bookcase, the contents of which I'd never scrutinised. Mum occasionally left a book on my bedside table with a particular passage marked so it wasn't as if I were intruding. But Rilke's words had cracked the nut of my curiosity and, in my current state of mind, I could think of nothing better than sitting out on our veranda overlooking St Ives Bay shimmering in the Cornish sun, with an inspirational book and a handful of tasty treats on my lap.

Typically, nothing was in alphabetical order. I pulled out a booklet, *Becoming Your Own Therapist*, which looked promising, as did a huge tome entitled *The History of Norse Mythology* but that was way too big to haul. Tucked in midway was a copy of *Letters to A Young Poet*. I pulled it out. Why had Mum got this book? *It's a classic, you idiot. Until last week you'd never heard of Rainer Marie Rilke.* There were several strips of ribbon tucked into the pages. I opened one at random. It was the seventh letter, the same lines that I had highlighted: *'For one human being to love another, that is perhaps the most difficult of all our tasks'.*

I sat down on the nearest chair, my thoughts tumbling. Did this mean something significant? Was it referring to my dad, or me and Bradley? There was no inscription or dedication, but on the bottom of the title page was a drawing of a circle. It contained an elaborate symbol, faded with time, and yet it was vaguely familiar. Feeling strongly that I'd crossed a line, I slid the book back in its place, picked up the booklet and the watering can, and closed the door behind me.

29

By Friday, I'd tied every loose end but one: my belongings at number 44. There was no reason not to pick them up, and unless Sebastian had changed the locks, which would have been a waste of money as he had to allow me access, I decided to collect the rest of my stuff. Whilst there, I'd leave an official *notice to quit*, along with a polite message to contact me with a moving-out date. Taking action felt good. I was moving on.

The mid-morning traffic was light. I resisted the habit to turn on the radio and reflected on the situation. In view of their current standoff, why would Harriet tell my brother about the breakup? Inadvertently, though, it must have increased the tension between them. Sebastian had spun events to suit his agenda and had manipulated my brother in the process. His artfulness made my skin creep. As for my parents they were in the middle of something, the contemplation of which was too unsettling to handle, so I parked that one on the touchline.

The front door needed a paint, and a push. I intended to get the door off its hinges, but Sebastian had said it could wait. There was never the right moment to carry out maintenance. As soon as he was gone, I'd treat the house to a thorough overhaul before renting it out. The grubby kitchen worktops and floor made me wince. Sebastian was fairly tidy, but as I had made a point of doing the housework, he obviously hadn't woken up to the responsibility of doing it in my absence. Merryfield Estate was a pleasant enclave, but the original thrill of living here was a distant memory I had no wish to retrieve. I could never move back here. Even Embla no longer felt like a haven, but that was because I was seeing the world through new eyes. Spending three weeks in Cornwall would, amongst other things, help to determine where my next postcode would be.

Except for a handful of DVDs, my gran's teapot, and a few out-of-date magazines there wasn't much to collect downstairs. As I trundled up to the bathroom, my nostrils protested at the lingering smell of Sebastian's aftershave. After gathering up a bag of toiletries and bath robe, I went into the bedroom. The wall-long fitted wardrobes provided acres of hanging space, but as Seb didn't possess many everyday clothes, he'd added a tiered shelving system to house his equipment. The stack was bulging with enough products to open a sports shop. My cursory rummage notched up two multisport GPS watches, five pairs of polarised lens goggles, bundles of neoprene swimming caps, socks and gloves, and untold tubes of anti-chafing lube. From a cost perspective, this eyewatering haul was negligible compared to the tally of Sebastian's bikes, seasonal wetsuits, and helmets which were currently under lock and key in Bradley's garage.

With my meagre bounty almost bagged up, the last item to collect were my trainers, little-used that they were, but of too good a quality to leave behind. Seb's footwear stash catering for every possible terrain. Each box was neatly stacked and labelled in rows along the bottom of the wardrobe. Where else would mine have been but at the bottom of the pile. As I pulled out the box, the tower toppled over and there it was, a folder labelled 'Project H'.

π

The letterbox rattled. I'd lost track of time, sitting there with the folder on my lap, stunned by its contents. The first section, *'Ironman,'* contained numerous dates and costings relating to the forthcoming competitions organised by the WTC. Sebastian had highlighted the Hawaii event which was scheduled to take place the following year. It was all there: how he and Bradley would split expenses, find the cheapest form of travel, start a comprehensive training programme. Harriet must have known that it was a definite, hence their blow-up. Since buying the house in Westwych, money had been tight. As the main wage earner, her 'baby savings fund' was meant to pay for an extended period of maternity leave when the time came, but the competition costs would, in theory, wipe that out. No wonder she was furious.

Next came the bank statements. Sebastian had squirreled away twenty grand over the previous two years! Every month, a cash deposit of on average a thousand pounds had been made at the Mercia Building Society. Many people were paid this way, so this was no big deal in itself, but I'd long suspected that Seb's client list earnings had left him with loads of spare cash, even after splashing out on his equipment needs. As the health club's unofficial bookkeeper, it was obvious to me that Bradley had been subsidising Sebastian's room-hire fee way beyond what was reasonable, but according to my brother, they'd made an arrangement, and as Max was onboard, so best I back off.

It was clever. Sebastian had been offsetting his events and holiday expenses by bunking in with Bradley and Harriet wherever possible. To mitigate any suspicion of being miserly or underhand, he offered family and friends free training sessions and massages, the result of which was that everyone else paid for his meals, drinks, and so on. It may have been a form of bartering, but he had lied about his finances, and most likely about other things, too. Collectively, we were bankrolling Sebastian Espie's lifestyle.

My snout was up. Last, but most disturbing of all were the music lists. Every family member's date of birth and specific anniversaries had been written down, the notable exception being my mother's. Beside each name, Sebastian had made a note of our favourite songs to further ingratiate him with the Hayles. My dad must have told him about the Glastonbury and Reading Festivals, as only he knew where those obscure tunes came from. Beside my name was Snow Patrol's song, *Run*. Seb had played it at my birthday bash in The Red Balloon, and I had sobbed in the loo for ages before Harriet came to the rescue.

During our last term at university, Emily Pagett and I had got drunk more than once in her digs whilst listening to the anthem. When her invitation to study at Cal Tech came through, the song had been my sole consolation after her departure. For all our promises to reunite, I never went to Pasadena, and neither had she returned to the UK, having no family here. The only person who knew about us was Bradley.

I sat back and sighed. In a way it was fascinating, but also deeply disturbing. There was no doubt about it, the Hayles had been played. As an insurance policy, I took several photos before putting everything back, although it occurred to me that excluding Mum, who else would care? Like stones and glasshouses, I couldn't say a word. If I confronted Sebastian, he'd twist it to make me the sly, desperate one who'd been sneaking around. It was unlikely he'd broken any tax laws, but his underhand, self-serving behaviour had crossed a line. Having discovered these documents it proved, if further proof were needed, that I had to distance myself. Fears of upsetting or alienating the tribe were irrelevant – Bradley and my father could fly off into the sunset with Sebastian Espie and his twisted ways for all I cared. The days of allowing myself to be manipulated and taken for granted were history.

π

That night, I had my first nightmare since the scoliosis. I was standing beside a pair of lock gates, waiting for the sun to set. One by one, familiar faces appeared as ghostly forms, clustered together on the opposite side of the bank: Dad, Bradley, Harriet, Raddy, Gita Nair, Sebastian. Their eyes were holes, and their gaping mouths revealed teeth like Tish's rotten bottom row. In the murky lock water, despite their frantic efforts to swim away from the enormous, splintered gates, my mother and Lise were gradually being sucked under the gushing torrent while

Kristian and Edmund tried in vain to stop the gates from closing – the paddles click, click, clicking …

My screams woke me up. Where the hell was I? Flailing around in the half-light, my hand landed on Little Ted. I sank back into the soggy pillow, clutching my childhood teddy bear to my wildly banging heart. It was Saturday; I was in my bedroom at Embla, soon to drive to Cornwall for three weeks. With my wits finally recovered, I got up and pulled back the curtains. The fresh morning sky was streaked with ribbons of pink and violet, heralding a glorious day. Early birds chirped for all they were worth, while a squirrel high jinxed from tree to tree. My spirits instantly lifted. As the grandfather clock chimed five, I padded downstairs. In one hour from now, I'd be on the road.

Mum had taken care of food and linen at the lodge, but I was to let her know as soon as I arrived. My suitcase, laptop, and snacks were on duty by the door. Apart from a charge/coffee stop, it would be a straight run through to Brightside Park. The beach could wait until early evening when the crowds had gone. I'd never actually stayed there on my own before, which was a staggering fact, bearing in mind that we'd owned it forever. It hadn't occurred to me to go alone. Now, I couldn't wait to get there.

30

Brightside Park was situated on the crest of a hill, bordered on one side by dense woodland, and surrounded by *ooh* and *aah* views. Only a local like my grandad would have known the ideal spot on which to build such a fine holiday park all those years ago. The small Cornish town of Hayle was definitely on the up, and with the drift towards eco-travel and staycations, numbers were increasing. Most of the lodges were privately owned, the season lasting from Easter to October, and only a handful were let out to holidaymakers, so it really was a home from home. They were built in a series of quadrants spread around the site, each with its own car/cycle park and recycling area which created a sense of community and a degree of privacy. Ours was the first of fifty lodges enjoying prime position at the top of the hill at the back, with the fabulous St Ives Bay panorama in full view.

I climbed the veranda steps, unlocked the door and set down my suitcase. Unbelievably, just a few hours earlier my entire family had been here. The lodge was sparkling, and there was even a vase of delightful wild flowers on the shelf. After opening every window, I went into the kitchen. Mum had stocked the fridge with insanely healthy food – even the double-mint-choc slices were sustainably vegan – and there were several bottles of wine in the rack. At first glance, it appeared that my bedroom hadn't been used, not that I would have minded as there were always extra bodies to accommodate. Inside the bedside drawer was Harriet's zip-up, what she called her 'odds and ends' bag. She and Bradley must have argued pretty badly for her to sleep in my room. With Sebastian's unpredictable behaviour and Bradley as his gate-keeper, Mum's presence must have helped considerably.

Tea and sandwich made, I sat out on the deck. Scarcely a cloud had appeared throughout the entire journey, and neither had there been a hold up, despite reports warning of blocked roads and traffic jams. It was my intention to keep a low profile for a couple of days, mainly to give myself time to adjust to this unknown scenario before venturing out to favourite haunts and to scout for new ones. Despite the initial euphoria, I was under no illusion that spending three weeks in my own company would be daunting, but this was meant to be the start of a new chapter, and there were important matters to consider, one of which was Kristian Michelson. As he inched his way to the top of my list, so swelled a state of anxiety and trepidation which was threatening to derail my marvellous sabbatical.

This was nothing new. Professionally and within the family unit I was confident and self-assured, but when it came to the personal, it took a lot of courage to ask someone out, so I rarely bothered. There had been a few short-lived flings before Sebastian, the most memorable being with one of Harriet's running club buddies, and the other, a covert liaison with a visiting auditor. My 'confession' to Kristian on that final morning was in all likelihood prompted by a quiet desperation, and as the days went by, and without any contact between us, I couldn't be certain of anything anymore. But he had offered friendship, and in the circumstances that was enough. Before I could even think about emailing him, I had to read the novel, as it provided a legitimate re-introduction to the inscrutable scholar.

π

I flicked through the competition schedules which had been pinned to Bradley's bedroom wall. Sebastian's team hadn't done as well as predicted. Mum was listed as a member of Bradley and Xander's winning beach volleyball squad – that was a first. Bizarrely, the final day's events column was blank. They must have abandoned the competition. Had it rained? Was it something to do with my brother's bust up with Harriet, or my parents exchanging words? Although I'd spoken to Mum every day, I specifically hadn't asked for an update.

Suddenly exhausted by it all, I leaned back in the chair. A sepia-tinted scene from our Eurocamp holiday in the Jura spang into my mind. We'd arrived at the forest, kitted out with our bikes and whatnot and were ready to hurtle off on a trail although my mum had plans of her own. Long after our session ended, she still hadn't come back from her forest ramble. My distraught father was about to call for help when Mum drifted nonchalantly out of the trees like a woodland sprite. She couldn't understand why we were so upset and told us off for making such a drama out of it. For the first and last time in public, my dad lost it. When his tirade finally blew out, she took his hand and we trooped silently back to the campsite.

As I scrutinised the programme, it began to make sense. The beach volleyball tournament was held on the same day as the little-league sandcastle competition. Mum loved spending time with the Haylings, as the babes were called. Unlike my suspicious aunts, my cousins had no problems asking for her advice – what was the most effective natural remedy to alleviate Kyle's stubborn cough, or to sooth Janina's inflamed skin. Mum would have insisted on keeping a close and caring eye on the little ones during Sebastian's warped idea of fun, and just as she'd done in the Jura, she had stayed on to hold my father's hand when it all fell apart.

Cheery voices and splashes rose from the swimming pool below. In the distance, a fleet of sailboats bobbed like corks on the ultramarine water. It was time for a stroll. I tore up the schedules and instantly felt better. Mum's idea of a break was meant to be just that – a break from everything and everyone. Whilst re-organising my beach bag, I remembered my promise to give Connie a call. She'd lived her entire life in Hayle and would know all the best places to visit. I was determined to meet her for lunch. No doubt she'd have been primed by my mother, but that was to be expected. A number of questions had been niggling away at me, questions that only Connie could answer. Besides, it would have been unforgivable to spend three weeks at Brightside Park without seeing Mum's far-out best friend.

31

Before I had even finished half of the humungous cream-lashed scone, Connie got straight to the point.

'I don't know what I was expectin' pet, but you look ever so well. How you gettin' along up there on your lonesome?'

'Better than I anticipated, Connie. I can't believe it's been a week already. My daily routine begins with fifteen minutes of Qi Gong with Wanda, via YouTube, out on the veranda. Then, after a fruit and yogurt brekkie I head down to the beach for a walk, followed by mid-morning coffee and honey toast at the Lazy Hazy Café. If I'm not going out, in the afternoons I rest, read, and try to catch myself when I'm not paying attention which is hilarious. Sometimes I have a paddle – oh, and a double scoop ice-cream cone from Trembath Ices, a different flavour each time.'

Connie cackled. 'You haven't lost your appetite, April, so I won't worry about you. Have you spoken to your mum?'

'Every day to begin with, but we've agreed that as I'm not about to throw myself off Godrevy Lighthouse, I'll call her if I need to.' Connie's steely eyes bored into my soul. Her sleeveless dress exposed wafer thin arms, the tattoos barely visible on her parched skin. Although Connie O'Hara was generally considered to be unconventional, I secretly admired her wild ways. 'How are you, Connie? Mum said you've been under the weather.'

'Take no notice of your mum. She's always on the lookout for a body to care for. Did she tell you about last week's shenanigans? No? Well, do you want to know?'

I couldn't help but smile.

'She decided to stick around, to keep an eye on Sneaky Seb. We agreed to look after the littluns, to give the mums a bit of down time. Your mum's team won the beach-volleyball, so that was the first thing to put Sebastian's nose out of joint. After that, it was the kiddies turn. But when they were tryin' to build castles with him on the clock, and little Janina started howlin', she pulled the whistle from his neck and blew it. *How can you set these babes off against each other and treat it as fun? It's bloody cruel.*'

'Mum said that?'

'I can't recall her ever losin' her rag, and I've known your mum since we were five. Your family beggar belief, April. Why do they have to make every friggin' activity a competition?'

I sat back, visualising the scene. It was just as I had predicted. Connie and Mum were right. Why couldn't a morning on the beach with a bucket and spade be enough? I was beginning to understand the consequences of our customs and behaviours, and I didn't like it. 'I'm so glad I wasn't there, Connie, but what you said about Mum is a concern. She hasn't been herself for months. It can't be the menopause as she's way past that. Is it the pressure of Homebodies? Do you think there's something going on with her and my dad? What's your opinion?'

Squeezing the last drops of tea out of the stainless

steel pot, Connie poured the dregs into her cup while contemplating how much to tell me. I wasn't surprised. After all, she and Mum were as close as any two people could possibly be, and I was under no illusion that she would give anything away, even to her best friend's only daughter.

'Do you want the other half of that scone, April? No sense in wastin' good food.' She wrapped it in her napkin and tucked it into her beach bag, after which she took out an envelope and laid it on the table. 'Before I forget, these are old holiday snaps I found knockin' around. You were after this sort of thing for your mum's birthday book.'

'Yes, sorry, Connie. I was – I am. She's already got the album, but it's not complete.' I slid the envelope in my rucksack. 'Thanks for remembering.'

Connie looked at me for a long time, scanning every millimetre of my face, searching for I don't know what. Her knobbly hand was unexpectedly soft on mine. 'Now, April, don't you go frettin' over your ma. She's tough enough to ride the biggest wave. Maybe her marriage is up against it, but that's the nature of relationships. Nothin' stays the same. What I can tell you is that she is relieved to find that you've finally come to your senses.'

'I wasn't aware of being away from them, Connie.'

'You mistake my meanin', pet. If I need to explain, then there's a ways to go yet.' She stood and pulled a tattered purse out of her bag. 'Anyways, you've got my number. Call me if you're feelin' blue.'

Her shell necklace tinkled as she bent to kiss me. In a flash, I snapped out of my strop and hugged her. 'I'm sorry, Connie. I didn't mean to be rude. Thanks so much for meeting me, and for looking out for me. It's really good of you. No need to pay for the tea.'

Connie ran a rough thumb across my cheek. Her ancient smile brought a lump to my throat. Then she flitted off into the hot afternoon with her turquoise/tangerine dress flapping in the breeze. I slumped back in the chair. How bloody ungrateful was I? It was ridiculous to have been offended at hearing the truth. Hadn't Manny and Sofie said that our perception sharpens when we tune into the world around us, but this awareness might only last a nanosecond before reverting to our unconscious and habitual behaviour, which was what I seemed to be doing at breakneck speed. My mother's optimism, however, might have been premature. With elation tilting one side of the seesaw and despair on the other, it would have been easier and much less painful to have stayed in the dark.

But as I slid the tray into the stack, something *had* shifted. The scene before me was a canvas of space, colour, movement. Around the bay, vibrant green hills sloped gently towards the sea as it lapped the corn-coloured sand. Overhead, bulbous clouds slipped silently by, unruffled by flocks of freewheeling gulls. Would I have noticed any of this before meeting Lise? Connie's description of Mum's *up against it* marriage confirmed I was on the right track. If my parents divorced, Embla would be sold, and everything I held dear would be gone. Tears stung my eyes. Mum would be okay as she had friends like Connie and Liz to love her, but my dad? I pushed the unbearable thought away and scooted on.

32

Sundown. I closed the laptop lid and stretched my arms out, feeling my back widen and release. While attempting to engage with my 'self', already a fortnight had been gobbled up. After abandoning several attempts to invent a revised 'happy life' mathematical formula, I resorted to making an updated spider diagram to help clarify my current situation. It was startling to find family and work subordinate to the Angel Ninebarks' community and philosophy, which I'd put at the centre of the sketch. It also highlighted the agonising business of 'home'.

During those heady days on the Anna Lee, we'd passed a number of attractive canal-side properties which had lodged somewhere in my mind as potential abodes. Embla was now out of the question. Without direct contact from my dad, who was allegedly concerned about me, just the thought of sharing a roof with him left me cold. Sebastian still hadn't sent a moving-out date, and that had made me angry. Fully motivated by these powerful emotions, my serious online search turned up three suitable waterside properties available to rent. It was a start.

I took my cocoa onto the veranda and watched the sun bed down. Recalling the fantastic art session with Sofie, it was tempting to buy a paint set and join the hordes of amateurs attempting to capture the Cornish magic on paper, but I didn't have to do it this time around. I could and would come back. As the burning disc plunged into the sea, I let the image fade, remembering what Lise had said about not clinging to it. There would be another. I went inside and was startled to hear my phone buzz.

'April! I didn't think you'd pick up.'

'Of course I'd pick up for you, Harriet.'

A pause. 'How are you?'

'If you want a truthful answer, I'm not sure yet. To begin with, it felt weird to be here on my own but now I like it. Brightside Park isn't nearly as noisy as I thought it would be.'

'That's because the Hayles aren't there to grab everyone's attention. April, I hope you didn't mind my using your bedroom. My cold had worsened throughout the week, to the point where Monica had tucked me up in your bed with one of her remedies. You know how Bradley is when it comes to catching germs.'

'I'm sorry to hear you were ill, Harriet.'

'Actually, I was relieved to sit out the last two days.' After another longer pause she said, 'I'm really sorry for not being there when you needed me. I should have known there was something seriously wrong when you didn't show.'

'You have nothing to be sorry for. I just need time to sort myself out. This may sound harsh, but I don't want to know what anyone else is doing or how they are feeling. Just for once, the focus is on me.'

'Yes, of course. Quite right, too. Monica said it was okay to call. It was important to tell you how much I care.'

'Thank you, Harriet It means a lot. Mum has finally got her mitts on me and is doing a great job. She must have put Connie on alert as when we met for lunch last week, she had some interesting things to say.'

'The sandcastle competition? It was truly awful, and Monica was right to end it. Your father, Bradley, and Sebastian took off for the rest of the day. I don't know whose idiotic idea it was, but there were unintended consequences. As a protest, Xander, Declan and a number of your cousins abandoned the programme in favour of a surf day and nightclub. Sebastian was furious to find his big finale scuppered. It was shocking to witness the family splinter like that. Monica drove me home as Bradley and I were no longer ...'

Harriet must have heard herself offloading and stopped. She was on the verge of tears, but I wasn't about to comfort her. I'd spent years worrying about my brother, and in any case, what could I do from three hundred miles away? 'It's good to hear from you, Harriet.'

'Yes, well, I'm glad I called. Goodbye, April.'

It was extraordinary to hear Harriet confirm Olly's prediction that my family would splinter, and yet in a way I felt intensely relieved. How could anything change if we didn't abandon the old ways of doing things? I was beginning to understand my own part in it all – not wanting to let go, needing to keep us all glued together, blindly treading in my dad's footsteps, but blaming myself would be counter-productive. It was difficult to hear Harriet's distress without offering consolation or solution as was my habit, but the fact that I hadn't given way to guilt was a huge leap forward.

Interestingly, she had noted the effects of the Hayle invasion on Brightside Park. Until tonight, she'd kept her observations to herself. The vibe here wasn't the same, but that was a bonus as far as I was concerned. I'd taken to hanging out at the pool in the late afternoon for a quiet dip. When was the last time I floated on a Lilo without being tipped off?

π

The warm shower washed away the last grains of sand from my toes. After drying off, I rubbed a few drops of Lise's neroli and pomegranate oil into my skin. The fragrance catapulted me to the Anna Lee, to those wondrous days that no longer felt real. I dressed for bed and set to, once again, with Kristian's novel. The closer I got to finishing *Niels Lyhne*, the more nervous I became. To be honest, I'd never been a great reader. Muddling Bs and Ds made it problematic at school, even with help, but as I excelled in maths and science and my English grades were respectable, no one seemed overly concerned. Having missed the literary boat during my extended adult education, nowadays there was only ever time for magazine and internet articles. Taking on this type of book was a first.

To begin with Jacobsen's themes were out of focus, so before continuing with the novel, I researched the fellow who had so enraptured Kristian Michelson. My findings made for grim reading. Jens Peter Jacobsen was a bright lively boy, and a 'lazy' student – that was until his parents finally accepted their oldest son's passion for the natural world as after that, Jacobsen charged full steam ahead. His

Darwin translations brought him fame, while his gifted prose writing ensured him a place at Scandinavia's literary table. But at 25, he was diagnosed with tuberculosis, which was, at that time, almost certainly a living death sentence.

While his intellectual mates were pumped with ideas of upending the strict conservatism of 19th century Denmark, poor old JPJ, as he was affectionately known, had to leave his treasured Copenhagen behind and return to the sticks where his fraught family, in particular his adored brother William, cared for him until his death at age 38. *Niels Lyhne* had divided opinion. It was generally agreed, however, that Jacobsen's prose style was unique. Shortly after his death, his works took root in Nordic culture, his poems became operas, and his books inspired the likes of Ibsen, Strindberg, and Rainer Marie Rilke.

Putting the man into historical context was helpful, but the novel was far from uplifting. The body count would have hoisted Jed Mercurio's pulse, and you knew the story was never going to end well. Every relationship that Niels embarked upon was a disaster, and his painful death, sustained from battlefield injuries, befitted the sombre denouement. And yet, Jacobsen's exquisitely detailed portrayal of his shrinking world had piqued my curiosity, particularly his descriptions of the natural world which were like paintings on the page. As an observer who wasn't able to participate – his 'self' truly estranged from life – there was no question that Jacobsen's senses were acutely and painfully perceptive.

In some ways, Kristian reminded me of his hero. His quiet and sensitive manner was not unlike Jacobsen's, and while he hadn't been condemned to a premature and painful exit, Kristian had suffered considerably at the hands of his guardians and still appeared to be affected. Wasn't it the nature of suffering itself that had tied him and Jacobsen together – didn't it tie us all together? Whatever it was, at least I'd have something to say however inarticulate as Kristian was now very much on my mind.

π

The following morning, I could hold back no longer. Knowing there was little point in me, April Hayle, a twenty-nine-year-old chartered accountant with a B and D quirk, trying to impress Kristian Michelson, *eminent scholar*, I wrote to apologise for not being in touch sooner and thanked him for the book. Although it hadn't been an easy read, *it had left me feeling melancholy*, there were impressive passages. I had made notes and would be happy to hear his opinion sometime.

After taking forever to decide how to sign off: *warmest wishes* (stuffy); *kind regards* (too formal); *all the best* (urgh); *lots of love* (really?) I opted for *April x* before clicking the send button and imagined it winging its way across nine-hundred miles to land in Kristian's inbox, (please, please, please not in spam). His reply was so swift to begin with I was far too nervous to open it. But of course, I did.

Dearest April,

Your breezy message has blown all the gloom from the
morning. I imagined you ensconced in the Loughborough
office counting your numbers, but there you are, under rousing

Cornish skies. I hope all is well? My sincere apologies for taking you back to school for all the wrong reasons, and yet your resumé of Niels Lyhne has cut to the heart of the matter. As an atheist in a religiously conservative society, JPJ's naturalistic prose and subject matter were ground-breaking, as was his passion for the natural sciences. I have no doubt that April Hayle, twenty-nine-year-old chartered accountant with a B and D quirk has so much more to say, and I will wait, with patience, to read it.

With warmest regards,

Kristian

Of course he didn't know where I was! Kristian had assumed I was at work. His formal reply was hardly surprising as that was his style. I'd have been alarmed to have received lots of love and kisses, but he had been playful, *and* he remembered I worked in Loughborough. Encouraged by his email, and ignoring the sensible voice that suggested waiting a while before sending another, I immediately bounced one back with an update on my circumstances ...

... so you see, Kristian, my perseverance has paid off, and I can tell the world I have read one of the great novels, even though I shan't rush to re-read it. As for my re-entry, as Edmund called it, it has been more than bumpy, but there are other possibilities so please don't think I am complaining in any way. My mum expects me to live at Embla, and of course I will, but to have an option in place will be such a relief, hence my online search. Anyway, enough of my woes. How are you faring? (Don't spare me the gory stuff!)

April x

After twenty-four hours of agony, the following morning was red letter day:

Dearest April

My landing was also turbulent. Thomasine continues to give me the cold shoulder (a wonderful expression) while your heart-warming friendship with Elkie provides some hope for a similar experience with the Siamese. Still, there is much to celebrate, reunited as I am with dusty relics and new projects. Your inspired suggestion to co-write a book with Sofie is in progress. This will entail a visit to Quietwater sooner than I had envisaged, but as there are dear friends to be reacquainted with, I shall bear the upheaval with good grace.

Like you, I often avoid the busy daytime streets in favour of dusk, when I walk or cycle the canals and think of the Anna Lee. Thank you for making my visit so memorable. It has re-awakened the pilgrim in me. The demarcation between earth and heaven is porous, as if one could reach out and touch it. Do you feel that too, April?

From your stirring description of Brightside Park, how could you not revive. I feel sure that upon your return to Embla you will be better placed to make the right decision with regards your dwelling. There is, however, a possible solution. Edmund will furnish you with the particulars in person, but until then …

As you know, Lise overwinters the Anna Lee at Quietwater. She has offered you the boat as a refuge, from September until the following Spring. There is no better 'liveaboard' than you. The only caveat is that you allow Elkie access. Whilst she is happily ensconced in the cottage, we Michelsons agree that Elkie would be unable to rest without checking the comfort of her charge.

April, I apologise for such a long message, but there it is. I shall await your reply, and in the meantime, I send you my warmest wishes.

Kristian

Stay on the Anna Lee – with Elkie! How I danced around the lodge that morning. With Edmund and Frieda nearby for assistance, and Tish for company, how could I refuse? Kristian must have contacted them immediately after my first email, which was why he hadn't replied sooner. If I hadn't have felt so giddy I'd have sobbed at the kindness of these relative strangers. There was no mention of what the rent might be, but it had to be cheaper than an apartment. Driving to the office wasn't too far – hey, with hybrid working a fixture these days, I'd ask Gita if I could work from home. As soon as Edmund confirmed everything, I'd arrange to see the boss.

Before dashing off a reply, I scrutinised Kristian's email, loving his subtle sense of humour, and mining every single sentence for a hint of something – a coded message, a clue to indicate he might want to see me again … *as there are dear friends to be reacquainted with, I shall bear the upheaval with good grace.* Was that it – a dear friend? Oh, well, it took the pressure off, and I could be myself. I wrote back, thanking him for the life raft. To finish, feeling brave, this is what I said:

Dear Kristian

It appears that by a strangely wonderful quirk of fate, my adventure on the Anna Lee is to continue. If you are in England during those months, you are welcome to stay onboard, or the very least, join me for dinner and a long walk under the blues and greens.

With unbounded gratitude

April x

33

Far from being sorry to leave Brightside Park, the drive back to Westwytch, via Quietwater, couldn't have been more uplifting. Kristian had arranged a meet between Edmund and me, and all was agreed with a friendly handshake, and of course, a cup of tea. Come the first week of September, my temporary address would be the Anna Lee, Quietwater Bridge. Clothes, footwear, and personal items were my only requirements as I was welcome to use everything on the boat, as well as the Heathcote's utility room for laundry and suchlike. There was no rent to pay, only electricity, and water usage. As to my offer of hospitality, Kristian had written back to say that while Quietwater Cottage was his usual place of rest, supper in the Anna Lee's welcoming hearth was not to be missed.

Why wouldn't Kristian stay with his aunt and uncle? He'd lived at Quietwater as a child, and as his visits were so infrequent he'd have considered nowhere else. I was too adrenalized to be embarrassed as it was looking increasingly likely that Kristian would visit before the end of the year. I'll admit that our daily email exchange had opened the door into the scary world of feelings, but without any concrete evidence of reciprocity, I let myself wallow in fantasy land.

In any case, Kristian was in the 'good friend' category along with Lise, Tish, the Heathcotes, Manny and Sofie. Having these wonderful people to call upon and a fabulous plan in place, this went some way to cushioning the increasing alienation from my kin.

π

I finished packing and went downstairs to the kitchen. It was my last night at Embla. Since returning from the lodge, I'd seen and heard from no one. Now that I was feeling upbeat, my family's apparent lack of concern stung. With the summer holidays over, their quizzes, competitions, and birthday celebrations were scheduled to go ahead as usual. Although I was moving out, there was no reason why I couldn't join in, if and when I chose to, although I probably wouldn't. Aware of being petulant, I forgave myself, just as Mum's *Becoming Your Own Therapist* booklet suggested, and set the table for three.

My dad had been away on business. We hadn't seen each other for an entire month so I was bound to feel anxious. Mum was pleased to have me home, but her tepid reaction to my new address had annoyed me. Still, I remembered what Connie had said, so I couldn't blame her for acting strange. Mum wouldn't want me to leave, but neither would she try to talk me out of it. 'When is Dad due back?'

'Soon. He said not to wait. Have you talked to Bradley yet?'

'Why should I? He hasn't been over, and he only lives two minutes away. Harriet knows I'm home. After her 'full of concern' phone call, you'd have thought she'd have flown here to see me as soon as I got back. What is their problem?'

My mother closed the oven door and sat down.

'Look April, I haven't told you anything about anything as you said you didn't want to know. But now you've had a break and look a whole lot better, would you like to know what's going on with your brother?'

'Why not. Bradley wouldn't demean himself by visiting the Anna Lee, and I definitely won't be at his birthday dinner if he has one this year, which is highly unlikely as his party planner – me – has gone AWOL. I wouldn't mind, but I'm as busy as Harriet and she's his bloody wife.'

Mum sighed the sigh of a weary parent. 'Harriet has discovered that Bradley and Sebastian have been making arrangements to go to Hawaii next year for the ...'

' ... *Ironman*. Yeah, I know all about it.'

'How do you know? It only came to light last week. Even your father wasn't aware of it, or that his son's marriage is in trouble.'

'I didn't tell you because I thought it best not to get involved.' At her insistence, I told my mother about the statements, the music lists, and 'Project H'.

'So, unwittingly, you and Bradley have been underwriting Sebastian's *Ironman* quest.' She crossed her arms. 'I knew there was something up when that man arrived out of nowhere with his broken heart and bashed up guitar. Does 'Project H' mean Hawaii, or Hayle, I wonder?'

'But who else will give a damn, Mum? Everyone thinks he's a super hero.'

My mother's phone pinged. She frowned at the message.

'Your dad has gone to see Bradley at the health club. My guess is that Harriet has kicked him out.'

'Wow! It's that bad?'

'She must have given him an ultimatum. You can't switch off from wanting a baby once your mind's made up. As if the family weren't divided enough.'

'No guesses as to who'll be on Bradley's side. Why are you still married to him, Mum? Y'know, I looked into Carrow Corp. Their environmental record is shameful, and they have the nerve to greenwash the rest of the world with their ...'

'April, I'm fully aware that you are hanging out with a bunch of worthies, but please don't pass judgement on my marriage.'

We ate in silence, both with our own thoughts and concerns, neither having the slightest idea of what was going to happen next. Then, the front door opened and closed. I breathed out, long and slow, in a bid to stay calm. Despite our heated exchange, I was so glad Mum was here. It would have been easy to avoid my father altogether, but I was feeling much more assertive, and besides, it was time to grow up.

My father came into the kitchen wearing an unreadable expression, but there was no disguising the utter exhaustion that hung about him. Mum served the lasagne while I poured a glass of wine. He sat down heavily in a chair and rested his fingers on the stem. After an age, he looked wearily at me.

'So, you've finally decided to come home.'

'No, Dad. I've come back to collect my things. I'm moving out tomorrow.'

The grandfather clock chimed seven. It was like a scene from a play, who was going to make the next move, and I was ready to exit stage left – pronto.

'Bradley is moving in with Sebastian. The lad was in a state. He and Harriet are considering their future together,' he said.

'How about that. Our son is moving into our daughter's house, the one that she has so generously let out at a seriously reduced rent to a man who has lived off the sweat of our children's brows for two years. As a result, April can't go back to number 44 until he moves out, and in the meantime she has had to find somewhere else to live, *and* she has to pay for the privilege.'

My father's stupefied gaze darted from Mum to me. He may have been unaware of recent developments, but this had been brewing, as much as he had chosen to look the other way.

'There must be a misunderstanding. This doesn't sound like the Sebastian Espie I know.'

'Well, Vaughan, I suggest you scrub your bloody eyes clean and get to know him soon, otherwise you'll have no family left to polish your pedestal.' She got up and kissed my cheek. 'I've work to do in the office, pet. Let me know when you're settled.'

We sat there, father and daughter – estranged, alienated. It was pointless to stay, so I left the room, and my father, behind.

34

1st October. A month had passed, and with the help of the Heathcotes, Tish, and Elkie, I began to find my feet. The first week on the Anna Lee was bewildering, neither holiday nor home, and it was a challenge to apply myself to anything for long. Never had there been so much time to kill. After finishing my newly-revised work schedule which, compared to being in the office, barely raised my eyebrows, I'd frog-march the local towpaths to the point of exhaustion. But with every passing day, my muscles began to soften, my wings remembered to flap, and I slipped into Quietwater's soporific pace.

Tish was my first official visitor (Edmund said I was to invite whoever I wanted). She'd not long finished the retreat, and even I, having known her for such a short time, could see a change. As she toured the Anna Lee, her appreciation was expressed through wide-eyed smiles and the occasional appreciative comment. We had lunch on the foredeck, sheltered by the recently fitted canvas cratch cover. It added another exterior space, the equivalent of a conservatory from where the views could be enjoyed throughout the colder months.

'How lovely to hear the redstarts chirping away. It's like

living in your own wilderness but with all mod cons on standby.'

'I can't quite believe it myself, Tish. Elkie seems to like staying here, and Frieda and Edmund have survived my weekly meal. It's the least I can do in exchange for letting me raid their vegetable garden, *and* their wonderful library. I've also been helping them around the house, sorting through old papers, the odd bit of cleaning, which is nothing at all when you consider I'm living here rent free.'

'It's typical of the Heathcote's generosity, and it's natural to want to show your appreciation, but if you overdo it, they'll push back. It's the same over at the house. Since moving in, I'm overflowing with gratitude, and as a result, I've been trying to 'pay back' by doing everything and anything, but the Ninebarkers won't have it. April, we need to take a chill pill.'

'You're so right about that. So, how was the retreat?

'Not what I was expecting *at all*. The only regular gatherings were at mealtimes. We were free to do whatever we wanted, which was *sooo* weird. Some people pottered in the garden, others went for long walks or made artwork. One day a week was set aside for silence.'

'The whole day?'

'Yep, after breakfast. It was tricky at first, but then I looked forward to it. Oh, and Manny showed me how to play the ukulele, that was before he and Sofie had to leave.'

'I was sorry to hear about that. I hope Manny's dad recovers from the stroke. How was Lise?'

'After four weeks in her company, you think I'd know more about her, but just being near her was amazing, if you know what I mean.'

'I do. Lise doesn't say much, but every word is meaningful, isn't it. When we were travelling, it was as if she knew what I was thinking and feeling – who I really am.'

'Yeah, and you want more than anything to be authentic when you're with her, which of course is stupid – if we were always our true selves, there'd be no need to impress anyone. Lise regularly took herself off, alone. Wise women never need an entourage, do they? Have you noticed how the mystic men always have followers – someone has to book their itinerary and arrange the washing. Not Lise. *She* was protecting *us* from catching guru-itis.'

'Ha! Talking of wise women, how is Ruth's course coming along?'

'She reckons I've a flair for hedgerow medicine and has asked me to assist at her next workshop.' She grinned. 'Have you noticed anything?'

'Wow! Your teeth look amazing, Tish. Was it painful?'

'The donation knocked me out much more than the injections did, and everyone on the retreat made such a fuss over me it was embarrassing. I still can't believe that a stranger paid the balance.'

'Tish Swanson, you are the epitome of generosity, so why *wouldn't* someone pay it back?'

'That's what Edmund and Frieda said, so I accepted without saying another word – not easy for me, eh?'

'Has Lady Nelly seen your box-office smile?' I knew Tish wouldn't mind my teasing her as our friendship had bloomed considerably since May.

'It's bonkers, really. I thought Nelly was only interested in her prize Saddlebacks and crested newts, but when she saw my dentistry she said, *Tish Swanson, I do believe you have the sweetest mouth in the county.* I could have curled up and died, but later that day she came to Ninebarks to apologise. Apparently, she liked me long before the dental work.'

'Hey, this has all the hallmarks of a fine romance, Tish.' To spare her blushes, I changed tack. 'Harriet has asked to visit but I put her off. I don't want to overrun Quietwater with my troupe.'

'Didn't Edmund say you can invite who you want? I bet this is about your brother. Harriet wants you to see his tail trailing between his legs.'

π

Tish might have been right about that. As yet, I hadn't been back to Embla, but Mum and I had called each other regularly. Despite my protests, she had insisted on taking over as landlady, and had given Sebastian, in person, a formal letter stating a three-month *notice to quit.* Evidently, his new house-mate had lasted less than a week. Bradley had returned home to sort things out with Harriet, and the bromance had cooled considerably since then. Despite everything that had happened, I couldn't imagine my brother ever wanting to discuss his situation with me.

Eva and Uncle Max had sent text messages: was I coming to the next quiz, the next race meet, the next this, that, and the other? I tactfully diverted them but agreed to meet Eva for a coffee at Jonty's Café (no, I wasn't coming to the Christmas Eve dinner at The Red Balloon, but I'd tell her how to organise Secret Santa; it was unlikely I'd go back to Brightside Park with the family, but she and I could go together next season). Apparently, during 'Unleashed'

Sebastian had bunked down at their lodge. Before the week was out, he'd asked Eva for a date and said that he'd only got together with me as a favour to Bradley, but my constant pressure for a commitment forced him to break it off, *for my sake*. Poor Eva was in a state. After telling her parents, Max had sprinted to the health club to tackle Seb, although Eva was too afraid to ask what the outcome was. The bad news was stacking up for Sebastian Espie.

Ironically, my dad was having a tough time at work. Carrow Corp had been on the receiving end of a bucketload of bad press after a whistle blower exposed a massive environmental cover-up that had left hundreds of villagers' crops devastated. This grisly trademark had been repeated elsewhere in the developing world and was now all over the news. Carrow had made such a fanfare about their environmental credentials, and while they would inevitably ride it out, everyone was under scrutiny. Manny's 'what goes around comes around' warning was coming to pass. With my mum supporting her kids, dealing with a rocky marriage and Homebodies, this latest incident wouldn't have helped.

I gathered up the coffee cups. 'My brother won't come, Tish.'

'What makes you so sure?'

'I just know him. Bradley never apologises, but then again, I've always let him off the hook.'

'It's easy to exploit a generous heart, April, but that's because you used to let people do it. Now, when you choose to see your family it'll be different, just wait and see.' Tish grinned, her new teeth sparkling. 'Anyway, how about showing me that new route back to Angel Ninebarks.

Elkie's had enough of our pop psychology, and there's cake for tea.'

We walked along the deserted footpath. Thick hedgerows shielded us against the windy chill that undercut the cloudless afternoon. A mesmerising half-moon was in clear view. By the time we arrived at the house, the kitchen was abuzz. I was getting to know everyone at Angel Ninebarks, and outside of the workshops, was welcome to come and go. While Tish went off to fetch the latest edition of *Mycelium*, I wandered from room to room, reflecting on her pinpoint observations which echoed those of Lise and Sofie. Generosity was a wonderful quality, but in the wrong hands it could be corrupted, spoiled. Was it any surprise that Sebastian had stuck around for so long with so much of it coming his way.

I went in search of Sofie's visionary window. The last of the autumn sun scattered shards of light through Pomona's gorgeous apricot gown and onto the dark floor. For thousands of years, stained-glass creations such as this had instilled a sense of awe in the millions of souls who, like me, continued to admire them. Satiated, I wandered into the drawing room to the Midgard tapestry. I stood there, examining each thread, wondering what area my mum had sewn. Little by little, the mythology drew me in – strong, loving branches wound their limbs around mine, the golden symbol poured its divine light over me ...

Tish popped her head around the door. The spell was broken. Ruth had laid out a batch of zesty lemon tarts for the staff and visitors who usually gathered at four. I'd initiated a similar ritual on the Anna Lee, and when

Edmund or Frieda were able to join me, it was even better. Of late, however, the same vague sensation I'd had at Brightside was back, nibbling away at my newly acquired equilibrium. It was like trying to reconcile an account when the numbers didn't add up. Maybe this fluctuation was inevitable as I harmonised with Quietwater's ebb and flow. Or was it that my body mind had become so accustomed to feeling anxious that in the absence of it, I was aware of its re-appearance, much like I was with the back pain?

Elkie, as was her way, nudged me out of my conundrum. Tish passed me a mug of tea and we joined the others at the table. As I munched on the warm citrony delight, once again the niggle disappeared into the dusty recesses of my inquisitive mind.

π

Another ritual was my 'one-a-day' email exchange with Kristian. I could have whizzed off countless messages, but I held back and got the feeling he was doing the same. By waiting until evening to write, I was able to summarise the day, taking care to choose the appropriate word or expression while revealing a little more of 'me' from behind the keyboard. It was thrilling, as were Kristian's replies, waiting in my inbox the following morning. We could have Skyped, Zoomed, Facetimed, or even had a real live conversation, but this way suited our nervous-around-intimate-relationships personalities.

Having met him in person, I wasn't fazed by his verbal and literary style. It may have veered into the archaic, but I liked it. It singled him out. Kristian's vast knowledge store began to fill my cavernous literary and historical cracks, and our regular correspondence improved my writing skills exponentially. When he anointed me Queen of the Subordinate Clause, I had laughed out loud at that. After finishing *Narrowboat*, I wrote enthusiastically of my appreciation for the inland waterways' innovative engineers and for the thousands of navvies' 'pick and shovel' hard labour, without which Quietwater, let alone the network, could have existed.

Was it wishful thinking, or was there a hint that Kristian's true feelings were buried within his text, hence my panning for gold? He was far too sensitive to send sonnets or love poems, but in his last email, the tempo had definitely moved up a beat.

Dearest April,

What fun you and Tish have together. In her you have found a good friend – the best in fact, as she is without agenda, and you are laden with qualities that others might easily, but mistakenly take for granted.

I was astonished to receive your parcel. You remembered how much I enjoyed the sweet orange chocolate and you have taken the trouble to send me a box along with the notes in Edmund's study. It is wonderful to rediscover ancient ideas, fleshed out in embryonic stage, and it was you who excavated them. These will be of enormous help with my research which is, I might add, coming along extremely well. So well in fact, that arrangements have been made to visit Quietwater.

I arrive on November 25th. After enduring considerable anxiety at the prospect of knocking at the hatch unannounced, I gave up the idea to surprise you. So you see, April, I continue to be plagued with psychological tics.

Finally, may I say that your candescent descriptions and fresh perspectives of Quietwater only hasten my wish to return. Perhaps you will show me this new view.

I remain your dear friend,

Kristian

He was coming!

Fourth Quarter

35

November was the month for visitors, but not all were expected. It was a Saturday, midday. Light rain tapped on the roof and windows and was in for the day. Elkie hadn't stuck around for long that morning, and as usual, she determined the agenda. Immediately after returning from a rain-splashed walk, she trotted off in search of Frieda's attentions, while I finished up an accounting job. Meanwhile, the butterbean stew was simmering nicely on top of the stove, while inside it, the hiss of burning cedar wood enhanced the cosy vibe.

Nicely settled, I picked up the James Brindley biography. Devouring anything and everything remotely connected to Lise and Kristian Michelson was a tendency I'd been watching closely. The distinction between natural curiosity and obsession hadn't occurred to me until recently, and I was mindful of Tish's suggestion to chill.

Tap, tap, tap.

The rain had picked up its run rate, accompanied by a stiff breeze which nudged the boat. With the exception of rolling under the covers with a certain scholar, there truly was nowhere else I'd rather have been. Just as I was about to get stuck in, muted music tones filtered above the wet weather and into my ears. Was that *Love Plus One*? The volume increased, and now sounded as if it were outside the window. I sat up, my antennae on high alert. There was only one person who could parody a Nick Heywood song like that. With a leaping heart, I threw off the blanket and skidded over to open the hatch.

'Permission to board, Cap'n?'

In a flash, Oleanna Irving landed on the bottom step: coal black undercut hair glistening with raindrops; grey tartan waistcoat over crisp pea green button-down shirt; skinny turn-up jeans revealing Adidas Atlantic trainers, and the whole shebang topped off magnificently with a *Top Gun* flying jacket. We were back at Danesford Vale's end of year disco, dressed to impress.

'Put the kettle on, Crooked Polly. It's positively murderous out there.'

We laughed and hugged, and instinctively Oleanna ran her hands across my shoulder blades.

'Hey, not so crooked after all.' She stepped back. 'In fact, I'd say you are on the up, April Hayle. Not what I was expecting *at all.*'

'Mum must have ramped up the jeopardy to get you here.'

'Well, it worked. Hm, something smells good.' Olly shucked off her jacket and threw it at me. Her tomcat eyes frisked the saloon. 'Not too shabby. Mind if I case the joint?'

'Only if your trainers aren't muddy.'

'Ooh, gone all wifey have we?'

'It's not my boat.'

She kicked off her three stripes and disappeared into the interior while I made tea. *Oohs* and *aahs* skimmed the gangway, widening my smile. Suddenly self-conscious, I mentally listed all the things *not* to talk about. This was a flying visit – Oleanna Irving had never sat still for long enough to catch the wind. She bounced back in.

'Custard Creams?'

I pulled out a packet of our go-to biscuits from the cupboard. 'Emergency supplies.' We cackled conspiratorially.

'So, who unclipped your wings?'

She hovered beside a stack of books, scanning the titles, half listening. I brought over the tea and sat down. 'Long or short version?'

'I've got all afternoon, baby.'

'Oh ... fab! Well, it happened when I stayed on the boat for the first time, back in May. Lise Michelson, she's the Anna Lee's skipper, gave me a massage – one of her many talents – and ever since then, my back feels as if it belongs to someone else.'

'And your brain, by the look of these.' She picked up the books, one by one. 'Lee Miller, Charlotte Mew, *Worpswede Women* – this one pops.'

'The poet Rilke met his wife Clara Westhoff there. It's been a thriving artistic colony since the 19th century.'

'Hey, get you! Finally sorted your Bs from your Ds, eh? Seriously though, April, you should talk to Ma. She's directing a play called *Women in Yellow* – y'know, about the Yellow Book? She wants to cast me in the lead as Mew but I'm totally swamped. We decided to premiere *Cod Pieces and Mushy Peas* at Mercia Arts, which is why I'm in town. I'll send you and your mum tickets for the opening night. Keep your toes crossed. It might turn out to be the biggest dud of my career.'

'That'd be a real shame. I'd have happily come out of hiding to see it.'

Olly examined my face for sarcasm, but finding only admiration, she grinned. Still the hint of insecurity, despite her colossal talent. She looked world weary, inevitably due to the stress of maintaining her lifestyle, or maybe the stony veneer had been cultivated as a form of self-protection against the industry's fickle mood swings. 'The books are in the custody of my landlords, the Heathcotes. They live in the cottage. Having time to read still feels unreal. Other than work, and flitting about with Elkie, there isn't much else to do.'

'Elkie, eh? Undercover lover?'

'Four-legged wonder-dog and girl's best friend. Technically, Elkie is the Anna Lee's skipper. She flits between the cottage and here and knows exactly when to keep me company but doesn't stay long enough for me to become dependent on her.'

'The perfect partner.' Olly sat opposite. She dunked a biscuit in her tea and popped it into her mouth, whole. 'I can't believe it's taken you this long to unhook yourself from the tribe. Are Vaughan and Bradley still digging for victory?'

'I haven't seen them in ages.'

'Sorry, darling, didn't mean to be a cow.' She was suddenly serious. 'April, what the hell is going on?'

Over bowls of herby stew and chunks of warm crusty bread, I told Olly everything: how I felt abandoned when she left Danesford Vale; betrayed when she married Dee; ashamed of my family's behaviour and miraculously rescued by the Quietwater community. She listened until there was nothing left to tell.

'So, any day now, Lise could turf you out, or Kristian might fly down the hatch and batten it behind him, gawd love us!'

'On the plus side, Olly, you are back in my life.'

'Damn right. Whatever happens, you've got a home for a few months and you'll never be out on your ear with a mother like yours.' She pulled off another corner of bread. 'I like the cut of Lise Michelson's jib. Any chance of an introduction?'

I shook my head. 'She probably doesn't even know who you are.'

Silence.

'Sorry, still fumbling over my words. Anyway, I want to hear all about you, Oleanna Irving.'

'You mean, you don't follow me on Instagram? For shame! Actually, I don't blame you. The trolling is painful, especially after Dee and I got spliced. *How could you marry that shallow drama queen; you've totally sold out*, and that's the well-mannered stuff.'

'You can unplug, Olly.'

My suggestion annoyed her, as if I had no idea how stupid it was.

Then, 'Nice grub. Wouldn't be out of place in Broadway Market.'

'Thanks. So, how is Dee?'

'It's just as well you don't read the tabloids. They'd have us reviewing the pre-nup any minute now. It's enough to drive me to LA – for good. Dee is there half the year anyway as she misses her people, and she whines if we stay away for too long. I can't make her out. One minute she wants us to have a baby, next minute she's taken another six-month stint on the other side of the globe. Ever since we made the Dickens film, the missus has become obsessed with all things Victoriana.' Olly took out a fob watch from her waistcoat pocket. 'Anniversary present. She'll have me wearing a monocle before the tide's out. I gotta tell ya, April, Dee Mulvaney is high maintenance.'

She mopped the bowl with the last of her bread. It was good to see her eat. It was good to see her – full stop.

'That was top scoff. Anyway, let's get down to business. I've an offer you can't refuse: *GirlMeetsBoy* is on the lookout for another bean counter.'

'You're asking *me* to work at Bafta Central?'

She laughed out loud. 'I heard on the vine that Forensically Feckless Fenella might trade her life on the waterways for a spell of book-cooking in the big smoke. We could do with some extra digits. The office is a riot, always a drama going on as you can well imagine.' She rolled her amber eyes. 'And as for your billet, there's acres of space in our four-storey gaff – massive guest ensuite – until you get sorted. Oh, and we're right next door to London Fields lido, which, according to Dee is 'quaint'. Not that we ever hang out there. Can you imagine it, April? We'd be mobbed by the paps and the public before I'd got my knitted two-piece and floral bathing cap on. Whaddya say, partner?'

My mind whirred at the possibilities. London: a fresh start, a new job, high octane thrills ...

'We've always had each other's backs, haven't we, A?'

'It's a wonderful offer, Olly, and I am genuinely touched,

but I'd prefer to stay on this side of the curtain, for a while anyway.'

I got up and pulled her taught body into mine, feeling her disappointment as my own. It *was* a wonderful offer, but nothing could have induced me to leave the Anna Lee. There were, however, few who would say no to Oleanna Irving and this would have hurt. I dabbed her damp face with my napkin.

'Thanks, but no thanks? Oh well, it was worth a shot.'

And that was almost that. Olly skidded off to the bathroom, while I waited by the hatch, still reeling that she'd actually come to see me. When she reappeared, polished and composed, the previous scene might have been a figment of my imagination.

'I'm lovin' the tub. Dee would die for a couple of nights on this tug. If you fancy taking us for a sail sometime, give me a call.'

She slipped on her trainers, zipped up her flying jacket, and ran her thin fingers through her thick hair. We both knew that this was a one-off visit, the end of an era.

'Best get a move on. The first dress rehearsal's coming up, and I've got a truck full of tranquilizers at the ready. Anyway, I'm glad I came. Your family might be sinking but you are most definitely riding the crest, April Hayle. Oh, and keep an eye on your ma. When we spoke last week I got the feeling something's going on, as much as she steered the conversation.'

'I will. She thinks the world of you, Olly.'

'And you, dummy. Y'know, I could never understand why you and Bradley hounded after the old man when you had a super-trouper ma like Monica Trembath to love you. I'd have pawned mine for her any day of the week.'

'I hope to put that right. Thanks a gazillion for coming. As you can see, all's well.'

A final hug, her arms tighter around me this time. Olly let me go and just as she was about to climb the stairs, she turned back.

'You did love me, didn't you April?'

'Always.'

Oleanna Irving blew me her best Marilyn Monroe kiss and in the next scene she disappeared over Quietwater bridge, singing *Together in Electric Dreams*. I felt lighter than I'd done in months.

36

The following week, after an emotional conversation with Harriet I agreed to see my brother. He insisted our initial meeting was to be just the two of us, so good old Tish invited Harriet to Angel Ninebarks for tea. It would have been wrong to let my dear sister-in-law leave Quietwater without having a nose around the Anna Lee, so if the reunion with Bradley went well, I promised her a tour, although that was more a case of wishful thinking.

Bradley had looked rough. The beanie hat and stubble gave him a ramshackle air, and to begin with he wouldn't take off his Puffa jacket even though the boat was toasty. I showed him around, taking care to keep it light-hearted – still the need to protect him, but aware of it this time. Back in the galley, before I'd even taken the mugs from the cupboard, a tide of confusion, anger, and guilt tumbled out.

'Dad won't come. I've tried to talk to him, April, but he just clams up. It's not like him. Always got an answer, hasn't he?'

It was a start. I made coffee, weak with half a sugar, (just how he liked it) and cut two slices of coconut cake, thinking he'd never eat it as he was always in training, but hoping, nonetheless. Bradley finally gave me his jacket and shifted awkwardly as he waited for my reply. I didn't want to talk about our dad. 'How are you, Brad?'

'Me? Oh, busy as per. The next meet is coming around fast, and I'm not nearly as prepared as I usually am. In fact, I might even swerve this time.'

A solitary tear rolled down his gaunt cheek, and my heart ripped open. He quickly wiped it away, but he couldn't hide those fingernails, bitten down to the quick, a stubborn teenage habit. I resisted the urge to comfort him and as I tucked into the sponge, a splodge of strawberry jam smeared my cheek. Instantly Bradley beamed, and was twelve years old, goading me to a cake race, the pair of us smothered in red coconut snow and choking with laughter. In two bites, history repeated itself. We were friends. Allies. Him and me against the world.

'You've no idea what it's like without you, April. And it's not just because you make everything run like clockwork, which you do, *obviously*, but the whole family's busting at the seams.'

He gulped his coffee, so unused to this kind of talk. I was desperate to hear more, to finally break open the barrier and reunite with my darling Brad.

'Don't think I don't know how much you sacrificed for me. You should have gone to Oxford. I couldn't believe you opted for Loughborough when you could have got away.'

'Loughborough was great, Bradley. I've no regrets, and that's the truth. I'm not saying it to make you feel better.'

'Well that's one less thing to feel guilty about. No one but you really understood how much the rugby concussion impacted me, and you had the scoliosis to deal with. I've wanted to tell you for ages what happened that day but it was so bloody terrifying, I just couldn't do it.'

I reached across the table for his hand. 'You don't have to tell me, Brad. It's enough that you're here.'

'I've got to get it off my chest.' He took a deep breath. 'When I was out, y'know, during the concussion, I could have sworn I was looking down at myself, a sort of 'out-of-body' experience. It was over in a flash, and the next thing I knew, the coach and the paramedics stretchered me off. After that, I was petrified of everything. Couldn't even sleep with the lights out until I met Harriet.'

'I'm so sorry to hear that, Brad. Why didn't you talk to Mum? She more than anyone could have helped. She still can, that is, if you are brave enough to ask. Those types of experiences can transform the way we look at the world.'

The previously unconsidered thought rolled around his mind. 'Yeah, maybe I will talk to Mum about it sometime. She's been brilliant these last few weeks. We've set up a programme of gym sessions for her Homebodies. The trial went really well, although we spent most of the time in fits. They know how to have fun, that's for sure.'

'Wow! You and Mum did that?'

'We were meant to get it up and running before Seb came along, but it was one of a number of projects that got side-lined. Did you know that Mum arranged a meet between Xander and Olly Irvine, of all people, at *GirlMeetsBoy*. Could he get a better introduction to the acting profession? When Declan saw the video of *Whose Shoes?* he told Xander that it was never too late to live his dream, and he'd support him, whatever it took. I had no idea Mum and Olly were in touch.'

'Always have been. Olly came to see me last week with a job offer. Mum told her I had hit the skids.'

'She came here? But you've got a top-drawer career, April.'

'I *had* a top-drawer career, Bradley. Now I have a work-life balance. Gita's convinced I've lost my marbles. D'you know, when I asked what was next on her agenda once F&N ruled the accountancy world, she looked at me as if I were nuts. Anyway, I turned down Olly's offer.'

'Why?'

'I don't need any more drama.'

'Oh, right.' A pause. 'How was the iconic producer/director?'

'Knackered, but totally fab, as you'd expect. Olly must have thought the entire family were going under after her conversation with Mum. By the way, she's also been amazing with me. It's shameful how much I underestimated our mother.'

'Yeah, me too. I've been such an idiot.' His eyes filled up. 'Look, April, I am truly sorry for taking your goodwill for granted. Without your help, I wouldn't have passed any exams, let alone have got the job at Uncle Max's club. You've always taken the silver medal so that Dad could pretend I was doing okay. Everyone knows it, and this is the result. We chased you away ... ' He wiped his eyes with the napkin. 'I only ever wanted you to be happy. When Emily Pagett left the country, you were on a massive downer. I thought Seb was a good bloke, that is, until I moved into number 44.'

'He told you?'

'About the money? Yeah, and how it was meant for *our mega trip to Hawaii*. He was acting as if I were single. We all thought he was joking and played along with it, didn't we? Seb was never going to make *Ironman*. But when he showed me the financial breakdown and training plan, it totally freaked me out. I said it was time to get real and for a split-second he looked as if he was gonna punch my lights out, but then he was all smiles. I could have lost Harriet over that git.'

'But on the other hand, without him you and I might never have had this conversation and I might never have found the courage to break away. Maybe Sebastian's done us all good. He held a mirror up to the cocky Hayle family, and let's face it, Brad, it was about time.' I didn't expect him to agree but I no longer felt angry, or betrayed, and that was good. 'So what now?'

'Seb's gone. Said his mother was sick, up in Crewe.'

'He has a real live mother?'

'So he says. He quit the club two weeks ago, left the members in the lurch. Uncle Max is going mental. He threatened to track him down, but we talked him out of it. Even Vikki is red-faced. Sebastian Espie took us all in, and no one knows how to make it up to you.'

'I'm still here, Brad, *and* I get my house back.'

'But not the shed – well, not any more. That was the only thing Seb left behind. I must admit, Dad came up trumps with number 44. He asked Max and me to help dismantle the shed, probably his way of saying sorry. Anyway, after that we re-decorated the house, and tidied up the garden as best we could.'

'You did that for me?'

'April, it was the least *I* could do. It was me who helped Seb put the bloody shed up in the first place *and* twisted your arm to reduce his rent. If I feel bad, you can imagine how Dad feels.'

At that point he let me hug him, and then, another miracle: Elkie tapped on the hatch. I let her in, and she immediately went to Bradley. Just as Manny had done, he lifted her up and she licked his wet cheeks. After a while, he gently put her down and was transformed.

'Mum didn't say you had a dog!'

'Elkie comes and goes, but mostly she stays with me. You might not believe this, Brad, but I've got used to my own company.'

'You're not coming back to Embla?'

'No. I think I've finally grown up, and it's got nothing to do with you, or Dad, or anyone else.'

'Mum said you might join us for Christmas. I really hope you can make it, and not just because Raddy will be there, although we could use a full squad to face the wrath of Pious Petra.'

Bradley was still smiling when he called Harriet. They agreed to stay for dinner.

'Hey, April, before Harriet gets here, I want to ask your advice. D'you think I'm up to having sprogs?'

'What, you? A parent? Do me a favour, Brad ...'

I ducked out of the way of the cushion, and we fell about laughing. 'You'll make a wonderful father. Just remember to follow Mum's lead rather than Dad's, and make sure the nipper gets a dog to play with.'

37

Another bridge had been crossed, and I was elated. Bradley and Harriet had reunited and were at last talking babies, and my dad of all people had helped to decorate number 44! After a week on the market, two offers had been made. With the house soon to be taken off my hands, it was time to put my permanent post code plan into action.

Edmund invited me to accompany him to Fereday Boat Yard. He wanted to introduce me to more *good people*, although I suspected an ulterior motive. His distant cousin Danny, and daughter Laurel were the team responsible for the Anna Lee's makeover and her ongoing maintenance. They'd been working on a refit, practically an overhaul, and were nearing completion when their customers had received bad news, forcing them to withdraw from the purchase. Danny showed us around the impressive yard, complete with huge work-shed and crane. He talked enthusiastically about present and forthcoming projects, and by the time we left, my head was spinning with possibilities.

Without needing Edmund's prompting, I had quickly calculated that with the equity raised from my house sale and my savings, I could comfortably buy the boat. According to Danny, it would be water-worthy by early

Spring, with only minor interior fittings outstanding. While I was talking with Laurel, he had suggested to Edmund that if I bought Mistletoe, I might want to lend a hand. Not only would it keep the costs down, but I'd learn a thing or two in the process. There was also a permanent residential mooring available, far enough away from the yard as to be quiet, but near enough to have 'good people' around.

As we drove back to Quietwater, Edmund was tactful. 'It's a fabulous opportunity, April. I hope you don't mind my asking if you have the funds.'

'As a matter of fact I do, but I don't want to jump in too quickly. Danny and Laurel are so nice and I wouldn't want to mess them around, but to live *and* work on my own narrowboat would be a dream come true. I don't suppose you told Danny about my thwarted engineering dreams, by any chance?'

'Whyever would I do that, my dear?'

We chuckled, and his earring wobbled.

'You don't have to make a decision yet. Regardless of the outcome, Danny will have no trouble selling a boat with up-to-date eco-engine and fittings.' Edmund sighed. 'The inland waterways will once again be transformed, this time with electric and hydrogen boats, and wildlife corridors. I only hope I am around to see it.'

'Edmund, didn't you say that your age is other people's problem?'

$$\pi$$

When we got back to Quietwater, he stayed for tea. There was something he wanted to get off his chest, but I wasn't at all nervous, as Edmund only ever instilled confidence in those around him. I got the feeling he wanted me to wait until his nephew arrived before making a decision, but even if another miracle happened and Kristian and I hooked up, it wouldn't change the fact that I needed a home of my own. Quietwater Cottage was to be left jointly to Kristian and Lise, which was as it should be, and I could afford to do this alone. Would I ever be so insecure that I'd need to be permanently moored to a partner? Fereday Boat Yard was a handful of locks from Quietwater, and no distance by car. I'd have friends nearby, and it was affordable. I was in the mood to listen to my gut, and this felt right.

As I poured the tea, Edmund examined one of the *vaniljekranse* before taking a bite. 'The biscuits look and taste good, April. Frieda's only happy when she's passing on her knowledge.'

'Lucky me! I'm learning new things every day. Thanks so much for taking me to the yard. Danny and Laurel seem happy at their work. They must get a lot of job satisfaction.'

'Now that Laurel has finished her apprenticeship, Danny will have capable hands to pass the business on to, but not for many years yet.'

'What happened to Laurel's mother?'

'She died of cancer, must be all of ten years ago. Danny's father can't do much. Old Pete shuffles around, sweeps the yard. Mistletoe was his boat but it was going to rust and ruin, so Danny persuaded him to let it go, to give it another life with someone who'll appreciate it.'

'It's good of his son to take care of him.'

'Yes, April, it is. Now, how is your mother? I understand she hasn't yet been to visit.'

'I can't seem to pin her down, but she has promised to come soon. Harriet and I want her to join us at Angel Ninebarks next year. Mum stayed there once before, many years ago, and she'll benefit so much from another visit.'

Edmund's expression was a mirror of Lise's, and suddenly the water shifted beneath my feet.

'I'm afraid you're mistaken, April. Your mother has been here on many occasions, the last when she was six-months pregnant with you.'

'Oh! But I thought ...' My mouth went dry. Mum came when she was pregnant with me? 'Didn't she make the tapestry before Bradley and I were born?'

'No. Monica and Connie came together that first time and after that, your mother signed up as guest helper as often as she could. She and Lise helped Frieda to plant the herb garden, and the Tibetan cherry tree.'

'You knew her?'

'As Monica Trembath, before she married your father. Lise pointed this out when you were here in May. Harriet had signed you in as April Hayle, as she'd done previously, and as Lise rarely comes that early in the season, your paths hadn't crossed. But as soon as she saw you there was no doubt you were Monica Trembath's daughter.'

'But why hasn't Lise said anything? We've spent days together. There have been countless opportunities for her to tell me. Did something so terrible happen that it had to be kept a secret?'

'My dear, we had hoped that your mother might have told you. It's important for you to talk to her. Your visits may have stirred up painful memories.'

'Edmund, she may not want to tell me. Whenever we speak, my mum only ever asks how I am, never about the Anna Lee, or what I've been doing at Ninebarks.'

My heart was racing. There were important things to know, and Edmund Heathcote wasn't the sort to break confidences, but I wanted answers and was prepared to push him. Then I remembered Connie's holiday snaps. They were a clue to solving this mystery, I was sure of it. After rummaging around for the envelope, I spread the black and white photographs across the table. 'I made a celebratory book for Mum, in lieu of her sixtieth birthday. Connie recently gave me these. Do you know who the other people are?'

Edmund put on his spectacles before organising the photographs into order. 'These ones were taken in Laugavegur and Thorsmörk. Connie and Monica accompanied Lise and her friends to walk the Icelandic trail. Monica was fascinated by Norse mythology. To see where the sons of Thor were born was an opportunity not to be missed.' He picked up another photo. 'Ah, this is the Montgomery Canal. Lise had the idea to buy a narrow boat. I suggested she try a holiday before taking the plunge. She and your mother spent a week there, and soon after they parted. They never saw each other again.'

Edmund was quiet for a long while, allowing me time to digest his startling revelations.

'Making the Midgard tapestry may have been your mother's way of forever being linked to Lise, and the house. If you look at it closely, you can see the letters A and E – Ask and Embla – embroidered in gold at the base of each figure. Do you know the meaning behind the myth?'

Yes, I knew it. Like jigsaw pieces falling from the sky and forming a complete picture under my eyes, finally I understood: Mum's garden, a replica of Angel Ninebarks, with the Tibetan Cherry tree, and Ninebark bushes; the Rilke book's A/E symbol, identical to the tapestry; 'Embla', our house name, and its proximity to Ninebarks; Mum's increasingly agitated state: *leaving Cornwall was the second most sorrowful thing I've ever done.* The most sorrowful thing of all was to have permanently parted from Lise.

'Edmund, do you believe that Lise loved my mother?'

He took my hand. 'I do, but something greater was calling her. Monica had the insight to accept that my niece wasn't destined for a conventional life. You may have noticed Lise's exceptional qualities, not that she would ever openly disclose them although others are quick to do that. It happens every year at Ninebarks. You'll have also seen this whilst travelling on the Anna Lee, I'm sure. It's natural to want to follow her, to learn from her, but Lise would say she is neither teacher nor healer. That's why she never stays in one place for long. These gifts can be a curse, April.'

After putting the photographs back into the envelope, Edmund passed them to me. Seeing my rising distress, he took my hand.

'Lise recognised your mother's goodness in you. There was no other motivation for asking you to join her on the Anna Lee than the wish to help a dear friend's daughter in her time of need.'

I couldn't speak. My darling mother, how she must have suffered for a life she could never have. Hearing me bang on about my adventures must have been agonising.

I made no attempt to mop the tears that spilled onto the table. Edmund fetched me a tissue and put a comforting arm on my shoulder.

'April, you must call your mother. In her current state of mind, I feel sure she will be ready to talk to you. In fact, she will want to release the burden of it.' After a while he said, 'Now, will you be alright? I don't like to leave you like this.'

'I'm okay, really. Elkie is here, and I'll come to the cottage if needs be. Thank you for telling me.'

38

It was as if she'd been waiting for me to call. We sat in a quiet booth at Jonty's Café, Mum with her oat milk *latte*, me with a *macchiato* and chocolate cruffin. She wore a frayed scarlet beret which had belonged to her mother, and fingerless woollen gloves, courtesy of an industrious Homebody. The temperature outside had plummeted, but the café was snug. A hum of conversation hovered like mountain mist above the espresso machine's industrial clatter.

'How's Dad?'

'Struggling.'

'Why?'

'Your father never expects to fail. He wasn't prepared when you moved away, and he's still loaded with guilt from being blindsided by Sebastian.'

'Dad hasn't failed, but I've changed. Seb had us all fooled, apart from you. There's no shame in that.'

'You should tell him.'

'I will, but not yet. I don't blame Dad, but it won't do him any harm to reflect on the consequences of his actions. His turbo-charged confidence may suit the workplace, but to have inflicted that on us was careless at best. When did we ever get to doodle during our weekends? Even our bike rides to Beacon Hill Country Park were set against the clock. I didn't know it then, Mum, but now I wonder why we didn't do more creative things with you.'

'You did, pet, but you don't remember them right now, that's all. Your dad can't quite grasp that his brilliant, steadfast daughter has stopped following his bike light. Give him time, April. You've always been your dad's biggest supporter, consolidating his ideas and rolling them out. He's bound to feel as if a wheel's fallen off. You know it was never about choosing your dad or me, don't you.'

'Actually, I do. That's why I don't blame him, or anyone else for that matter. When it dawned on me that my life was – is my responsibility, I had to leave Embla, to untie myself from everything I knew as how else could I work it all out? At first I felt really down, like an exile in my own family, but after a while, it felt as if a yoke had been lifted. You understand what I'm trying to say, don't you, Mum?'

'More than you realise, pet.'

'What I've not been able to work out is why, being so completely different, you and Dad have stayed together for so long. You're a humanitarian whereas he is ...'

'There's a side to your father you'll never see. I'll admit that his engagement with the world is from the head rather than from the heart, but we share the same passion for positive change. Carrow's electric vehicle fleet rollout, ahead of everyone else's, was one of your dad's initiatives. He has been a good husband and father,' she said wistfully, 'but yes, there have been times when I've wondered what might have happened if I'd taken another path.'

My insides somersaulted, but I was also strangely excited. The mystery was, at long last, about to be solved.

'I was kicking my heels in Hayle, waiting to start a new job at the hospital. A friend had been raving about a place she'd been to. Never ones to miss the chance of an uplifting adventure, we took off for Angel Ninebarks in Connie's clapped out Mini. As soon as I saw Lise, it was like a thunderbolt. She was different, special. Connie and the other guests felt it, too – it wasn't my imagination. We hit it off,' she clicked her fingers, 'just like that. I went to the house as often as I could. Lise came to Cornwall and we stayed in the lodge. She met your grandparents, we travelled around for a bit. When she mentioned test-driving a narrowboat on the Montgomery Canal, nothing was going to hold me back, and at that point, I'd have given it all up to follow her. That week changed my life.'

A shiver ran down my spine. Wasn't that how I had felt? My mother had carried this around for so long, and yet it was still so raw, like a bruise, or a newly formed scar. If I had the courage to ask her what happened, she'd be able to let it go, to move on. 'Why didn't you stay together, Mum?'

'Before I answer that, you must know that Lise didn't lie or break any promises. She was never going to drop anchor despite my hopes and dreams. It was like finding a precious jewel, but you could only ever look at it, never keep it or wear it. Lise knew how much I wanted children. *You must follow your heart, Monica. If you give this up, you will always regret it.*'

'There never was any possibility of a life with her, was there?'

'I knew it when we spent the week on the boat. It was Lise's way of letting me down gently. The yearning was solely on my part, and I suspect there have been many others who have felt the same.'

I silently thanked her for not asking if I were one of them, even though she must have guessed. 'But Edmund said you went back to Angel Ninebarks, when you were pregnant with me.'

'To say goodbye. I wanted you, my unborn daughter, to absorb that unique energy. It wasn't possible to go when I had Bradley, but when Connie did a crystal pendulum divination, she told me I was carrying a girl and I had to go back. The visit would be closure. I never expected to see Lise again. She went back to Denmark as her brother was ill.'

Mum knew about Kristian! I let this revelation settle while we silently finished our drinks and the café released more of its warm customers into the cold afternoon.

'When Harriet first talked about going to Angel Ninebarks three years ago, it all came flooding back. I couldn't tell you not to go, April. What right had I to stop you benefitting from a wonderful experience? But when Lise's name wasn't mentioned, I assumed she'd moved on.'

'So, when Harriet told you about her back in May ...'

'I'm ashamed to say that when it came to it, I couldn't take my own so-called wise advice.'

I wasn't about to blame my mum for that, as it showed her for the fallible human she was. 'But what about Dad's part in all this?

'When I met your father at the festival, he was convinced we had a connection – his surname was Hayle, and I was born in Hayle, that sort of thing. Connie thought he was high and told him to bugger off. She said I was nursing a broken heart, and he was wasting his time. But he kept coming back, bearing gifts of drink, food, and even a daisy hair band.'

'That's so typical of Dad, to sweet-talk you into seeing him again.'

'It's called free will, April. I liked him, and in time I came to love him. Embla was your father's idea. It was the perfect place to raise our family. You have to remember that Grandma Raddy's parents fled Germany at the start of the war for a new life in Leicester. That's why she kept her children so close. I was an only child of much older parents. The opportunity of being part of a large, close-knit clan was a dream, and of course having my own babes would, I believed, release me from the past. But when this came up again your father expected me to leave him. He said that he'd known all along I'd go.'

'Dad knew about Lise?'

'Of course. Back then, your father was confident we'd make a good team, and we have. But of late he was convinced that there was unfinished business between Lise and me, and rather than deal with it, we – I let it push us further apart.'

'At least you didn't lie, Mum.'

'Why would I lie? Lise is an extraordinary woman. I was privileged to have met her, and now that you've spent time with her, you know exactly what I mean.'

'Everyone I've met feels the same way about Lise, so I guess nothing's changed. She's extremely skilled at giving her would-be disciples the slip. Actually, it's her brother ... I'm not sure if he feels the same way about me, but we've struck up a good friendship and I'm happy with that.'

My mum sat back and laughed.

'Well, there's a turn up for the books! Kristian Michelson, of all people. I assume he's recovered from his illness.'

'I believe so. We got to know each other during the second boat trip. Kristian is coming back soon ...'

'And you will know what to do, but if you are left in any doubt, not for a single moment do I regret you and Bradley. Lise was right about that. My only regret is that I didn't tell you sooner, pet.'

She held me tight, and was, as she had always been, my beautiful, loving mother.

39

Elkie kept watch on the towpath while I hovered in the galley. 'Nervous' didn't cover it – my stomach contractions could have bagged me a Commonwealth silver. Kristian had arrived earlier that morning and had been with his aunt and uncle ever since. Darling Elkie had trotted from the cottage to the boat and back again, reminding him to get a wriggle on.

Before leaving Copenhagen, he'd written to ask if he might join me for dinner on his first evening. I predicted he'd spend a few days with Frieda and Edmund and had tried not to read anything into it. Since visiting Fereday Yard, events were moving fast. Having emailed the briefest of details, my plan was to share the news with him in a cool, calm and collected way. Now it was on the cusp of pouring out.

Two barks. Elkie let him come down the stairs first. Swaddled in a metallic blue padded jacket, Kristian's pink cheeks peeped out of a midnight blue polo neck sweater. He took off his walking shoes and I waltzed into his arms for all of ten seconds before Elkie nudged in. She wanted a biscuit. He gave her a treat from the tin, after which she curled up in her basket, job done. We laughed to be totally at her mercy.

'It's so good to see you again, April. Your metaphorical baptism has been good, I think.'

'Fantastically exciting, *and* I've managed to stay dry.'

He gave me a parcel, tied with string. To hide my embarrassment, I offered to take his jacket. 'Sit by the stove, Kristian. You look so cold.'

'The Heathcotes have the constitution of polar explorers, although they make allowances for me, and have lit the fire. It's been a while since I was on the Anna Lee in winter. I'd forgotten how cheerful it is. Now, let me look at you.' He moved back, as if admiring a painting. 'Edmund is right. Quietwater suits you.'

'I feel good, inside and out. There's so much to tell you, Kristian, but I promise not to blurt it all out in one sitting.'

While he poured the jasmine tea from his favourite teapot, I abandoned all attempts to hold back. He must have known about the friendship between Lise and my mother, but he made no comment. I assured him that my parents would sort themselves out, given time. He seemed pleased to hear that Bradley and I had reunited, and when I filled in the details about Sebastian, I could have sworn his eyes brightened. 'And you, Kristian. How are you faring?'

'You used that very word in your first email, sent from Brightside Park. I wondered if you had lost my details.'

'Oh, no. I always intended to write, but it took a while to adjust to my changed circumstances before I could get started on *Niels Lyhne*, as that was a legitimate excuse to contact you. Yeah, it sounds silly, but I didn't want to come

258

across as desperate.' Kristian's smile was like a gazillion firecrackers exploding simultaneously. How could I not smother this totally fabulous man with affection?

'Desperate you could never be, but we are, I'll admit, a little foolish. Do we have each other's permission to launch our emails indiscriminately?'

'Yes, but we'd best agree on a word limit. You'll have seen how much I like to natter on.'

'But that is what I like, April. Now, why don't you open your parcel before dinner.'

With shaky fingers I untied the string and lifted out of the box a pale green/blue pair of woollen mittens and a hat, edged and bobbled in ivory faux fur.

'Quietwater can get cold in winter. I hope you don't mind.'

'No! These are beautiful, Kristian. Thank you.' I carefully pulled on the hat. 'What d'you think?'

'The juniper wool complements the colour of your eyes, just as I had hoped.'

He wanted to match the colour of my eyes! 'You knitted these?'

'With a lot of help. One of the neighbours is a magician with knitting needles. You'll be glad to know that Edmund approves of my new hobby.'

The oven pinged, sparing my blushes. We talked, ate, talked some more, and he wished me goodnight. A warm hug. No kiss.

What did I expect? Lying in bed that night, I asked myself that same question, over and over. Kristian was a strange brew: on the one hand, detached and self-contained, and on the other, bold enough to choose his mitten wool to complement my eye colour. And yet, the chemistry *was* there, as it had been in July, I could feel it. He also seemed relieved to hear that the business with Sebastian was over, and my family situation had improved. Like Lise, he offered no advice, comment, or judgement, but in the telling of my tale, I was aware of having done the right thing.

As the following afternoon's weather forecast promised to be dry, we agreed to go for a ramble once my work was finished, and he'd made inroads into the books and papers stack in the study. Without wanting to wish a second of my brilliant new life away, nevertheless, I couldn't wait.

π

The days that followed were sacred – to me, at least. We were getting to know each other, quietly and without fanfare. During a light hearted evening at Quietwater Cottage, it was reassuring to be in the Michelsons' affectionate company. If I had been expecting tension between Kristian and Edmund, there was no evidence of it. It was time to revise my storyline of the estranged and sad nephew scribbling away in an attic. Our growing intimacy enabled me to confess these immature idlings, but this agonising question of his future plans remained unanswered. Unable to sit with the uncertainty any longer, I decided to tackle him over dinner.

'I had a chat with my mum earlier. She wants to know if I'll join the family for Christmas. My grandma has invited herself, which is a miracle as she only ever spends the holidays with Pious Petra.'

As was his custom when I spoke, Kristian put down his

knife and fork. 'I feel another saga coming on. 'Pious Petra' is …'

'Ha! You'll wish you never asked. Petra is my dad's little sister: very controlling, easy to upset. Apparently, Grandma Raddy is of the opinion that Mum, Dad, Bradley, and me need her the most this year, so she is coming for the day to dispense her wisdom.'

'But you have reconciled with your family.'

'Almost. When I met my folks in town, Dad and I got through lunch without having to see a shrink or call the cops. So, yes, in the spirit of reconciliation I've decided to go.' I refilled our glasses, Kristian's with a smidgen, as he wasn't much for wine. 'How are you spending the festive season? Do you actually celebrate it – in fact, how long are you staying at Quietwater?'

'The answer to your second question is yes, I celebrate Christmas on the 24th of December, as is the Danish custom. We go to church in the afternoon.'

'What on earth would JPJ say!'

Kristian laughed out loud at that. Was he a teeny bit impressed with my knowledge of his hero?

'Let's make sure he doesn't find out. Being of sweet tooth, April, you would appreciate our dessert: rice porridge, blended with chopped almonds, vanilla and whipped cream. Whoever finds the single almond is given a gift. I believe your tradition is a sixpence in the Christmas pudding. After that, we exchange gifts, and sing songs. Carols come alive when sung under a domed ceiling or around a tree, don't you think?'

'I've never had the pleasure. Mum and Dad's biggest hurdles were religion and vegetarianism. Rather than argue, they agreed that if he didn't insist on us attending a religious school, she wouldn't stop us from eating meat, if that was what we wanted.'

'Your parents are wise.'

'I'm only just learning to appreciate just how wise they've been. It can't be easy to see our conditioning if we don't even know what it is, let alone how it has influenced us.'

Kristian smiled at that. He cleared the table, and all the while a sweet tension had insinuated itself around us. Elkie stirred in her basket, her legs twitching in sweet dreams now that she'd enjoyed her last walk of the day. I adored our dark-sky rambles, no matter what the weather, and was becoming accustomed to the night sounds. They were no longer spine-chilling, and I could sleep with the lights out.

When he returned to the table, Kristian's expression was unreadable. 'In answer to your other question, April, I will remain at Quietwater until the seventh of January.'

'Oh, so you've extended your visit. You'll be here for ...'

I can't recall who moved first, but it was as certain as Newton's mathematical equation for the gravitational force between two bodies.

$$\pi$$

We lay in Lise's warm downy bed, engulfed by a profound silence. From the shelf, the tea lights' flicker illuminated the box of truffles that he'd brought the day before, and a Rumi poetry book, unearthed in the study. Of the ten days that had passed, this was our fifth night together, and already we were relaxing into the other's vulnerability, like snakes that had recently sloughed off their skins. To be physically and mentally undressed with Kristian was new and exciting territory.

His finely tuned hands traced the bends and curves of my spine, triggering quivers and tingles.

'My sister has helped you.'

'In so many ways. My spine has reset its compass and is now heading north.'

'And in which direction is your heart travelling?'

I rested my hand on Kristian's heart. 'In darts, we call this a bullseye.'

'My darling, you have reinvented the language of love.'

When we stopped laughing, he said, 'You will find much to inspire you in *Bridge to the Soul*. After seven centuries, Rumi's words still resonate, and may continue to do so for all eternity. In his introduction, Coleman Barks gives an evocative account of the Khajou bridge in Isphahan.'

'Tell me what it's like there.'

'I haven't been, but perhaps one day we might go together.'

'That would be awesome, but to be honest, Kristian, a walk along the towpath with you is more than enough right now.'

'Well then, for the time being we'll content ourselves with Barks' introduction. That alone is worthy of your attention, and my re-admiration.'

'You want *me* to read to *you*? My guess is you already know the book inside out and can quote any number of poems.' I reached over for the book and passed it to him. 'Why don't you read to me unless you're ready for sleep.'

Kristian's eyes twinkled. 'What care I for sleep when the lady doth ask for poetry?'

π

There were so many tender moments, so much affection. In the depth of winter, the natural world was abundantly beautiful: frosty mornings, where dew drops clung to blackthorn branches; moon-bright nights, where reflections of trees lay like ghostly fretwork under our boots.

Under Christmas Day's cold morning sky, wrapped in chunky-knit jumpers and hunkered by the stove, we exchanged gifts. Kristian was enthused by his 'one hundred local walks' book, and I cried at his mother's exquisite rendition of *Who Knows Where The Time Goes* as it crackled on the turntable. Apparently, to celebrate Katrine's recovery, Jerry had persuaded her to record a number of songs written and performed by her favourite female artists, Sandy Denny being one. The vinyl was never intended to be sold and was given only to loved ones and was by far the most moving gift I'd ever received, particularly as many of the songs were my mother's favourites.

Dressed in my new hat and mittens, we set off for Embla. Unlike those few occasions when I'd have been too nervous to bring someone home, not so that day. As a forty-eight-year-old academic and keen knitting student, Kristian was way past garnering parental approval, and at this stage in my life I couldn't have cared tuppence for anyone's opinion.

Dad was the first to greet us – a firm handshake for Kristian, a tentative hug for me. It was a big moment.

Mum's 'confession' had prompted me to revise our father/daughter script. His cherished wife's love for Lise must have been incredibly unsettling. Had he, Vaughan Hayle, felt like the runner-up during their marriage, or had he accepted that the very essence of love was unlimited? For the first time, I felt my dad's fragility, while equally admiring his staying power. As for my mum, she looked unbound. She held Kristian's face for as long as was polite, and he didn't mind in the least. He was already one of the family.

Over bubbles and nibbles, we gathered by the fire, swapping presents, making jokes. Dad gave me a complete handbook of narrowboat building, which provided ample opportunity for quips. He and Mum appreciated their 'special weekend voucher' to stay in a New Forest hotel, courtesy of Bradley and me. Harriet had regained her sparkle. She now had two boys to adore. Believe it or not, Bradley had taken my advice and had persuaded her that what they really needed before leaping into parenthood, was a rescue dog. Finley's antics had us in fits. The bouncy Patterdale's steeple jumps over my delighted brother's back made for fun festive entertainment.

Equally as impressive was the charming two-legged newcomer who had totally won over Grandma Radka, particularly as Kristian spoke fluent German, and she was a young child again. And for once, no one mentioned quizzes, competitions, or prizes.

40

The big freeze had lasted long enough to muffle the Staffordshire landscape under its thin white crust. Inside the Anna Lee, the decks had been cleared for Kristian's last morning. He still hadn't said when he was coming back, but that was okay – ours was unlikely to be an everyday relationship, but that was good. With the sale proceeds of number 44 ready to be transferred to Danny Fereday's business account, I had finally settled on a name. 'Wingspan' was to be hand-painted in burnished copper across the bow of my new home.

'It's the perfect name, and the perfect solution, April. You will have two permanent addresses: Quietwater and Fereday Yard.'

He put down his coffee and gave me that look. Kristian's range of expressions were becoming more familiar. This one indicated there was a question coming. I tried not to smile.

'Taking everything into consideration, I will rearrange my commitments with the university in order to spend more time in England. How would that work for you?'

'Are you asking if you can stay with me on Wingspan when you come back?'

'Frieda and Edmund's generous hospitality is open-ended, and I consider the cottage my home, but as we are,' he coughed, 'together, I would very much like to spend a portion of the week with you, that is, if it's not too much of an inconvenience with your work schedules …'

Overjoyed by Kristian's awkwardly declared intentions, I slid my arms around his waist. 'Wingspan is your home for as long as it is meant to be. The only proviso is that you bring back a box or two of those delicious raspberry truffles.'

π

Kristian would return in six weeks, for our first Spring together. Frieda had suggested we try our hand at gardening. She was willing to teach us her skills, as not only was it something for us to share, but it would be of immense benefit when he and Lise inherited the cottage. How could we refuse such a generous offer? While still several years from officially retiring from academia, Kristian had already begun to consider other options. Offering his services as Edmund's apprentice was the quirkiest, as neither of us could picture him up a ladder, or as he once said, carving fluted wooden dowels from reclaimed oak, but working with Frieda was an opportunity not to be missed.

He wondered if later in the year, he might introduce me to Jacobsen's beloved city. We'd sit by Soren Kierkegaard's statue near the Royal Library, meet his friends, visit the university and his mother's coastal home. While I wouldn't say that Kristian was feverish with excitement (an adjective and a noun too far), I had no trouble in expressing my joy at his invitation to go to Copenhagen.

Far from floundering in his absence, a strong sense of purpose spurred me on. As well as updating Kristian on the everyday stuff, whenever I witnessed an extra-spectacular natural event, I couldn't wait to recreate it on the page. His name for our correspondence was *Notes from Quietwater*. My first 'note' reported on the snowdrop explosion. During an afternoon walk, Frieda had led me to a cluster of the modest white flowers under whose heads were exquisite green/yellow petals. Their arrival marked the end of winter, a significant moment. Embarrassed by my ignorance, I said nothing, but those delicate rays of hope exploded into my consciousness, and were no longer invisible, or so I had explained enthusiastically to Kristian.

Then there was the 'morning fire' note. I woke up to find the boat's interior filled with a vivid purple/red light. The sky was aflame, and from every window, the colours morphed from one psychedelic hue to another with electrifying speed. Bemused, Elkie watched me sprint from stern to cratch and back again as I attempted to throw on coat and boots for a real live look. After yet another marvellous encounter, I wrote the following:

Kristian

Elkie and I walked to Monkton Woods after lunch. It might not have been the best idea as it was blowing a hoolie, but I just had to get out there, to feel the power of it. Did you know that trees made a sound like the sea? 'Tempestuous' is the only appropriate adjective in my limited vocabulary to do it justice.

Enormous clouds were piling in, and suddenly a gap appeared, and in that gap was a blanket of blue. I followed it for as long as it lasted. It struck me that those clouds were a metaphor for the Hayles, rushing headlong to who knew where, while behind them was the bigger perspective. Like the blue you see when flying above the clouds. Like Lise.

Anyway, Kristian, my note may be a long way from the JPJ prose department, but it's from the heart.

April xxx

... and as always, his reply was warm, and succinct.

My dearest April,

Be in no doubt that JPJ is a very happy particle/wave right now. Not only has he found a new and appreciative reader, but one whose sensitivity matches his own. I continue to be delighted when your 'Notes from Quietwater' drop into my inbox as they bring me ever closer to you. 'Hoolie' has a fine metaphorical ring to it. The blue: yes, if it were possible to capture the spirit of my sister, then this you have done.

Yours,

Kristian

This is how I assumed our exchanges would continue, but the reality was that my wants and expectations were deeply ingrained and as a result, constantly being challenged. If I hadn't received a reply to an email after a day, I'd tail spin – did Kristian still want me; had something happened; when would he reply? My overabundant outpourings must have engulfed his insulated personality, despite their arrival through the barrier of a computer screen. After forensically re-examining my sparse romantic history, the pattern had been all too familiar: giving too much, doing too much, wanting the same in return, and getting desperate when I didn't get it. So far, so enlightening. But that wasn't the only thing to rock my boat.

Tish's predictions of a push back had already materialised. Danny Fereday was impressed by my enthusiasm and was happy for me to chat to Old Pete about the waterways, but he had a yard to run. Without having to spell it out, I could see that he and Laurel were far too busy to entertain me on Wingspan every afternoon, and there were only so many things I could do without their help. Similarly with the Heathcotes, and Tish, as they would often be happily alone. After finishing work, and reading boat manuals and books, keeping my own company was a challenge, even with Elkie by my side. Wasn't this supposed to be what humans yearned for – more 'being', less 'doing'? The theory was marvellous, but the reality was something else altogether.

π

The weeks went by, and slowly my cloudy senses began to clear, just as Connie said they would. As I observed the manner in which my new friends related to their environment and to each other, an increasing awareness of my connection to the earth, to whom I owed my existence, began to crystalise. Subsequently, a collection of submerged memories appeared to re-balance my distorted backstory. Far from trailing my dad everywhere, there *had* been many quieter, creative moments with my mother and my grandparents.

We had rambled around Heligan and Trelissick henges and gardens; delved into rockpools, made sand pies. We'd hole up on Grandpa's workshop on rainy afternoons making all sorts of weird and wonderful things. On one such magical occasion, Bradley and I created Trembath Island. It had a sandpaper shell beach, a rickety rope bridge, (made from balsa wood and garden twine), a blue paper bay, and as a final flourish, a bright yellow 'Trembath Ices' van on standby. Just as my mother had said, it was nothing more than selective amnesia that prevented these treasured memories from coming up.

Numbers continued to be important, but even that relationship was changing. Gita Nair, bless her generous heart, had kept the faith although mine had forever abandoned wanting an associateship. How could she not struggle to recognise the current version of 'April Hayle' when I had to double check it myself. When I offered to resign, Gita generously offered me a forensic accounting contract at twenty-hours per week, as an interim move. I grabbed it. Not only was I spared the trouble of finding another part-time job, but this arrangement freed up more time to work at Fereday Yard on the allotted afternoons. How I relished swapping loungewear and spreadsheets for spanners and overalls, and using calculations to measure wood, metal, and paint.

Laurel and I had hit it off immediately. Occasionally, Danny would hop aboard Wingspan to find out what we were cackling about. When Laurel described the Fereday's lack of business acumen, I helped to clear their backlog of invoices after which, at my suggestion, F&N were hired to do their accounts. At last I was learning to spread the load.

41

By the time Kristian returned to Quietwater, I was considerably less goggle-eyed, and much more aware of my habitual patterns and behaviours. My image of him as a fragile intellectual convalescent in need of rescuing was permanently thrown overboard. Far from sitting out his lonesome nights with Thomasine for solace, Kristian went out to dinner and to concerts, spent weekends cross country skiing with his friends, and was having fun in the apartment block's knitting circle.

The familiar wintry canal-scape had been superseded by warmer days and lighter nights during which we resumed our treks in and around Quietwater. Frieda's gardening sessions were inspirational. Through her profound love and knowledge of the natural world, we felt the earth through our soil-encrusted hands, we cheered the appearance of ladies smock, and we puffed like proud parents to see the trees fattening up. Could we have been any more thrilled to witness a molehill expanding and contracting under our very eyes while a host of worms wriggled to the surface? The heart-stopping finale was the rapturous appearance of two tiny pink paws and a nose.

As Kristian settled into his Quietwater days, he suggested we venture into our neighbouring counties, using his new book for inspiration. We began our quest by exploring A.E. Houseman's exalted Shropshire hilltop vistas. In what became another ritual, we completed every outstandingly beautiful trek with a scrummy pub or café lunch, during which we'd reimagine the Roman's experience of seeing Wenlock Edge's *winds through woods in riot*, and sigh with pleasure at the wistful wild horses grazing meditatively on The Long Mynd. But best of all, our mutual feelings were still aligned.

π

Mid-April. My new home was ready. Kristian and I brought Wingspan from Fereday Yard to Quietwater, where Edmund, Frieda, Elkie, and Tish waited on the jetty for our arrival. The Anna Lee had gained a fine-looking companion. Wingspan's copper coloured hull contrasted beautifully against her mid-blue superstructure, and the polished brass tiller bar sparkled in the morning sun.

The galley was of a similar design and layout to the Anna Lee – lots of natural wood and light. Without the need for a bath (the Heathcotes gave me a free pass to use their tub), a shower room and separate cloakroom were sufficient. The guest berth doubled as an office, allowing me to close the door on the working day. Harriet had been overjoyed to choose the upholstery fabric. Where else would she take her inspiration from, other than Angel Ninebarks.

To maximise on saloon space, I opted for a smaller table in order to incorporate two armchairs and a footstool, which Harriet had covered in William Morris' *Blue Strawberry Thief*. And with Little Ted in his newly knitted 'Wingspan' sweater safely on board, the effect was of warmth, comfort and style.

π

I hadn't planned to celebrate my birthday. Reaching thirty no longer felt like the scary milestone I'd previously imagined it to be, but the days of balloons and bottle corks belonged to another era. Since moving to Quietwater, every day brought something in which to rejoice, and I felt no need for more, but Kristian and Tish had other ideas.

The Heathcote's previously redundant dining room was recast into a Copenhagen-esque candlelit salon, *circa* 1850. Kristian had noted the dishes I'd enthused over whilst out rambling, and with Tish's help, served me in style. Frieda and Edmund gave me six embroidered napkins enclosed in hammered silver rings; Lise had organised a basket of delectable bath oils and soaps; Manny arranged for a bottle of his favourite Burgundy to be sent, and Danny and Laurel gifted me a selection of Old Pete's tools which had been cleaned, sharpened, and polished, and placed in a new toolbox. Apparently I looked like someone who would make good use of them, and who was I to argue?

The grand finale was Kristian and Sofie's circular stained-glass window which had been specially designed for my bedroom. It was hard to believe that for months they had secretly collaborated to create Wingspan in her gorgeous colours, with Elkie and me at the helm. When Danny and I fitted it in place, the effect transformed an already wonderful cabin into something super-special. Never before had I received that kind of overwhelming attention. That was on Friday.

On Sunday, we drove to Westwytch. Mum had sent through a package containing a batch of birthday cards from my family, which shouldn't have been a surprise, but it was. I'd insisted there were no gifts, and no celebration this year. I'd seen my aunts and uncles for the briefest of Christmas present stops, and exchanged the occasional message, and as yet I hadn't returned to the fold. I wasn't sure if a) I wanted to or b) if I wanted to, how to go about it. The truth was, I hadn't missed the get-togethers *at all*. Maybe I was still in the Quietwater honeymoon phase but the thought of triathlon weekends and quizzes really did feel like yesterday's news.

Bradley and Harriet's invitation to a low-key birthday lunch with Mum and Dad as special guests was, however, impossible to refuse. Later that afternoon, the four of them had arranged to enter The Red Balloon's annual fundraiser quiz which was fine by me. Kristian and I would be on our way home by then. Although our Christmas Day reunion had gone well, I was aware of taking it slowly. As Rilke said, it was my responsibility not to torment loved ones with my new way of looking at the world. But during the drive to Embla, Kristian was in the mood to challenge my view, and his comments touched a nerve.

'You haven't considered the possibility that you might enjoy a reunion with your family. After all, you haven't argued, you've simply taken time out to rethink the nature of your relationships. How can you know the outcome unless and until you meet them again? Rather than digging in your heels, April, why don't we go to The Red Balloon. If it's too much, we can leave.'

'Kristian, how can you of all people want me to do that? Friday night was the best ever birthday, and I don't want to spoil the memory of it. I've never liked being the centre of attention, and the Hayles *always* go over the top. Let's just have lunch and come home.'

We had driven the rest of the journey in silence. I was aware of digging in, of clinging to the remembrance of a fantastic night now dust and ashes, but I hadn't anticipated for Kristian and I to be in conflict over what I considered to be a fundamental issue – namely my overpowering family's tendency to want to control me. I may have been actively freeing myself from old patterns, but the Hayles would be the same as they always were. Naively, I had expected my perfect world to last. Fortunately, Kristian was infinitely more mature. He had no idea why I felt the need to apologise, and was happy to talk it through, but not whilst he was driving.

π

By the time we reached Bradley and Harriet's house, which was mercifully without balloon or banner, all was well. While I tussled with Finley's exuberant welcome, Kristian was whisked off into the kitchen by Harriet. I played down the Quietwater dinner party and thanked Mum and Dad for their generous gift (they paid for Wingspan's solar panels – not especially thrilling for them but *sooo* exciting for me).

With lunch almost over, Bradley leaned back in his chair, locked his hands behind his head and grinned. 'So little sister, exactly how much did you love my chocolate/banana/walnut cake?'

'Yours? OMG, he's had another seizure. Call the paramedics.' Bradley's laugh made my heart leap. We'd exchanged lively banter throughout the afternoon, the result of which had sprinkled the air with a heady nostalgia, and I was super-chilled. 'Actually, Brad, to use Harriet-speak: *yum, yum.* Thank you both so much for a wonderful birthday lunch.'

'Yes, thank you, Bradley and Harriet. You created a nutritious *and* a tasty meal, which is no mean feat. An excellent choice of brain food which is extremely useful when under pressure,' said Kristian.

'And guaranteed to get the neurons firing at full pelt. It's essential to be first off the starting blocks, no matter what the occasion.'

'I agree, Dad. When the clock's ticking, and the answer's on the tip of your tongue, you need every advantage available, especially when Uncle Max is looming large on the next table ...'

'Okay, okay, I'll join the flipping quiz.' A cheer went up. There had been a conspiracy, and I was delighted that Kristian had been involved in it. 'Right then, Dad, what's the plan.'

With moist eyes, my dad passed me the list of teams. I squeezed his hand before scanning it. We were in for a tough afternoon. Everyone was out to score big as every point raised more money for the charity.

'As you can see, Max and Russ are fielding strong squads apiece, but we've a secret weapon in Kristian, and your mum has been known to throw a few curve balls.'

Mum laughed. 'Anything to wipe that lovely expression from your aunt Vikki's face. Shall we go get 'em, pet?'

Under apple blossom and afternoon sunshine, we walked through the village to The Red Balloon. Arm in arm with Kristian, I pointed out our childhood landmarks while Finley bounced alongside Bradley, so pleased not to have been left behind. I'll admit to feeling anxious, but I was also quietly excited at the prospect of a reunion under these circumstances.

As soon as we entered the pub, an explosion of ticker tape, party poppers, and cheers bowled me over. Like a gold medal-winning Olympian, I was engulfed in an ocean of well-wishing. Vikki had arranged an enormous birthday cake, while Petra placed a captain's hat on my head, with 'Wingspan' emblazoned in scarlet across the cap. Uncle Max had hold of the mic, his face beaming.

'Before firing the starter's pistol, I'd like to say, on behalf of Planet Hayle, how much we've missed you, and how chuffed we are to see you here today. Everyone's booked their week on Wingspan, which should take you nicely to next Christmas (laughs). You didn't think we'd let you sail off into the sunset without us, did you, Apple? Now, in the unlikely event you've forgotten how to ride, we've something to remind you.'

From behind the bar area, Eva wheeled out a bicycle. It was a tailor-made fold-up, perfect for the towpaths, and a neat stowaway. Fortunately, I was excused the embarrassment of giving a speech as shortly after, the Hayles went on to do what they do best.

It was late – very late, but that was good. Kristian and I were breaking rules here, there, and everywhere. Entwined under the heavy duvet, we admired the tiny silver cup, *Winners of The Red Balloon Annual Charity Quiz*.

'That was a close call. Brad was firing on all cylinders, and as for Mum … did you catch my dad's expression during the Green Giants round when she named every founder of the main environmental organisations? And you were totally amazing, Kristian. I couldn't believe our luck when European History came up. Why wouldn't we play our joker on that round? Uncle Max was gutted to be runner-up, but he gave me the biggest hug, and said I was welcome anytime, but not to bring you.'

Kristian chuckled. 'It was touching to hear him call you 'Apple'.'

'Apparently, I couldn't get my two-year-old tongue around the word 'April', so Max taught me to say 'Apple' instead.' I sighed. 'You must wonder why I made such a fuss.'

'Not at all. In spite of the tension, there was no mistaking their admiration and affection for you.'

'You noticed the tension?'

'Universities aren't exactly temples of calm, are they, April? Having sat in many exam halls, you know better than anyone what happens to the mind and body when there is a lot at stake. How can the atmosphere and everything in it not contract?'

'You are so right about that, Kristian. The longer the quiz went on, the tighter my shoulders got, and the less fun it was. I've enjoyed months of minimal back pain, and this just goes to prove that specific situations act as triggers.' I snuggled into Kristian's warmth. 'I'm sad to say that most of my life has been like that.'

'But not now, April. You have a clearer understanding of causes and effects and henceforth, when you see your family, it will be how you want it to be.' He kissed me and said, 'It took courage to go, my darling. Thank you for indulging us.'

42

Not so long ago, Lise Michelson had stood beside me in Angel Ninebarks' kitchen, and we talked about our brothers. So much water had passed under the bridge since then, and although I was looking forward to the anniversary celebrations, there was no quelling the anxiety. Lise was back, and my mother had been invited.

With the help of former staff including Manny, Sofie, and Iris Kyler, the house and gardens looked a treat. Elkie's composure was temporarily displaced as old friends popped up to make a fuss, and she had taken to flaking out under the old lime tree. Lise had returned the day before with her mother. The ethereal Katrine Michelson was so unlike stout, cherry-cheeked Frieda, and yet to even the most untrained eye, they were sisters. Kristian said she wanted to meet me before the party, on Wingspan. At last I was to be introduced to the mother of the Michelson siblings and the owner of that heavenly voice. It was a nerve-wracking moment when Katrine floated onto the stern, her divine eyes a gift given to her children. With her faded hand resting on my cheek she said, *Your mother had Lise's heart, and now you have my son's.* According to Kristian, that was the ultimate seal of approval.

Later that day, Lise appeared. I hadn't seen her since leaving the Anna Lee which, when added to the emotional encounter with Katrine, I had to fight to keep myself together. For all the changes I was undergoing, she was the same. Lise rested her hands on my wings, and after appearing reassured, she toured the boat. By the time she came down to the galley, her smile could have split the atom. We drank tea as we had done before and would do again.

'Danny and Laurel have excelled themselves. Wingspan is the perfect name for this finely built craft. Unlike the universe, April, we humans must remember to expand. My brother appears to have caught on, at long last.'

'I'm so glad you noticed, and it's not my over-active imagination. There is a change in Kristian. He and I are so unalike, but somehow we seem to fit.'

Lise nodded. 'And the nightmares?'

'Nothing since March. Does this mean that Kristian is finally healing?'

'How could he not, dearest April. Now, this season we are taking a trip along the Trent and Mersey Canal through to Derbyshire. Why don't you join us? We'll make a flotilla.'

'Wow! I'd love to. I'll invite Tish. She's itching to travel the waterways.'

'You are a good friend. With Kristian and you on Wingspan, perhaps Tish will travel on the Anna Lee, with our crew. She may prove a little too enthusiastic for my brother.' Lise took my hand. 'Edmund told me about your generous gesture. The dentistry is exceptional. It has given Tish confidence.'

My cheeks burned. 'Does she know it was me?'

'Tish would never embarrass you, even if she knew, which is unlikely. It's better for her to have received this magnificent gift without feeling beholden to you.' Lise got up to go. 'Elkie may not be such a frequent visitor while I'm here. A tug-of-war with her as the prize would be a waste of our energy.'

The thought of Elkie dividing her affection between the Anna Lee and Wingspan was comical. 'That dog has been the cherry on the icing on the cake, Lise.'

We fell silent, but I was okay with that. Listening to other voices was infinitely preferable to hearing my own, as it was much more interesting to encounter fresh viewpoints. I hadn't expected to discuss anything remotely reflective that day but as usual, I was caught unawares.

'A year has passed since we were first together, April. Your views on certainty and security may no longer be what they were.'

It was a while before I answered. Lise had once said that it had taken courage to accept her invitation to stay on the Anna Lee. She'd known all along that my beliefs would be well and truly upended, even if I hadn't. Clinging to numbers had been my way of keeping control while my teenage spine went hurtling off into the stratosphere. It had been my *modus operandi* until last May. Clinging to my family had, unwittingly, stunted my psycho-spiritual growth, although according to Mum, my inner light was only ever temporarily obscured, but of course she would say that, bless her.

'By removing myself from the familiar, the only certainty I can count on is the changing landscape, Lise. Whatever was driving my life before, be it ambition, success, or social pressure, it appears to have disappeared down the plug hole.' It was hugely gratifying to hear her laugh once again, and I was desperate for her to stay longer, but it was to be a brief visit. 'Shall I see you at Ninebarks tomorrow?'

'Of course. We will raise a glass. I understand Monica has received an invitation. Has she visited you on Wingspan?'

Lise was asking about my mother – at last! 'Yes, and she loves it. I invited her many times onto the Anna Lee, but she never made it. I guess it was a step too far.'

Lise's eyes were fathomless pools. After an infinity of almost drowning, I came up for air. 'I'm not sure if she's coming to the party. The only thing I know about Mum is that she's unpredictable. A free spirit, if ever there was one.'

Lise's silence confirmed it. As much as I longed to know about Iceland, and that pivotal week on the Montgomery Canal, she was never going to talk about it. Even if she had, what made me think I would understand the depth of what she and my mother had shared? It was an immense privilege not only to have met Lise Michelson, but to have the continued good fortune to be in her company. Then I recalled what my colleague Maureen Umber had said, when I asked what she had wanted. *'To love and be loved'.* Yes, Mum and I had definitely experienced that.

'*Hvad der vil være, vil blive.* This is Katrine's favourite expression: what will be, will be. I must go to her. No doubt my mother will be fussing over my brother, and you know how he doesn't like a fuss.'

After she left, I sat for a long, long while, thinking about the things Lise hadn't needed to say, but that was the

Ninebarks way – less is more – and in a world consumed by its own noise, it was a blessing to be out of it.

π

We stood together in the bountiful gardens: mothers, sisters, uncle, nephew, niece – and me, the new arrival, but no longer an outsider. Tish was in her element, serving mint and mango iced tea in a *Make Me Smile* bubble gum T-shirt while Nelly Monkton, one of a hundred and fifty guests, looked on admiringly. The rain clouds had passed, leaving the last droplets to dry under an obliging sun. Angel Ninebarks' burnished stems would have made Marguerite Monkton glow with pleasure.

I was beginning to wonder if my mother would come, but then she appeared, weaving her way through the crowd towards me. She was radiant in a plum paisley dress and raffia beach hat, tied with a lime green scarf. An image of a confident, virile Vaughan Hayle, his heart back-flipping at the sight of her at Glastonbury Festival filled my mind and my eyes. The previous twelve months had almost submerged us, but the fabric that wove our family together was much stronger than even my brilliant, insightful mother had anticipated. Her children were healthy and happy, her marriage, for the moment at least was intact, but it was time to lay those old ghosts to rest. As I stood with the Michelson family, we silently and collectively acknowledged Mum's courage to have come to Angel Ninebarks, alone.

Before I could say hello, Lise went towards my mother. Hand in hand, they walked to the witch/wizard bench, to sit beside their Tibetan cherry blossom in the secret herb garden, planted over thirty years ago. It suddenly struck me that it was never me who was going to crash and burn. Connie had known it too, but she had faith that all would be well with her best friend. Monica Trembath had carried an unattainable dream in her heart, and now, finally, she was ready to relinquish it. I may never know what passed between my mother and Lise on that gorgeous afternoon, but it didn't matter. I'd come to realise that there were times when an unsolved mystery was just as enthralling.

The Inland Waterways –
Then and Now

The canals we see today owe their existence to the Romans. Originally constructed to improve drainage and irrigation, they have been evolving ever since. It was during the 16th and 17th centuries that Britain's canalisation began in earnest. In the early years of the Industrial Revolution, it was estimated that a horse-drawn barge carrying coal or iron ore was thirty times more efficient than a horse-drawn cart. As the need to serve the heavy industry in the midlands and the north picked up speed, so traffic intensity and pollution increased. Although known as the first 'Golden Age', the reality for both the 'pick and shovel' navvies who built the canals and tunnels, and those that worked the boats, it was another story altogether.

In 1761 James Brindley built Bridgewater Canal, the first of its kind, linking Worsley to Manchester. It was named after the 3rd Duke of Bridgewater, one of a number of wealthy mine-owners and industrialists who financed the transportation of essential raw materials to feed the ever-expanding machine. The Bridgewater Canal incorporated the first navigable aqueduct and was heralded one of the seven wonders of the canal age: the era of 'canal mania' was born. Brindley's pioneering techniques resulted in an explosion of building, covering 4000 miles and lasting sixty years. It was his softly flowing lines and charming brick and stone bridge designs gracing the Staffordshire and Worcestershire canals that inspired Quietwater Bridge and cottage.

With the expansion of the road and railways in the mid-1900s, the canals began to fall out of favour and into disrepair. In its heyday, around fifty thousand people worked on the waterways, transporting goods such as timber, tea, foodstuffs and even ice. To fill the gaps left by the war effort, and to cut rising costs, many men were joined by their wives, taking turns to work through the night and generally sharing the heavy load. Families were raised in the tiny cabins in which these industrious women washed, baked, and decorated the dark interiors with 'roses and castles' folk art. As competition intensified, inevitably the numbers of boat families dwindled, and with them went a harsh but independent way of life.

Although acts of parliament prevented the closure of canal companies, by the end of the Second World War, the newly nationalised network was suffering from serious neglect. Tom Rolt's seminal book, *Narrowboat* helped to turn the tide. Whilst travelling the dilapidated waterways systems on 'Cressy' he captured the remnants of a culture on the cusp of disappearing while alerting the reader to the ailing network. The book was published at a critical time. Enthusiasts ready and willing to save this wonderful heritage began to make their voices heard. In 1945, literary agent Robert Aickman read Rolt's book, and after meeting him on Cressy, a year later they formed the Inland Waterways Association. It had two goals: to stop further canal closure and to persuade the government to invest for future preservation. A series of countrywide promotional efforts were organised, the most significant was in 1950, in Market Harborough. This national rally attracted hundreds of boats who carried thousands of people on their first waterborne trips. Major publicity campaigns followed, further amplifying the plight. This led to a new generation of enthusiasts who rolled up their shirtsleeves to begin the restoration of canals such as the Kennet and Avon and the Llangollen.

In 1963, The British Waterways Board was set up in recognition of the canals' potential in the leisure and recreational arenas. But decades of grant and funding instability led many waterways users to demand a reliable and secure future for the network. After several years of cross-party debate and consultancy, the transfer from public corporation to a not-for-profit charitable trust was granted, and in June 2012, the Canals and Rivers Trust was launched.

There is no doubt that the drive and determination of visionaries such as James Brindley, Thomas Telford and Tom Rolt, along with the thousands of devoted volunteers has accorded us a second, *sustainable* 'Golden Age'. Benefits to wildlife and the economy through conservation initiatives, urban regeneration, heritage architecture, and leisure are on the increase. Our fascination with, and love of the inland waterways remains undiminished. For my part, *Quietwater Bridge, mid-morning* couldn't have been written without experiencing those glorious narrowboat trips and unforgettable towpath walks with family and friends and may inspire you to discover the magic of the waterways.

Acknowledgements

Special thanks to Benthe Mathiassen and Benthe Ravn for your generous guidance and advice which substantially enhanced the novel's Danish flavour; to Sue Keen, for your eagle-eyed, honest feedback; to Jane Gregory, Louise Wilkinson, Sally St Ledger, Mal Neate, Sue Warrington, and Sandra Waller for your unwavering belief in my storytelling abilities; to Linda Storey, thanks once again for sharing your tremendous skills and talent. Immense thanks to Erik Bellamy for your detailed technical assistance, and to you and Yvonne Walters: your company on our memorable trip along the Shroppie (for all the right reasons) was fab. Finally to John – life-long lover of narrow-boating – a thousand, thousand thanks.

By the same author

Marianne Bly

Hawkweed Cove

The Sandglass

The Roundhouse

The Smallest of Dreams

Quietwater Bridge, mid-morning is Deborah Rowland's sixth novel. She lives in Shropshire with her husband.